My Year Zero

a novel by rachel gold

Bella
BOOKS

2016

Bella Books, Inc.
P.O. Box 10543
Tallahassee, FL 32302

Printed in the United States of America on acid-free paper.
First Bella Books Edition 2016

Editor: Julia Watts
Cover Designer: Kristin Smith
Cover Illustration: Alexis Cooke

ISBN: 978-1-59493-482-7

About the Author

Raised on world mythology, fantasy novels, comic books and magic, Rachel is well suited for her careers in marketing and writing. She has an MFA in Writing from Hamline University and has spent the last 14 years working in marketing and publicity—but if that makes her sound too corporate and stuffy, you should know that Rachel is an all around geek and avid gamer. For more information visit: www.rachelgold.com

Other Bella Books by Rachel Gold

Being Emily
Just Girls

For Alice
Love, always.

Acknowledgments

Infinite thanks to Alice, to whom this book is dedicated, for loving me, for your sense of humor, for being further down some paths than I was and grinning back at me so I knew it was okay.

Immense gratitude to the many wonderful readers who improved the story and the prose. My alpha reader Alia Whipple and my apex reader Stephanie Burt—I can't express how much your input and edits helped this book. My beta readers: Melissa Trost, Virginia McCoy, Ha'Londra Welch, Wendy Nemitz, Kim Nguyen, Laina Villeneuve and Sara Bracewell.

Special thanks to my team of experts: My dad, Bob Gold, for explaining the mathematics of infinities to me more than once; Heather Anastasiu for fixing the ending; Lin Distel for nearly-incomprehensible handwritten notes that deepened the characters and themes; Cyn Reuss for the bi-squared joke (awesome!); Mara Burr for letting me steal her cool job; Carrie Mesrobian for many conversations about sex in YA novels; therapists Tina Kohfield and Brian W. Brooks for their help on the topic of bipolar disorder; Natasha Tracy for vetting Blake's scenes; and Gidget Houle for everything you did then and now.

Thanks to Linda Hill at Bella Books who told me to write this one next, to Katherine Forrest who ensures that my secondary characters are all wearing clothing, and to editor Julia Watts. Also thank you to my cover designer Kristin Smith, the cover illustrator Alexis Cooke and her partner in crime Mandie Brasington who helped with manga recommendations.

Thanks also to my fantastic writers' group: The Agents of Pantyliner (a pantser vs. outliner joke): Juliann Rich, Aren Sabers, Heather Anastasiu, Eva Indigo and Dawn Klehr.

Great love and gratitude to the members of my household, four-legged and two-legged: you make me better.

"There was no year zero… At first glance this style of numbering might not seem so bad, but it guaranteed trouble."

—From *Zero: The Biography of a Dangerous Idea*

CHAPTER ONE

When I met Blake, I had no idea that she would destroy my life. She was this small person, darkly incandescent, vibrating with nervous energy. Eyes blue-gray like a kingfisher's wing (moving as fast). I should have known by the way she went on about infinities and zero. Who falls in love with zero?

But I'm ahead of myself. The story doesn't start with Blake. As with most great stories, it starts with sex.

A few months after I'd turned sixteen, I figured it was time to have sex. Almost half of American teens have had sex before they turn seventeen, so if I could get laid this year I'd be a little ahead of the curve. And I'm talking about girl-girl sex here, so it wasn't like I had to worry about getting her pregnant.

I didn't want to *just* get laid. I'd settle for it, but I wanted the whole deal. I wanted holding hands and making out and gifts and movie dates. I wanted to fall in love.

This was a hundred times harder than I wanted it to be because I lived in a town of eighty-six thousand that felt like a town of eight thousand.

My plan was to get myself down to the Twin Cities for the Pride festival that summer. This meant six months to get into pickupable shape. My best getting-picked-up asset is my body, which resembles a department store mannequin, except alive, stretched out longer than it should be, and with a bit of muscle. My face is cubist art: long, blocky nose that would look okay if I had well-defined cheekbones, but I don't. My cheeks are shapeless and prone to blotchiness.

If I had any chance at getting hit on, it was going to be in a tank top.

Which is why I was in the weight room of the gym during fourth period while everyone else was playing volleyball. Also I hate team sports. First off, I hate sports. And I hate groups, so team sports are double the hate.

I told the gym teacher I was getting over an ear infection brought on by Duluth's teeth-freezingly cold wind. I shouldn't run around a bunch—could I go to the weight room instead?

I liked lifting weights. (I mean hand weights, not some massive deadlift Miss Universe thing—wait, Miss Universe is a beauty pageant. But Mr. Universe is a muscle guy? That's messed up.) The thing about weights is that it's me against myself and frankly, I'm pretty easy to beat, so I get to win a lot.

The weight room smelled like dirty socks that had been ground into a manure pile by an asphalt truck, but I had it to myself. That was more than I could say for any other part of my school day. I was sitting on the end of a weight bench doing bicep curls and humming along with my iPod. Okay, I was singing. Not loud and certainly not on key.

The song blasting through my headphones was Halestorm's "Break In." I switched from the well of self-pity (I'd never have anyone to make me feel defenseless and known like Lzzy Hale was singing about), to feeling like it had to happen eventually. The last few lines might have come out of my mouth at an audible volume.

I finished the set and glanced at the clock over the door. A woman was leaning against the frame, grinning at me—not mean-grinning—amused, eye-crinkly grinning. She had purple-streaked hair and a short, curvy body, emphasized by the charcoal and pomegranate sundress that clung to her hips. Over the dress was a worn leather jacket and below it heavy black motorcycle boots; very much like no one I had ever seen before.

It's not like I'm prone to hallucinations, but I have a vivid imagination and I figured it'd finally gone over the edge. It made sense, school was that dull this year and my possible sex life was that arid.

She jerked her chin at me and said, "Hey, I'm the Queen of Rogues."

"Oh," I said. "I *am* hallucinating."

She laughed. "Nah, this is my hair's natural color."

I realized I was holding the (five pound—totally not impressive) weights up by my shoulders and put them down.

"I'm Lauren," I said, still not sure she was real, but it's never a bad idea to be polite. "Are you lost?"

"I came to meet a friend for lunch," she said.

"And decided to wander into the weight room?"

"I heard singing," she replied with a smirk.

I blushed and looked away, which is when my brain started to kick in. This might be a real human being and I was missing my opportunity to say something clever like: *I always thought the rogues were a democracy.*

"Where's the cafeteria?" she asked.

"It's across the hall from the big gym," I told her.

Instead of leaving to find said cafeteria, she sat on the weight bench across from me. I didn't think she was that much older, but she seemed elegant and cute and edgy, compared to my lanky, awkward and moist. Her hair was a honeycomb brown with thick streaks of dark purple that made her alabaster cheeks seem even whiter. Shoulder-length messy curls, plus the round shape of her face, gave her a mischievous fallen angel look.

"How did you get to be queen?" I asked, uncomfortably aware of my damp T-shirt and sports bra, all gangles and sweat. I added, "I mean, I thought the rogues were democratic."

The words sounded much stupider coming out of my mouth than they had in my head.

She laughed, a lips-mostly-closed chuckle, like someone took a bigger laugh and compressed it into her mouth. Or like she'd learned to laugh in a way that didn't mess with her candy apple lip gloss.

"I'm Sierra," she said. And in a somber tone she added, "It's not a democracy."

"Yeah, of course not. Do you want me to walk you over to the cafeteria? Give me a sec to change."

"Sure."

I intended to walk sedately into the locker room, but it was more like drunken weaving since I was so thrown off-balance from this conversation. Girls with orchid-streaked hair didn't just show up in my life. Had I conjured her? Certainly not with my singing (that was more appropriate to banishing), but with my wishing for someone to be in my life.

She was probably straight I told myself as I threw on jeans, a non-damp bra, an undershirt and a flannel. I patted my hair down with wet hands so it wasn't so frizzelated. Statistically, most people were straight.

I jammed my feet into my Doc Martens and, while I tied them, went over her appearance like I could puzzle her out: the sundress was pure straight girl, but not the boots. They were heavily scuffed in the toe, like she'd had them forever. The leather jacket was worn too, that had to be a good sign. Her hair—what did that mean?

When I came back into the weight room, Sierra was still there, existing. She followed me into the hall.

"Where did you come from?" I asked, and it sounded all blunt and weird so I added, "I mean, you don't go here."

"I'm really from another galaxy," she said. "But that's a long story. I'm up from the Cities with my family. A friend of mine goes here and we told the office I'm a senior considering a transfer so I could come hang out."

"You're not?"

"First year of college. I figured it'd be fun to hop on a bus and come out for lunch and maybe sit in on a class of hers to remind me why college is a thousand times better."

"Fun to hop on a bus in the snow? In December? In a sundress?"

"Wool stockings," she said, the smirk back on her lips. "There's my friend. You want to eat with us?"

"Uh, I have to...I'm in the next lunch period."

"Maybe I'll see you later," she said.

"Yeah."

She was already walking away, waving to her friend, some senior-looking girl I didn't know. I wandered back into the hall trying to remember what class I was supposed to go to and wondering if all that had actually happened.

CHAPTER TWO

When I got to lunch, I expected Sierra to have vanished back into my overactive imagination. Not only was she there, but she was holding court at the end of a table, leaning against the wall, talking with a group of girls that included my not best friend Jenny.

Jenny was golden: blond, cheerleadery, all that. Sierra's effortless loose curls made Jenny's pristine golden ringlets look like they were trying too hard. (Jenny always looked like she was trying too hard, but no one seemed to care.)

I met Jenny in fifth grade but we grew apart in junior high. Everyone grew apart in junior high. Last year she started hanging out with me again. By some miracle—or by the power of Jenny's evil mastermind leadership—instead of kids turning on her for hanging out with the school's one out lesbian, they left me alone because the queen bee found me useful.

I was supposed to get my tray and walk over and say hi, like it was nothing. But I froze. I shuffled out of the doorway and away from the serving line. Sierra's glistening red lips moved, Jenny and the other girls laughed. They hadn't seen me yet, I could still run.

An arctic blast of air hit the side of my face and I turned toward it. So did everyone else in the cafeteria.

A tall, skinny kid had one of the windows open and was climbing in. From the outside. With no coat on, despite the fact that it was ten degrees out, too cold even for snow to fall. Everything weird that happens at my school happens in the winter. This is because winter in Duluth is fourteen months long. In the depth of that winter, with only eight hours of daylight, everyone loses their mind eventually.

Winter holiday break was three days away and already in December we'd had a kid eating bugs throughout my entire English class, two guys caught jerking each other off in the bathroom, and a fistfight over chess. There was a rumor that one of the seniors had run away from home with an older girl, and four pregnancy scares. Oh and a prank involving a bucket of urine that backfired spectacularly.

When I saw this kid shove the window open, I figured it was more of the same.

He had waxy, buff-colored skin with too prominent bones, short, greasy mud-colored hair and amber eyes. I recognized him but I couldn't think of where I'd seen him. Sure he was a senior at this high school, but I'd seen his photo someplace specific, if I could remember it.

He put one long leg in through the window, bent low and pushed himself over the sill. He was talking, muttering at first, but when his head came into the room his words got louder. Maybe this wasn't a prank. I put a few more feet between us.

He was saying, "Drones. Drones! Micro-drones, spies, in everything, need a microscope, you can feel them watching, recording." He pulled his other leg over the sill and stood up.

He held something in his hand, rectangular and compact, with metal and wiring, and he started waving it over his head.

"It's a bomb!" someone behind me screamed.

A hundred students moved at once, knocking over chairs, dropping books, running for the doors and getting stuck with the other students trying to shove their way out.

A few of us didn't move. Most of the stoner kids' table stayed seated, watching the guy with half-lidded eyes. A couple of guys who seemed like they might know him stood in the middle of the room looking nervously from him to the nearest door. The kids at the back of the line for the doors had turned to watch. Sierra was among them. She was composed, patiently waiting to exit, watching me.

I shrugged at her. My heart was going fast and I felt light-headed. Some of the people shoving through the doorways were yelling, one girl screaming. I wasn't eager to join them.

The kid held the metal box in front of his face like he could see into it and then waved it around again. I could almost read the writing on the side. It was printed; clear words that should make sense.

"They're after me," he said. "They've implanted me with the drones, I know it. Can you see them? Come here and tell me if you can see them. I know you can. They'll get you too. You can't run. They'll get you!"

I remembered where I'd seen his face. It was in a photo of the robotics team.

The security guard came up next to me. Brown shirt and khakis, walkie-talkie in her hand, dark hair back in a tight braid. "Come with me," she said.

"He's on the robotics team," I told her.

Her wide eyes and raised brows suggested either that she had no patience for me or thought I was as crazy as he was. I couldn't tell which.

"That might not be a bomb," I said. "It looks like a hard drive. See the printing on the white side?"

She blinked at me a few times and called across the room to him, "Son, is that a hard drive?"

"They're in my data," he yelled back. "They want what I've got. It's all here. Can you copy it? You have to save it for me."

He lunged across the room and shoved it at her, but she didn't take it.

"What kind of drive is that?" I asked.

He pulled away, pressed it to his chest, looked hurt. "You're testing me. It's a Western Digital two terabyte SATA drive. You think I'd trust my data to anything else? This is cutting edge, this is over the edge, beyond the edge, this is the future times a million, that's why they want it. They need this tech. You have to take me out of here. They're going to find me."

With the drive this close, I could read the words "Western Digital" along the side. He was right. How could he be ranting about drones and at the same time know exactly what he had in his hand? Did crazy work like that? Part of the world in focus and another part wildly out of control?

Sirens outside. He glanced back at the open window. A light dusting of snow, lifted up from the ground and blew onto the radiator where it fizzled.

"Oh man, the drones are here. They're in me. They gave me away. Shit, help me hide."

He ran across the room and shoved himself into the closet with the napkins and ketchup.

"You should evacuate with the other students," the guard told me.

Two cops were pushing their way in through the crowded cafeteria doors as I reached them. They passed me and I heard the guard tell them, "We think he might be holding a computer hard drive."

More than half of the doors from the hallway outside the cafeteria were closed like they were supposed to be in lockdown mode. Further down the hall, doors were still open. Everyone with lockers away from the cafeteria was told they could get their coats and go home or wait in the far classrooms for buses. We were two periods from the end of the day.

I found Jenny and Sierra in one of the big classrooms at the far end of the school. They were standing by a window that faced the parking lot with all the cop cars. One of the clone girls that always follows Jenny around was with them. I didn't remember her name.

When she saw me, Jenny ran over and fake hugged me: the kind where your arms go around the other person but there's no real contact. The clone girl patted my shoulder. She was very pale with limp, wheat-blond hair, as if when they copied Jenny they turned the exposure up too high. Sierra stayed where she was by the window, turned to watch us.

"Weren't you scared?" Jenny asked me.

"I guess so," I said. I felt shaky now, ripples in my hands and my legs. Wasn't that how scared felt?

"What do you mean you guess?" she asked, voice rising. "You stood there staring at him. Did you know he was going to do that?"

"Of course not. But everyone was going through the doors at the same time and, I don't know. Isn't it good to not panic?"

I went over to the window to see if they'd brought the kid out yet. Jenny followed, rolling her eyes at me. She said, "When there's a bomb you're supposed to panic. You're really weird sometimes."

She'd told me that before. Half the time it was because I didn't agree that a guy she liked was cute, so I ignored it. Yeah, I didn't cry at sad movies, but that's because crying makes you appear weak. And I didn't gush over new clothes or groan when we got extra homework, because why bother. If that made me weird, I guess I was.

I told her, "It wasn't a bomb. It was only a hard drive."

"He was totally mental, though," the clone girl said. "Like schizo or bipolar and completely off his meds."

Sierra straightened up, seeming inches taller than the clone girl, even though she wasn't. "Not cool," she said. "I have a friend who's bipolar. It's not like that."

"He's *crazy*," the girl insisted. She pointed toward the parking lot.

The cops were leading the kid out to the squad car, his hands cuffed behind his back. He kept shouting. The wind carried hints of his words across the parking lot and through the glass of the window. I heard "drones" a few more times. He tried to run when they reached the car and they had to wrestle him into the back.

We stayed silent until the car drove away. School was optional for the rest of the day. Half of the students were already gone. With break a few days away, we'd take any excuse to leave.

Jenny and her clone left me and Sierra standing by the window.

"What are you doing next?" I asked, feeling more nervous about asking that than facing the kid with the wild hard drive.

Sierra shrugged. "I guess I'll catch the bus back to my aunt's."

"When they let me back to my locker to get my coat, I can drive you back."

"You have a car?"

"Yeah," I told her.

"That'd be super sweet." She glanced out the window again and back to me. "You were very coolheaded in there."

I didn't know how to tell her that cool had nothing to do with it. I didn't react to a lot of stuff. Sometimes I'd get scared or angry for no reason and other times when I should have been completely freaked out, I didn't feel it. My father was an attorney and he taught me and my brother to make logical arguments as soon as we could talk. I figured it came from that; I could see things logically and not get all wrapped up in them.

"I'm afraid of centipedes," I said and wanted to kick myself because of how stupid it sounded.

But Sierra laughed and the whole inside of my torso dissolved into jittery static.

"So if he'd come in waving a centipede?" she asked.

"I'd have been the first one out the doors," I told her. "I'm just not afraid of hard drives. Did you get to eat?"

"I started to but it was terrible. I haven't had a school lunch in a year and I can't say that I miss them in the least. How long do you have until they spring you from this place?"

"What, until I graduate?"

She nodded. Her eyes were super blue. Winter sky cobalt blue when it's too cold for clouds.

"I'm a junior," I told her. "Though I'll have enough credit to graduate next winter. You know, there's a pizza place not far. If I can get to my locker…"

"I'd love to," she said.

* * *

Sierra didn't disappear before I got back. She followed me out of the building to the parking lot and the car my father got me a few months ago for my sixteenth birthday: a carbide gray Subaru Legacy. The name was ironic since I was so not his legacy, that was my brother Isaac. I was his failure.

"This is yours?" Sierra asked when she got in.

I braced myself in case this was the start of one of those stinging Jews-with-money comments and said, "Um, mostly. We got it used and technically it belongs to my father, but it's mine to drive."

She nodded and didn't say 'must be nice' or the stupider things that started with 'you people…'

I drove along Superior Street to Sammy's Pizza. It was filling up with out-of-school kids, but we got one of the little black tables against the wall and decided to split a cheese pizza with extra cheese. Sierra contemplated the black and white tile, the metal stools, the gooseberry green wall color, the overall mashup of kitsch and modern. I couldn't tell if she thought it was cool or ancient.

Did it count as a date if you met a girl by accident and ended up getting pizza because of a bomb scare?

I wanted it to count as a date. I'd come out as lesbian about five seconds into the first time I kissed a boy. To be fair, I kissed him a few more times and kissed another boy, all in all pretty boring. Like Jell-O. Not the texture of the kiss, but the way that when I see Jell-O on a table at a buffet, I'm not drawn to it. I might take some if there's nothing else sweet, but most of the time I'll skip dessert. It's hardly worth the effort it takes to eat it.

Maybe you love Jell-O, I'm not saying it's across the board the worst dessert ever (that award goes to unripe fruit), I'm saying it's not my thing. Sierra, on the other hand, I could thoroughly get used to watching her eat pizza.

"I hope he's okay," I said. "What do you think happens if the cops have to take you away like that?"

"They lock you up in the psych ward for a while," Sierra answered, super matter-of-fact.

I looked at her and she shrugged like "what?" I wanted to ask how she knew that, but it didn't seem polite.

"I don't think it was bipolar, though," she said. "Blake's never like that. She's my best friend. She's deeply cool. She has a character in the story I write with a bunch of other people. Do you write?"

"A little. I mostly draw."

I'd managed to get a bite of hot pizza into my mouth and was trying to figure out a graceful way to chew and swallow. Most of the time I knew how to function like a normal human being, honest.

"What?" she asked.

I swallowed and gulped some water.

"Mostly comics," I said. "Not the superhero kind. Do you read manga?"

"Not really. Should I?" she asked and took another bite of her pizza slice, as if talking then chewing was an easy skill to master.

"Uh, yeah, everybody should."

She laughed. "Will you lend me some?"

I reached into my backpack for Nakamura Asumiko's *"Adolte and Adarte"* and slid it across the table to her. She flipped through it.

"I'll mail it back to you when I'm done. Do you like science fiction?"

I nodded, hoping she'd look away so I could swallow. The bite of pizza seemed so small when it took it, but it was expanding in my mouth.

"You should join us, the story group. We only have one illustrator."

She glanced down, riffling the edge of the manga, and I gulped down the mass of pizza.

"What's the story about?" I asked.

It could have been a grinding tragedy about garbage collectors on Mars and I'd have said yes.

Nobody here wrote group stories. Almost nobody here wrote stories as far as I knew. Most of the students were either obsessed with grades so they could get out of here for college, or obsessed with drinking and hooking up. My father considered my comics and my illustrations to be a kid thing that I'd grow out of when I finally decided if I wanted to be an architect or a corporate marketing goon.

"Our story takes place in this galaxy that's ruled by four old gods but there's this race of Illudari—like high elves—who are fighting to replace the old gods with their own leaders, the kings and queens of the galaxy."

"The Queen of Rogues?" I asked.

"That's who I am. In the current story, she's actually allied with one of the old gods, Lord Stone, to go against the most powerful of all the old gods. But some of the other kings and queens are upset so there's fighting between them."

"How do you write it?"

"There are a bunch of different ways you can submit your posts, or write in the group document we have going. Dustin, he's Lord Stone, he compiles it all with the art and puts it on the official site. And we talk about it when we're together or on chat—about where the story is going next so you kind of know what to write. Your pizza's getting cold."

I managed a few more bites as she told me about the story background because she peered across the restaurant while she talked. I could only half listen. When I listened too much or looked at her, I started to feel all full of static again and forgot how to eat.

When we'd eaten half the pizza and boxed the rest, she gave me directions to her aunt's house. It was a normal-sized house on the west side of town, where we used to live. I parked by the curb and wasn't sure what to do next.

Sierra took my hand off the wheel. She ran her thumb along the edge of my index finger, burning and tickling my skin.

"Ink," she said.

I nodded because I usually had ink on my hands and with her touching me, I couldn't figure out how to form words.

"Give me your address for the comic and your email. I'll have Dustin send you an invite to the story."

I wasn't going to pull away from her touch, but she let go, so I reached into the backseat and got my bag. I tore a sheet of paper out of my notebook and wrote down what she wanted.

She folded the paper and said, "Thanks!"

She was out of the car and moving up the shoveled, stone walk to the house, the bottom half of her dress seeming out of place between leather jacket and boots. She let herself in and shut the door. After I'd put the car in drive, I realized that I had none of her information: no email, no phone number. I didn't even know her last name.

I couldn't get out of the car and go ask. I hated myself, but I couldn't. My heart pounded and some (smarter, tougher) part of my brain was yelling at me to run up the front walk, ring the bell and ask. The slower, dopey, well-behaved part of my brain drove us away from the house.

I got home and sat for a while in the garage rubbing my thumb against the side of my index finger (it didn't feel the same, not even close) and wondering if I'd ever hear from her again.

CHAPTER THREE

After two weeks, I gave up on hearing from Sierra. Then something would remind me—ink splatters on a page or the gap in my library where that one manga was missing—and I'd go back to hoping that she'd email me.

You would think that once you shared a bomb scare with someone, they'd get in touch with you. I guess the Twin Cities was that much cooler than Duluth, so when she got home she wasn't curious about a random comic geek up north.

The cycle went on: remembering, hoping, giving up. The sun came up and went down again too soon. Snow fell white and turned brown. Days happened, and weeks and months.

And then she emailed!

She wrote: *So sorry! Busy with work/school/holidays/family/bullshit! I still have your comic, haven't forgotten. Talked to Dustin this weekend. He'll add you to the story. Watch for an email with details! Can you forgive me?*

I read it a half-dozen times and typed a casual reply: *Hi, how are you?*

No, that sounded stupid. I deleted it and started again: *Hey, good to hear from you.*

Too eager. Delete, try again: *Hi, I thought you'd forgotten...*
Omg, too needy!

I sent back: *Hey, thanks. No worries about the manga, send it whenever. I'll watch for the invite. Sounds cool.*

That also sounded daft, but whatever, I had to send a reply. I stared at my laptop like anything would happen right away. It didn't. I put on my iPod and went to clean the bathroom in an attempt to distract myself and because it was on the chores list for tomorrow.

When I was done, I tried to do homework but I was checking my email every three-point-four seconds. After long minutes, two messages pinged into my inbox, almost at the same time. I opened Sierra's first:

Oh! I'm glad you're not mad. It was so fun to meet you. I wish I'd had you draw me something that I could show Dustin. You're going to like everyone on the story. They're all amazing. I can't wait for you to read it.

She gave me her chat info, I put it in and saw her pop up as online. What should I say? I'd already opened the email to her with "Hey" and that was my usual start. Might as well stick with the classic.

I wrote: *Hey, this is Lauren.*

Her reply showed up in seconds: *Hi! Did you get the invite?*

Yeah, but I haven't read it yet.

Sierra said: *You need to pick a character and set up a page for them. The craziest things have been happening in my family. I'm sorry I didn't email you. I forgot where I put the paper and it was in the pocket of that dress. I never wear that dress. I had to go searching through everything to find it.*

She went looking for my info! That had to mean something, right? Like not only did she remember me but she liked me enough to go out of her way.

I asked: *Is your family okay?*

Sierra wrote: *My sister got fired again and everyone is freaking out. They think it's her boyfriend, like she's not the bad influence. I should probably go totally lesbian so they won't panic about me.*

Had she meant "totally go lesbian"—like she wasn't now but could go there—or actually the way she typed it, like she was already partway there and could maybe go the rest of the way? Please let it be the latter. I figured coming out was the fastest way to see.

I said: *That's my plan.*

Lesbian or not panicking?

Both.

Sierra replied: *Cool! You can give me tips. About lesbians. I don't panic.*

My heart stopped or was teleported out of my chest and was replaced with pressurized helium. The cursor and I blinked at each other. The cursor seemed as befuddled as me.

I typed: *You should probably start by kissing girls. See if you like it.*

As soon as I sent that, I thought it sounded too flirty, but Sierra replied: *Oh, I've kissed girls before. I was sort of dating one but then I met Dustin and we clicked.*

Heart-fluttery what? She'd already kissed a girl?

So you're bi? I asked.

I'm whatever, you know, love is love.

And you're dating Dustin?

Sierra said: *Something like that.*

Did she think I was hitting on her? Had she been trying to figure out what my orientation was? Was she flirting with me? What was "like" dating?

Sierra wrote: *Dinner's here. Got to go.*

Okay, I'll check out the story.

Bye!

I couldn't focus on anything except the line where Sierra said she'd kissed girls, and dinner sounded like a good idea, so I went down to the kitchen. When my father got home in a few hours, he'd have eaten at his law office or gone out to dinner with a client. He wouldn't bring food home for me. I had a credit card and an allowance and he expected me to get what I wanted as long as it was reasonably nutritious and as long as I also got whatever he put on the grocery list.

The grocery list was a small whiteboard hung in the upstairs hallway. It read: oranges. It belonged on the fridge, but nothing was permitted on the fridge. That would detract from the handcrafted cabinetry.

When Jenny's parents divorced, her father bought a Porsche. I get that. You're trying to get away from someone, you want a fast car even if it is metaphorical. When my mom left my father, he bought a house. Not any old house but a cabin-mansion overlooking the lake through two-stories of enormous windows (as if you want to see more frozen lake views during Duluth's fourteen months of winter).

Did I say cabin-mansion? I meant METICULOUSLY BUILT cabin-mansion. That's what it said in the real estate brochure, full caps. Back when I was ten, I had to look up "meticulous." It meant careful and precise, which was my father's perspective on everything that year. After that he reeled it back to suspicious and exacting.

My mom got a job working for the President. I'm not even kidding. She's the Assistant U.S. Trade Representative for South Asia so she goes around to all those countries and makes it easier to do business with the U.S. She loves to quote Roosevelt's famous line, "If goods don't cross borders, troops cross borders." I don't blame her for leaving; when you get a chance to work for the President and represent the whole country, how could you say no? But because of all the travel, she couldn't take us with her. And if kids don't cross states, bullshit crosses states.

For a year before the divorce my parents were extremely shitty to each other. They stopped talking except for short, ugly-sounding sentences and there was a lot of door slamming and one of them driving off around dinnertime and coming back after I was in bed. Isaac is five years older than me so he was more in tune with it. I'd ask him, "Why aren't Mom and Dad talking?" and he'd say, "Because they hate each other," which made sense to him but curdled my kid-brain.

After the divorce, Isaac got a new TV and an Xbox, I got every art supply I could ask for and a drawing table, and my father got his cabin-mansion. You might think I'm mad at the house because I'm mad at my parents, but I assure you, I am not mad at the house and its PRICELESS VIEWS. (It was an intensely shouty real estate brochure.)

The house has huge cedar beams throughout the two-story living room with its wall of windows. There's slate tile floor full of golds and grays, browns and silvers. I used to sit in the entryway and run my fingertips over the tile to figure out if the different colors had different textures. The gray was finer than the browns and golds, and the silver was like silk.

After she left, Mom sounded happier right away and my father stopped talking to us except to say, "Isaac, take care of your sister." I figured any day we'd be moving out east with Mom. But her job kept her too busy going to places like Kyrgyzstan and Tajikistan. (She got points for sending me a postcard from Middlefart, Denmark, but still). We spent the whole summer with her every year from when I was ten through thirteen. Then Mom's job got busier, and Isaac went out east to college.

Me and Isaac did okay together. We actually like each other and I didn't mind hanging out by myself, so he'd make sure we had dinner on the nights our father worked late and he'd get me up for school in the morning. He'd send me off with a little pep talk that I think he got from his coach. (There was an age-inappropriate "slaughter them" in the middle plus a lot of swearing.)

Did my father know he was going to have to keep me and Isaac when he bought the cabin-mansion? It does have four bedrooms and a ton of space. Isaac thought it was badass because he and his friends could hang out in the woods behind the house's ornate gardens. I wasn't as excited to have friends over. I had friends then, Jenny and two other girls, before I got tall and weird and awkward and queer.

Speaking of awkward and queer, along with buying the cabin-mansion, my father started dating not long after Mom left (or maybe a little before she left, based on some of their fights). Around fourteen I'd started to wonder if he'd had this whole plan in his head for how the divorce would go: that it would be okay because she'd take the kids and he could work as much as he wanted and spend his spare time asking out Duluth's small population of hot, eligible women. The house is perfect for bringing dates home. The whole first floor is this giant great room situation with a handcrafted dining table and huge couches.

He didn't bring women back to the house until after Isaac went to college. The first time I walked into the kitchen and saw him on the couch laughing with a prettied-up woman, I think we were all shocked. Maybe he'd forgotten that he had a daughter. I said, "Hi," nuked dinner and went back to my room like it was all normal, but after that I started keeping candy bars in my room, just in case.

It's mortifying to walk in on your father's date. Profoundly worse were the rare times I thought his date was hot. There was this one woman, tall as me, mane of brown-blond hair, not too much makeup, freckled and sunshiny face. Looking at her, I forgot how to make words. I spent the rest of that weekend at the library even though in the pre-car era it was a two-mile walk in the snow. This was another reason I needed a girlfriend of my own.

* * *

I wanted to tell someone about Sierra, to have an excuse to talk about her and to debate what she might have meant by telling me she'd kissed girls, but who?

Not Jenny and her clone army. Maybe Mom would be a little happy for me, in a perplexed way. We mostly talked about world politics and shopping when we talked every week or two.

Isaac? Was it weird that I liked my brother more than just about anyone in my life?

I wrote out a text to him: *I met this girl. At my school. She had purple hair and wears dresses and kisses girls and I don't know what that all means. And she's dating this guy, but…how do you ask a girl out?*

I deleted that because it was stupid.

But I couldn't say nothing.

I sent him: *How do you ask a girl out?*

He texted back a few hours later: *Is she into you?*

Maybe, I wrote.

Get that to a "probably" and ask me again, he said.

I wanted to ask him how to do that. How do you go from maybe to probably to yes without being a creeper? I guess that was up to me to figure out.

CHAPTER FOUR

I stayed up until after midnight finding my way around the story, reading until my eyelids were heavy and hot. In the morning, my father rapped on my door because my alarm was going off and I hadn't hauled myself out of bed yet. By the time I was up and dressed, he'd left.

The only evidence that he'd been home was the whiteboard in the hall that now read: oranges, coffee creamer.

I dragged through the school day, but when I got home I was fully awake. Calling up the story site on my laptop, I picked up where I'd left off. The main characters were from a human-like race called the Illudani, a cross between elves and vampires. They had metal-hued skin, from inky, graphite tones to shimmering silver.

Sierra came back online while I was reading.

Whatcha doing? she asked.

Reading, I told her. *And looking at this art.*

That's Bear, she's fantastic.

What kind of girl called herself "Bear?" Or was that what her parents really named her?

There's Kings and Queens and Gods, right? I asked.

Yep. And the Kings and Queens can appoint their court. Do you want me to give you a rank and a character to be?

That'd be cool, I replied.

I've got a Knight who's in a few of the stories who doesn't have a real person behind her. Or we can make you a new character. But you'd have to start at the outside and work your way in if we do that.

What does the Knight do in the stories? Is she awesome?

She's the best thief in the galaxy, Sierra replied.

Should I ask if Sierra's character was also bi in this fictional world too—before I agreed to a female role? That seemed too forward. Like, why would I be asking unless I wanted her to like me?

Starting as a Knight in the Rogues' Court put me as close to Sierra as I could get.

That's cool, I can be the thief, I wrote.

My other Knight in the story is Blake, I mean in real life—in the story she's Cypher. She's like my best friend, the bipolar one, and super smart. You should meet her sometime, you'd like her.

I considered the words, ran back over them, thought about her mentioning Blake that day at school with the crazy kid. Did she say "bipolar" every time she brought up this best friend? Or was she saying it because of the conversation after the bomb scare, because that's the way she'd first talked about Blake? Would Sierra start introducing me as her "lesbian friend Lauren?"

Did it have to alliterate…lesbian/Lauren, bipolar/Blake? What title did Dustin get? (I wanted it to be "douche.")

In a side window on the computer, I did a quick search. Bipolar disorder: dramatic mood episodes, intense emotional states, depressive lows, manic highs. Maybe this girl Blake didn't give a shit what people knew about her. Super-outgoing, confident, emotional people scared me. Should I be picking a character who was paired with someone like that?

Of course if I changed my mind now, I'd be the dick who didn't want to run with the bipolar girl.

"Dick" also alliterated with Dustin…nah, that was too easy.

Okay, I typed to Sierra. *Do we run around thieving together?*

In one story you do, but most of the time the thief is on her own because she's a thief and all. Blake's character Cypher is the Master of Secrets.

Oh, right.
The thief's name is Zeno. I let Blake name her. It's some math thing.
I'll tell the group you're coming in as Zeno the First Among Thieves and
link you the doc with her backstory, it's only a paragraph right now. You'll
want to add to it.

Minutes later she sent me the link and I clicked it:

Zeno was born to a noble family but she didn't like it so she ran away and joined the Rogues. She's loyal and an okay fighter but really good at breaking into places and stealing things. She serves the Queen of Rogues directly.

I had work to do. Had the mysterious Blake written that? If so, I wasn't impressed.

I messaged Sierra: *How much room do I have with this character?*
Can I change stuff and kind of reintroduce her?

She wrote back: *That's a great idea! Do it! I can't wait to see it!*

There was a black and white drawing of a slender but chesty woman with hair pulled back in a short ponytail. If I put my hair up like that, would it come out that neatly? I didn't put my hair up. (If you have to wear your hair long because your father would freak if you cut it, why not keep it to hide behind, right?)

Zeno was about six feet tall with pewter skin and narrow eyes. There were notes about her being a werewolf and the artist had drawn her with a wolfish face: mouth and nose protruding a bit like a muzzle and light-colored eyes.

Sierra's character, the Queen of Rogues, stood at six and a half feet, which put her a foot taller than Sierra herself. She had silver-platinum skin and sapphire-blue eyes, plus a mane of black hair that sparkled like the night sky.

Blake's description of Cypher made me laugh:

Cypher is short, way shorter than you'd think she should be, so she's always eye level with people's chests. Not that she minds. She's got short pink hair and it's not the least bit stylish. It looks like a paintbrush that got jammed down into a jar for too long. And her eyes are indigo, no wait, dark gray, or a combination of those two colors that we'll call "grindigo." Did you know "greige" is a real color? Anyway, her eyes are grindigo. Except when she's peering into the zero point energy and then they're black.

I wanted to rewrite Zeno's description immediately and say something clever or cute, but I had to think about it. I had to let her permeate into my head so I could feel how her character wanted to expand. I read the three stories where she was a side character. Zeno walked on scene, said a thing or two to move the plot, and wandered off to steal things.

* * *

I dug into the story more, even though some of it was pretty bad. I mean I'm no J. K. Rowling, but I can write in complete sentences. At least one of the writers was given to having every character gasping and exclaiming and once even ejaculating, but not in the way that would have made the scene interesting.

I was working on ways to reintroduce Zeno as a machine-based life form when I saw Sierra back online.

Pounce! She messaged. *What're you doing?*

Working on reintroducing Zeno.

Want to write it together?

Yeah, cool, I wrote, *but how does that work?*

Get in the shared doc and write a paragraph or two, or a few lines of dialogue, and then I do the same, in turns. And we stay on chat so we can talk about where the scene is going if we need to, so it all makes sense. Go ahead and start it, write a little with Zeno reintroducing herself to the Queen.

Staring at the blank document, I told her: *I don't know where to start.*

Okay, what's your new Zeno like? What's different?

I thought she should be a little taller and, I don't know, stuff about being part machine maybe.

Got it, she said. *Can I run with it?*

Please do.

Sierra:

The Queen was in her throne room polishing her barbed daggers when a tall stranger came through the doors and bowed low. She was familiar. But not in a way the Queen could place.

She walked up to the stranger. A tall, beautiful woman with long, dark hair, and complicated metal armor over her legs, body and arms. The Queen appreciated the armor. It looked deadly and effective.

"Who are you?" she asked. "I feel that we've met."

On chat Sierra said: *Okay, you go.*

Lauren:

"I'm not surprised you don't recognize me, but it's me, Zeno, your thief. I stole an artifact that changed me. It's in my bag if you'd like to see it."

Zeno set down a leather pack at the feet of the Queen with a heavy thunk. The servos in her armor whined and hissed as she moved.

I told Sierra: *I don't know what the Queen would do.*

She wrote back: *Hang on, I've got it.*

Sierra:

The Queen walked slowly around Zeno, her fingers tracing the hard curves of the armor.

"My thief," she said. "I like how you say that. Who sent you so far away to get this thing? It wasn't me. Was it Cypher? She's too curious, that girl."

She stopped in front of Zeno, radiating an aura of danger and power. Zeno trembled a little but then stilled because she knew the Queen would never hurt her.

The Queen put her hand on Zeno's arm, or rather on the metal over her arm.

"Is this part of you?" she asked.

Lauren:

"Yes, now it is. It happened when I grabbed the artifact. The metal came out of nowhere and protected me, but I don't know how to make it go away again," Zeno said. Her voice dropped to a whisper. "I'm afraid I'm no longer certain that I know what I am."

Sierra:

The Queen moved her hand along the metal armor covering Zeno's arm. Her fingers reached its edge and brushed the skin at the base of Zeno's throat, making her shiver.

"We'll have to find a way to get this off you," she said.

Lauren:

Zeno found her mouth suddenly dry. She licked her lips, not knowing what to say. The Queen was so many ranks above her, it would be improper to take her statement as more than a practical suggestion.

Sierra:
The Queen of Rogues grinned at her thief's discomfort. She'd always liked teasing Zeno but now in this new form of hers, there was something else about her. What did she look like under all that armor?
"We should ask Cypher how to deal with this, she'll know," the Queen said. "But not yet. Come and sit by me. Rest. I'll have the servants bring wine and you must tell me all about your travels. You've been away too long."

Okay, Sierra messaged while I was reading her last part. *I have to run but there's an opening for you to keep writing. If you need, you can have Cypher come in with new info. Blake won't mind as long as she sounds decently smart. I'll read it later. Isn't this cool?*

Yeah, it's awesome. See you soon.

She signed off and I read back through what we'd written. Writing together made me feel more in the scene than when I was writing on my own. Going over it again was like reading over a memory. I could feel Sierra standing in front of me, touching my armor, touching me. I wanted that to be real.

Sierra had a confident way of moving. Even if she was a foot shorter in real life, it was easy to picture her as the Queen, stalking around the throne room. Her dramatic and compelling and me... she'd described Zeno as "beautiful." Did she actually think that about me or was it merely storytelling?

Were we flirting? I didn't even know how to find out. I hated how far away she was.

CHAPTER FIVE

Over the next few days, I finished reading through the existing story and, of course, cleaned the house. At the start of the week, my father showed up, checked the fridge for his oranges and coffee creamer, and asked me how school was. He listened for two minutes before reminding me that we were going to temple for Purim on Wednesday evening.

By Wednesday, I'd forgotten. There were space elves, for goodness sake, and an elegant Queen of Rogues offering to take off my armor. I couldn't be expected to remember that this boring human body of mine, marooned on the frozen ass-end of a nowhere planet, was expected to dress up for temple.

A quick, sharp rap of knuckle on wood.

"Lauren," my father said. "Fifteen minutes."

He would want me to wear a dress. I put on loose gray pants, a favorite sweater, little gold earrings and a necklace. He was waiting at the top of the stairs in one of his innumerable suits.

"It's a holiday," he said. "Don't you want to look nice?"

My father comes from centuries of warrior Jews. If Masada hadn't been a total massacre, I'd say those guys were my ancestors.

He's six feet tall and broad-shouldered with thick, curly black hair and the eyelashes of a movie star. Women literally flock to him, like birds around a full feeder in the dead of winter.

I'm pretty sure that in his copy of the Hebrew Bible—not that he's observant at all—the commandment "honor thy father and thy mother" includes a footnote that reads "by making thyself look thy best all the time, as defined by thy father and thy mother and lo unto pain of death never by thine own sense of style, which is an abomination."

I went back into my room not wanting to look nice at all. Skirts aren't nice. Dresses are not nice.

Okay, truthfully, leggy sixteen-year-olds with giraffe knees don't look good in a dress. Sierra in a dress and motorcycle boots: very nice.

I wedged myself into pantyhose that felt like they were sagging and trying to crawl up my crotch at the same time. Add boring flats, because in heels I was taller than my father and I tended to fall over a lot. (He never tried to catch me. You might think that was penance for being taller than him in heels, but in truth it was his strongly held belief that I had to master gravity all on my own. He didn't teach me to ride a bike either, that was Isaac.)

Because I was tall and people often mistook me for being older, and because my father was handsome, and because in a plain black dress I resembled a matronly funeral guest, I had been at times mistaken for his girlfriend. I tried not to think about what that meant about the women he dated.

I hadn't seen the latest girlfriend. He'd been staying at her place and leaving me the house to myself, which was sort of neat except that I had to keep it spotless and there was never anyone I wanted to invite over to hang out in the big, empty great room with me.

We only went to temple for the holidays, when it was packed. My father would circulate in his fashionable suit and shake hands and look important. He's a partner in the local branch of a big law firm so he is sort of important, I guess. Lots of people know him and laugh at his jokes (which are not funny).

As holidays go, Purim's awesome. (Also a fan of Sukkot, because no holiday that gets joyful over lemons can be bad, and Yom Kippur, even though it's the most serious business holiday. Not big on Hanukkah; all the Christians think it's a much bigger deal than it is and it's a pain in the butt to keep explaining that I do *not* get a gift for each day.)

Purim is all about kids running around the temple in costumes and everyone eating. This year there was even a boy in a Queen Esther dress along with half the girls because everyone wants to be Esther (except me when I was little, the dress thing). Having all the kids there means that the rabbi keeps the service short and we get to the eating and partying more quickly than omg-will-this-Hagadah-ever-end Passover.

I spent the service gazing in the direction of the rabbi but in my mind trying to work out how to draw the Queen of Rogues with Zeno. I wanted to get the shadows right so that you'd naturally focus on her fingers at the edge of Zeno's armor, tips brushing Zeno's bare skin. In my purse (hate having to carry that thing), my phone buzzed and I prayed it was Sierra texting me.

After the service I snuck off to the restroom.

You home? Come write, Sierra had texted.

Can't. I typed and paused. She hadn't said anything obnoxious yet about me being Jewish so I figured I should go for it and see. I added, *I'm at temple for Purim.*

What's that? she asked.

It's a holiday. Kids dress up and there's a big party.

There was a long pause during which I washed my hands and then stood in the hall outside the bathroom holding the phone.

Oh, there are costumes? What are you wearing? she asked and the question sent a tingling, lurching feeling down my legs.

I'm not a kid, I don't dress up, I typed back.

So you're in jeans and a flannel like when I met you?

No…I'm in a dress. I couldn't stop grinning; she remembered what I'd been wearing when we met!

I bet you look great in a dress, she said.

I have to go mingle, I typed and slid the phone into my purse. I went down the hall trying to not look like a leering horndog who wondered what it was like to rub your pantyhose-covered leg against someone else's pantyhose-covered leg. By the time I'd walked back to the sanctuary, I had my smile contained to a reasonable level.

"Ah there she is," my father said as I approached.

He was standing beside a man with sandy blond hair, a neatly trimmed beard and a small child perched on his hip. It was cute to see a guy holding a kid like he did it all the time, like if he had the chance to put the kid down or hand it off, he'd decline.

They were talking with two dark-haired women. The one in the ruffled tawny blouse seemed more into my father than the one in the turquoise sweater.

My father introduced me to them and I immediately forgot their names. He told tawny blouse, "Lauren goes to the same high school as your son. Is he here? How's he doing this semester?"

"Oh great," she said and scanned the crowd. "He's enjoying hockey. You two must know each other."

We didn't, but I said, "I'm sure we've met. But I don't follow much hockey."

"Lauren is an artist," my father said with an inflection that made the word a boast and an insult at the same time.

"Is that what you'll go to college for?" the woman asked.

Of course, I replied in my mind, but my mouth said, "I'm thinking about design, maybe architecture."

Or, you know, disgusting corporate law so I could protect polluters and shred class action suits like my father. So not. Isaac might be in law school but he was leaning toward International Human Rights. An evil part of me wanted him to go into Environmental and come up against our father someday and win. (Sad fact: Isaac probably wouldn't win.)

Springboarding off the fact that I'd be the one nonlawyer in the family, my father was going on about Isaac. Tawny blouse's son came over to us after she gave him a wave so wildly enthusiastic that orbiting satellites must have noticed.

"Travis, this is Lauren. She goes to your school," she said.

"Hey." He nodded and held out his hand, not making eye contact. I was a good five inches taller than him. He had a long face with thick eyebrows that would look great sketched in charcoal.

We stepped to the side and compared the classes we were in, though I already knew we had none together. My memory for names might suck, but I'm great at faces. The other adults had wandered off, leaving Travis's mom and my father leaning in close and chatting. She was in high flirt mode.

My phone hummed and I itched to pull it out and see if Sierra had more to say about my dress. I couldn't do that in sight of my father. I'd never hear the end of it later if he saw me texting in a social setting. He already thought my social skills were exceedingly fail.

"Do you want to get cake and find someplace to sit?" I asked Travis.

He gazed longingly across the open middle of the synagogue to where a group of boys were shoving each other and laughing.

"How about you cover for me?" I upgraded the offer. "Let's walk across the room together and you can drop me off at those chairs so I can text my friends."

He chuckled. "It's a deal. I'll tell my mom."

We turned back to where our parents were talking.

"...her teacher called us in for a meeting because she was concerned about Lauren's reading level," my father was saying.

Sick dread and falling inside. Heat up the inside of my spine, in my cheeks. Blood hot in my skull. This story again; always this story, or one like it. He never told the stories I'd want him to tell. Nothing about art, about teachers praising my sense of perspective or visual narrative, about the local comic anthology I was in. He told stories that made him laugh, that matched with his ultra-narrow view of the world.

"In second grade, the teacher thought she couldn't read because she wasn't picking up any of the books," he said. "When they had quiet reading time, Lauren sat by herself and the teacher thought she was slow. We had to take her in to see a specialist. Turned out because she was reading those cartoon books, she didn't think the books in the classroom were real books. After all, they didn't have cartoons in them. She thought only books with pictures were real books."

They were both laughing, my father genuinely because he thought this was one of the funniest things he'd ever heard. The woman because she was going to laugh at everything he said.

"Wasn't that funny?" he asked me. "Do you remember that?"

"Yep," I told him. I didn't remember it. Why would I? As if a story about people thinking I was stupid and how he got me checked out for learning disabilities was funny. I remembered how he'd locked up my comics for months and asked me if I wanted people to think I was stupid.

The weirdest part of this whole business was that he thought I'd want to laugh about this with him. The hot, sick feeling was inverting itself in my chest, sucking away into a nothing place of numbness. I forced a smile.

He put his hand on my shoulder; he only ever touched me in public. When people could see, he was the loving father raising a successful if physically awkward daughter.

I said, "Travis and I are going to get cake and go hang out with his friends over there, okay?"

The cake sat at the far end of a long, blue-and-white decorated table loaded with food, way more than the usual *oneg shabbat* on Fridays. Plate in hand, I walked Travis to his friends and dropped down into one of the empty blond-wood chairs that made up the body of the sanctuary. I set my phone on the chair next to my leg.

No text from Sierra. I had a note from Mom wishing me a happy Purim. I sent her a quick message: *Thanks, you too!*

I texted Sierra: *So what are you wearing?*

The reply said: *Black, like always…but I'm not Sierra.*

It was Sierra's number. Was this a riddle? A flirt? Or someone else with Sierra's phone?

I wrote: *I don't like puzzles.*

Nor dresses, I gather. No prob, this is Blake. Sierra's in the shower. I'll tell her to text you when she's out.

What are you doing with Sierra's phone? I asked.

What I wanted to ask was what she was doing hanging out at Sierra's house with her phone while Sierra was in the shower. Was that a regular thing friends did? Jenny never handed me her phone and went to take a shower, but then I was her lesbian friend and we just did homework together.

She said to say hi if you texted, that you're bored, Blake replied. *She says to tell you she's wearing nothing but a smile, which isn't true, she's got a towel and is about to put on sweatpants that make her look like my grandmother.*

I have to go, I wrote. *I'll see her online later.*

I wandered around the cavernous room, got a plate of cookies to pick at, stood by my father until he started another embarrassing story, went to the bathroom again. I ended up watching kids acting out the Purim story with far more martial arts moves than the original. (Queen Esther, Persian Jewish Ninja, owned all her scenes!)

When we'd been there long enough to seem socially awesome, my father waved to me and we left. He dropped me off at home: pulled into the garage, saw me safely through the inner door, put the car in reverse and left. It was midweek so he could have been going back to the firm to work, or to go see whatever girlfriend he had going.

I checked my computer but Sierra wasn't online. Hanging out with Blake? Had they gone somewhere together? I made bad microwave popcorn that tasted like burnt packing peanuts and tried to watch a movie.

"I wasn't reading cartoons," I said to the empty living room. "I was reading comics."

My words trailed off into nothingness.

When I got into bed later, the nothingness was still there. In the dark, the ceiling seemed to stretch away from me forever. I stared into the vastness of space, as if I could see to the edge of the galaxy and beyond it, to all the galaxies.

I didn't know how to tell people—on the rare times I participated in conversations like "stuff that scares me" or "what's worse? Zombies or demons?"—that pictures of outer space scared me worse than anything else. Monsters, zombies, demons, death, destruction, serial killers, I didn't care. But one image of a spiral galaxy on a black background spotted with space dust and other galaxies and I stopped breathing.

What was out there? Where did it end? What happened at the end? My mind zoomed out beyond the Milky Way, beyond the other galaxies that were all expanding on spacetime like an unbelievably huge balloon. I'd read a book on the universe trying to get over this fear but that had made it worse.

What were black holes? What would happen if I fell into one? The gravity was so strong that even light couldn't escape the event horizon—so what did that mean for consciousness? If I fell into one, would I be wiped out forever?

What was it like to cease to exist? Now that I thought about it, I had to try to imagine it. My whole body got freezing cold and started shaking. I sat up and turned the light on again, wrapping my blanket around me. I got out of bed and distracted myself by reading at my desk until my face was falling onto the page.

CHAPTER SIX

On Sunday afternoon with the chores done, I went back to the story to take up Sierra's prompt and fill in more about Zeno. I'd been thinking about her—about Zeno, and also about Sierra. I couldn't stop thinking about Sierra. She was so different from everyone around me. Not like colored hair was that rare, but the way she put herself out there, the way she'd introduced herself as the Queen of Rogues that day we met. She and the story swirled together in my mind.

Who did I want to be in that world? What should I make Zeno into? I didn't want to be a Mary Sue, a character with disproportionate power who could get out of every conflict without effort. Zeno had to have weaknesses, insecurities, fears. But not the same as mine.

I should start by answering the questions posted by the first part of the scene, like, what *was* in the bag?

Lauren:
Zeno lifted her bag. She accompanied the Queen up to her throne and sat in the cushioned seat at her right side. Servants brought an ewer of wine and poured it into chilled cups.

"Tell me where you've been," the Queen said.

"I went in search of an ancient artifact that Cypher said has the power to reduce matter to its true form, but I only found half of it. When I touched it, this armor came over me. I don't know what it means. I have always been proud of my past, being one of the race of wolf-shifters, but I fear I'm something else."

"Cypher will know," the Queen said and closed her eyes in concentration as she telepathically called to the Master of Secrets.

Cypher teleported into the center of the throne room. For the race of immortal ones, the Illudani, she was small in stature, the height of a human, with tousled pink hair and eyes like chips of lapis rolled in gray dust.

In the other stories, Cypher tended to appear out of nowhere and say whatever was needed. As Master of Secrets, she was a perfect plot device. What did I *want* her to say?

I got a pop out of the fridge and made myself cinnamon toast. When I got back to my room, my chat window was flashing. I'd put my screen name on the account I created to post as Zeno so anyone else in the story could contact me. But I was surprised to see the line:

Hey this is Blake, did you survive your thing the other night?

I remembered sitting up in bed the night of Purim shaking because I felt like I was sliding off the edge of the universe. Did that count as surviving? Either way, I wasn't going to tell Blake.

Yeah, I wrote back. *What did you end up doing?*

Dustin and Kordi came over, she wrote, but didn't elaborate. Instead she added, *Do you want me to write a few lines for Cypher?*

Sure, I told her because now I wasn't thinking about the story. I was thinking about Dustin and Sierra and wondering if I had no chance or less than no chance.

Blake:

Walking up the length of the throne room, Cypher bent to the worn leather bag at Zeno's feet and unlaced the top. She peered inside.

"This is only half," she said. "But it was enough to begin unlocking the secrets of your past. We must find the other half. Also I don't recommend anyone touch this."

"What secrets?" Zeno asked. "I'm a noble wolf-shifter, that's all there is to it."

Cypher laughed. It was clear that Zeno had been memory wiped at some point. Although Cypher didn't know everything Zeno had lost, she wanted to help figure it out.

"You were given to that family to raise, but wolf-shifter isn't all that you are," Cypher told Zeno. "That's not your true family. Didn't you ever wonder why you left that life so readily? Why you took to thieving as the most natural pursuit in the galaxy? Why you're so good at it?"

As I read the words, my eyes burned. I liked it. Of course I liked it. But it also made me grind my teeth. Maybe it was the fact of a new person, someone I didn't even know, talking about me.

But this wasn't me. Zeno was a character, not even one I created. She was made up, even if it felt real: the part about being memory-wiped, the part about not being from this family, not being what I thought I was.

Lauren:
Zeno seemed confused and troubled by Cypher's words. "I always felt there was something different about me," she said. "But where does this armor come from? And if I was given to the family that I've always believed was mine, who did that?"

Cypher said, "Someone went through a lot of trouble to make you think you're not what you are. We can expect that your true nature is deeply hidden."

Zeno flexed her arms, watching the neatly-assembled parts of her new armor slide over and around each other. It was part of her. She asked the armor on her right arm to recede, and it did. The metal plates and connectors rolled away from each other into nowhere. The Queen put the tips of her fingers on Zeno's bare bicep.

"Still flesh and blood under all that," she said.

"Am I?" Zeno asked.

I posted that much and then I had to stop and think for a while. Did I want Zeno to be a person or a machine or a combination of the two?

I got out my sketchpad and started drawing her arm with the metal pieces on it dissolving into nowhere. The first few tries came out looking like crap. Literally. On the first one the metal armor bits resembled poop floating in air. On the third attempt, I managed a bit of the effect I wanted.

I put down the sketchpad and went to get more Pepsi. When I got back to the computer, I saw that someone else had posted in the Queen of Rogues' Court story thread.

Dustin:
Lithos, the Lord of Stone, burst into the Queen of Rogues' throne room. The Queen was on her throne, radiant as always, with Cypher at her feet and in the chair to her right a strangely familiar woman, half encased in armor, who reminded him of Zeno the thief.

The Queen rose to greet him with a kiss. "My Lord, what brings you in such a hurry?"

"I've made a great discovery," he said. "Our war on the High God is not lost as we thought. If we can find the locus of the High God's power, we can become the High God."

"That legend has circulated for centuries," the Queen said. "But no one has ever been able to find this locus."

"Yes, because they've been searching for it in the wrong way. The locus isn't hidden in a specific place, it's hidden in time. The locus of power is in the future."

Everyone gasped.

He continued, "Its power reaches back to our time and empowers the High God, but if we can redirect that power, it will be ours. We can finally end the tyranny over the galaxy. I'll need Cypher to help me find the precise time in the future where the locus is located and then Zeno must prepare to go forward to that time and redirect its power."

"What's mine is yours," the Queen said. "If we're to rule this galaxy, you may use Cypher and Zeno as you see fit."

Blake:
"Employ," Cypher said into the surprised silence of the room. "You may employ us. No one uses me. Zeno, up to you if you like being used or not."

Before Zeno could speak, the Queen drew herself up to her full height. "Of course my Knights are *always* under my protection."

Dustin:
"I meant no offense," Lord Stone said. "Quite the contrary. You have the most accomplished infomancer and thief in the entire galaxy. My own court is many times the size of yours and yet I cannot replicate what you have here. I merely seek to move us forward speedily to our goal. I protect your people as my own, as closer than my own, as my own heart."

Ugh, sappy. Dustin went on from there, detailing a bunch of stuff about time travel and how we were all supposed to get the locus from the future. I could scan that later.

I had to give Blake respect for putting Dustin in his place. But I wanted the two of them to wander off in another story direction so I could write with Sierra alone.

CHAPTER SEVEN

I worked on my sketch: an image of Zeno standing near the throne, holding her arm out as the armor receded. The Queen was at the foot of the throne with her hand on Zeno's arm.

There were two illustrations of the Queen already online, drawn by Bear, and a few photographs of Sierra dressed up as her from last Halloween. She'd put on high boots that laced up to her knees with huge soles so she was almost tall. She had gray jeans tucked into the boots and a tight, oily-looking black shirt. On top of that was a dusky overcoat covered in buckles and lines of safety pins. She'd spiked her hair and frosted it white-purple, done her eyes in heavy kohl and gold eye shadow.

She was leaning on the arm of a stringy guy with coral-red hair, dressed in tan and brown robes that reminded me of Obi-Wan Kenobi from *Star Wars*. I resized the photo in the preview window so I could see her without him.

I waited impatiently to catch her online without the others. Would there be more touching of Zeno's armor or more... developments in that direction? Days later when I finally saw her online, I had an attack of shyness. She added to the story but only more detail about the plot with the High God.

Later in the week when my sketch was good enough to show, I messaged her: *I did a sketch of the Queen and Zeno. Do you want to see it?*

YES!

Don't post it or share it, okay? It's not done, I told her.

I promise!

I sent her the sketch and seconds later she was typing into chat: *This is AMAZING! I love the look on my face. You're really good at this. I'm jealous, is that silly? You can draw and write. I can only write. I wish I could do that. This armor effect is so cool.*

Thanks, I said.

You should post it. And write more in the story. You left your scene hanging, you know.

I did? I asked. It didn't feel like I'd left it hanging. It felt like Dustin hijacked it.

Sierra wrote: *You never answered Cypher's question.*

What question?

If Zeno likes to be used, she said.

I could feel myself blushing. The kind of blush that goes nuclear across your face and tingles up your scalp. Thank God I was sitting in front of a computer and not a live human being. I took a sip of my pop but it wasn't cool enough to help with how hot my face was.

I guess it depends, I wrote.

On what?

On who's asking and what they mean, I said. *I mean, there's the gross kind of used and there's the other kind.*

The sexy kind? she asked.

Was it possible to die of blushing? I wrote, *Um, yeah. But I haven't...I mean, I wouldn't know. I guess Zeno might...*

Hahaha, relax. I'm just teasing you.

Oh, sure, I typed.

Her words flashed up on my screen and the heat in my body turned into nausea. I hated being teased. I hated that I let her get me all flustered and we were only bullshitting.

* * *

I stayed away from the story for a few days, then got too curious and went to catch up on the action. There was a bunch of scheming between Dustin/Lithos and Sierra as the Queen. It included wondering about if Zeno might really be from Lithos's court. I had to shut down that idea.

Hey, Sierra messaged me. *There you are. Where have you been?*

School and stuff, I told her.

I missed having you in the story. It's more fun when you're there. I'm dying to know what you're going to do with Zeno.

My backstabbing heart forgot all about feeling led on and stupid in the power discussion days ago. She'd missed me! (Settle down, stupid heart.)

Not make Zeno from Lithos's court, I said.

Hahaha, of course not! She can be whatever you want. And we should totally get her a girlfriend.

That would be cool.

At least one of me would have one.

I've always wondered if someday the Queen and Zeno would hook up, Sierra wrote.

Heart beating all fast, my fingers feeling like hot sausages on the keyboard, I typed: *Isn't the Queen with Lithos?*

She doesn't have to be exclusive with him.

Can I ask you a question? I asked.

Of course!

When did you come out to yourself? You said you were kind of dating a girl, when did you know?

Sierra paused for a bit and wrote: *I guess when I got together with her. Last year of high school, which was last year, we were in this band together and we started hanging out and then we were more than friends. But we didn't officially say we were girlfriends. I don't feel like I have to define myself. Love is love, you know.*

Not really, I said. *I'm not into guys and I figure people should know that, especially guy people. I guess definitions work for me. But that's great about you, I mean, you have a lot of options.*

She replied, *Not as many as you'd think. I'm not interested unless someone's smart and compelling.*

That's your type? Smart? I asked, hoping that didn't make it too obvious that I thought she was ridiculously cute and was trying to figure out what she liked.

She wrote back: *Lol, no, I also like tall and a little skinny and artsy, and they have to like the same kinds of music I do. Why?*

Tall and artsy I had in the bag. I wanted to say something clever and brilliant, but I had nothing so I backed up a little.

Just curious, I wrote. *It's not like I'm planning on seducing you. I'm not the type of person who goes around seducing other people because, you might have noticed, I'm quite introverted.*

Have you tried? she asked.

Seducing people? Uh, no. My primo seduction time is all occupied by me sitting around pitying myself.

Sierra wrote: *Maybe you're afraid of getting hurt.*

I said: *You wouldn't say that if you saw what my options were here in Duluth.*

Hey!!! You should come down to the Cities. Do you think your parents would let you?

I can ask my father. He'll probably say yes. He mostly doesn't care what I do.

We'd love to have you come down. You can stay here, there are lots of couches to crash on. You can meet everyone in the story.

Are you sure? I asked. I felt like if she asked me to, I'd get up from my desk, go to my car and drive down to the Cities right then.

Let me check with my roommate, she said.

I didn't take it too seriously. But over the next few weeks she kept bringing it up. She also returned to the idea of Zeno and the Queen hooking up. To be on the safe side, I had to assume she wasn't really flirting. But I kept getting fluttery when I'd see her log in. I had to go find out.

CHAPTER EIGHT

Spring break in two weeks would be the perfect time. It was less than a three-hour drive from Duluth to the Twin Cities. I impatiently waited for my father to be home on a Sunday afternoon and seem relaxed, and then asked him if I could spend spring break with friends in the Cities. Of course he said no.

I persisted. The debate went on over a few evenings, in measured tones, points and counterpoints. I wanted to raise objections and ask to approach the bench, but those jokes weren't funny to my father who would accuse me (accurately) of mocking the legal profession.

In his mind law is the noblest of all professions and possibly the oldest. I agree about that second point. Someone must have hired another person to argue for them way before people figured they could sell sex for money. I like to think that bazillions of years ago people had sex for fun, but argument was already serious business.

I might not have won *Lauren vs. Father 916 Great Room 2015*, except that he seemed to be on the outs with whatever woman he was dating and had to keep coming back to the house. He insisted on talking to Sierra's parents on the phone. He might have gotten a cop friend to run background checks on them; I wouldn't be surprised. But he finally agreed!

I could spend spring break in the Cities at Sierra's house as long as I texted at least once a day and let him know I was okay. And no drinking or drugs. He didn't mention sex. Either it didn't occur to him that I was old enough to be having sex or, because I was a lesbian, he couldn't figure out what he should worry about in that department.

Or maybe, like me, he thought I wouldn't be lucky enough to get laid this week anyhow.

I left at dinner time on Friday before the official week of spring break (and before my father could get home and change his mind). That gave me nine days in the Cities if Sierra didn't get sick of me. After school I packed, ate a frozen dinner (the turkey one with the little cup of cranberry sauce because I felt celebratory), and got on the road.

I got lost in the Cities. Twice.

I'd been to the Cities with my family when I was a kid. (After Mom left there weren't any family trips.) I vaguely remembered the zoo and the mall. But the duplex Sierra rented was near the University of Minnesota. I overshot my exit and ended up in South Minneapolis, turned around, got on the wrong freeway and found myself north, but on the wrong side of the river from her house. I didn't want to double back again (and risk ending up in downtown), so I meandered north until I could cross the Mississippi and worked my way back down to her address.

I found Sierra's house after ten p.m. I parked in the back and texted her from the car because it was late and I was having an attack of shyness. She opened the back door and stood silhouetted in golden light, curvy and unfamiliar. I wanted to draw her like this, with the shadows stretching out in front, detailing the uneven edges of her hair in long, sharp points like knives.

Grabbing my bag and suitcase, I hopped out of the car and crossed the short backyard. She held the door open for me.

"Glad you could make it," she said.

The kitchen would have horrified my father. Everything in here was older than me. The floor was so worn that the pattern stamped into the linoleum had rubbed away in a darkened path from the outer door to the interior of the house. The cabinets bore at least five coats of paint: a hard-chipped corner showed sunshine, avocado, citron and taupe under dirty-napkin white.

The kitchen led to the dining room with Sierra's room to the left and a bathroom to the right. Next came Cyd's room. Cyd was the very straight girl who rented the place with her. Sierra introduced her like that online, very straight, like there was another orientation on the far side of hetero from us.

On the far side of the dining room was a substantial living room with mangy berber carpet and two sagging couches, all shades of gray in the dim light. The molding on the door to Sierra's room had chunks taken out of it from decades of being banged into (all the molding in the duplex looked like the setting of multiple kung fu sword battles).

Sierra's bedroom was almost twice the size of mine, with a bed, a desk, a couch and a dresser. I only half noticed because she'd grabbed my hand when she pulled me into the room. She pointed to the end of the couch and said I could put my stuff there. I didn't move. She was holding my hand. We both stood there until she dropped my hand and walked back out into the kitchen.

"There's pizza, you want some?" she asked.

I was still trying to figure out why a person would put a couch in a bedroom and where I was expected to sleep. I dropped my stuff where she said.

"Sure, what kind?" I asked, walking back into the kitchen.

She was standing in front of the open fridge. "I've got part of a Hawaiian and part of a pepperoni."

"Oh, I'm okay."

"You don't like either of those?"

"I don't eat pork," I told her.

"Why?"

I saw curiosity in her wide eyes, but that was it. She wasn't staring at me like a total weirdo. I decided she could get the long answer.

"It's not like I keep kosher, but I think that not eating pork is a good idea. It keeps me mindful, you know, and also pigs are pretty smart."

"Oh that's cool. When we first met, I wondered what you were. I mean, you know," she laughed. "That sounded dumb. I thought maybe you were something exotic, like Arabic."

My brain stalled out, unsure how to explain that Jews and Arabs have a common genetic heritage but, you know, a few thousand years of cultural baggage. Did she know that Jewish was as much an ethnicity as a religion? Probably not. Did I want to have to explain that tonight? Clearly not.

I recovered enough to say, "That's me. Totally exotic. Sometimes clueless people try to talk to me in Spanish. I mean, not that there aren't Spanish Jews, but we're not. My family isn't. Um, and it's not that I'm calling you clueless."

"You'd better not be," she said. "Do you want anything else? I've got…toast."

"I'm fine. I snacked on the way down."

"Hot chocolate?"

"Sure."

She got two mismatched mugs from the cupboard and dumped water and cocoa packets into them, then put them in the microwave for a few minutes. When they were steaming, she set mine on the counter and carried hers into the dining room. Mine was a tall, white mug, scuffed all over, that said "Random Mutation," on the front. I lifted it in both hands and followed her into the dining room, watching the floor so I wouldn't trip.

A huge, ruddy wooden table dominated the dining room, thoroughly pitted (knife throwing target practice?), surrounded by six chairs. Three of the chairs matched, warm oak with a darker grain; two were lighter ash with orange cushions; and the last, at the foot of the table, was dark brown folding metal. Sierra sat in the oak chair at the head of the table and I took the chair nearest her.

"We have to keep it down," she said and pointed at the closed door across the room. "Cyd's sleeping. She's not a light sleeper, but no yelling."

"I was utterly about to yell," I said.

Sierra smirked and sipped her cocoa. "What do you think of the story?"

"It's fun. And awesome."

"If you don't want the Queen and Zeno to hook up, let me know," she said.

In the dim lamplight the greenish part of her blue eyes took on a golden hue. With the purple streaks in her hair, the color of her eyes seemed beyond real, like she was herself and the Queen at the same time.

I forgot if she was talking about two characters in a story or the two of us. I forced myself to unclench my hands from around the Random Mutation mug and rubbed my damp palms on my jeans.

"No," I said. "I mean yes, I think they should, it's, um, good character development. But…I don't think I can draw that."

Her carmine lips opened in a soundless laugh. She reached across the table to touch the back of my hand, a light tap with her fingertips.

She said, "I have faith in you. But you totally don't have to. Can you draw something cool for the locus of the High God? Like circles and spheres and galaxies and stuff?"

We talked about the story for almost an hour, until I was fading with exhaustion. She made a bed for me on the couch in her bedroom. It was ancient in a way that made it more comfortable once I found the right position across its sagging cushions.

After Sierra turned out the lights, I listened to her soft breathing and imagined that I could feel Cyd across the hall in deep sleep. It had been years since I'd tried to sleep in a house with anyone other than my father, who never made a sound. Isaac used to mumble in his sleep sometimes and I'd hear him if I was awake. I followed Sierra's breathing, like the gentle waves on a lake shore, and fell asleep.

* * *

In the morning I met Cyd and she offered to show me around the Cities. She was as tall as I am and impossibly statuesque. She had the kind of high, sharp cheekbones that I'd kill for and a hawkish, elegant nose. Her skin was a shade lighter than mine, reddish hair cut stylishly short and swept to one side. I wondered what people mistook her for, but I was too chicken to ask.

Sierra and I got into Cyd's beat-up Honda, me in the front with Sierra leaning in from the backseat, her hand on my seat's backrest and the tips of her fingers tickling my shoulder. Cyd drove us over the bridge and through downtown, up past Loring Park where the Pride Festival is each year, past the Walker Art Center (that looks like the head of an angry robot ready to rise up and defend Minneapolis). We went through Uptown, around a bunch of lakes, along a pretty, winding creek to a park with a waterfall and a sandwich shop.

I got a crawfish salad sandwich and, holding it up said to Sierra, "See, not kosher."

She gave me a puzzled look (that made her nose crinkle adorably), but Cyd said, "A girl in my class calls all the McDonald's breakfast sandwiches 'McTreif.'"

I laughed and almost got part of a crawfish up my nose. "Treif" was the Yiddish word for not kosher and it was awesome to hear Cyd use it.

After sandwiches, Cyd drove us to Dreamhaven Books and I browsed blissfully until Sierra started standing next to me. Cyd dropped us off at the house and went to a lecture by one of her acupuncture teachers.

Sierra wanted to run out to pick up snacks for tonight when other folks from the story would come over. Plus she had to stop by the secondhand fashion and artsy gift shop where she worked to pick up her paycheck. She asked if she could borrow my car and I figured why not. She'd had an old car that died last fall, so she had to be a better driver than me.

"You can stay here and get comfy," she said. "You don't need to come on my boring errands."

I'd happily have done all kinds of boring stuff with her, but she seemed to want to go on her own, so I stayed. I read and dozed off on the couch in her bedroom. When I got up, there were unfamiliar voices in the living room. I heard a woman and a man laughing: hers was a husky, open-throated sound and his a light chuckle.

Was that Sierra's boyfriend Dustin? If so, I was pre-intimidated by the evidence of his sense of humor. I went into the bathroom and contemplated my hair. Frizztastic. I wet my hands and ran them over the frizz. It lay down restlessly, like a dog who hasn't been for a walk yet.

The woman's smoky voice carried through the bathroom door: "No. The Greeks didn't *believe* in zero. That's what fucked up their mathematics."

"You're such a geek," another guy's voice said. Not the same as the guy who'd been chuckling, this voice fell in the bass range but with a grating overtone.

"Ah the sound of envy," the girl replied.

The first male voice (the chuckling one), said, "The Greeks were dicks. Are you going to play?" His voice was silvery without being too light.

I flushed the toilet, so I missed what came next, and went into the kitchen for a can of Pepsi. There wasn't anything else to do; time to check out the living room.

The wide room had two ancient beige couches and a heavy, ebony-stained oak coffee table that had been shoved against the couch to the far right. Three people sat on the floor in front of the nearer couch with cards spread out between them. Not regular playing cards. Against the backdrop of the smokestack-colored carpet, bright illustrations of monsters, swirling magic, mutated forms, and armored warriors stared up at me.

A guy with a barrel-shaped body in a navy hoodie sat cross-legged, his back to me. His dense brown hair, made a stark contrast to his eggshell skin at the back of his neck and all down the heavy, furred calves showing below his gray cargo shorts.

Across the room, sat a taller guy with chestnut skin and a broad, flat nose. Close-cropped midnight hair, a diamond-shaped face with defined cheekbones and arched brows gave him a careful, pretty look. He wore black-framed hipster glasses, the only noncolorful part of an ensemble that included powder-blue sneakers, jade jeans, and a periwinkle shirt covered by a vibrant indigo vest, fully buttoned.

By comparison, the girl sitting perpendicular to him, leaning back against the couch, was a shocking absence of color: jet-black hair and olive skin, obsidian jeans, coal button down shirt, onyx suit jacket with the sleeves rolled to her elbows. Her bare feet rested on the outstretched legs of the colorful guy.

I remembered texting at Purim, "What are you wearing?" She'd said, "Black...like always" and I felt the off-kilter disorientation of knowing her without knowing her.

She looked up me with slate-blue eyes. Her gaze flicked away and back, away and back, then held mine. Her eyes reminded me of a busted smartphone: screen cracked with a spiderweb of lines, shattered, indecipherable text shining brightly through. I thought she was like a torch: the kind angry villagers use to set windmills on fire.

The barrel guy saw her staring at me. He lumbered to his feet and held out a hand. "I'm Roy."

It wasn't like we were meeting at a lawn party. What was the protocol for meeting people in a strange house where you'd already been napping? I shook his hand, to my regret, because his palm was damp and he held mine for way too long.

"Lauren," I said.

"Oh yeah, from the story? Then you already know Blake and Kordell."

Blake was shorter than I expected. I could almost see her making a good master of secrets, except that her nose was broad and kind of cute, not the least bit sinister. Maybe that was a tactic to set people off guard.

"Join us," Kordell said with a gesture to the wide open center of the room between their game and the coffee table. I folded myself down to sitting, equidistant between Kordell and Roy.

"How do you like Zeno?" Blake asked.

I pushed a drop of condensation down the side of my Pepsi can and said, "She's…uh, I think she should have more of a power than she does."

"More than being a werewolf?"

The werewolf thing didn't match at all with the science fictiony nature of the story. It was hard for me to picture Zeno turning into a wolf inside of a giant spaceship—like that would be an asset. Maybe that was Blake's point. Maybe she wanted to make a character with a fairly useless power.

"Why did you pick a werewolf?" I asked.

"Irony," Blake said.

She looked away again, and back, her compact, rose lips forming a half smile. Was the expression meant for me or was she smiling to herself?

Blake said, "The original Zeno developed a paradox to prove that motion was impossible so that he could argue for a changeless universe. I thought it would be funny if this Zeno, the thief, could change shape. Maybe I should have called her anti-Zeno, but that doesn't make for a very good name and I was getting obscure enough already."

The words came out of her mouth clear and rapid. There were so many of them that it took me a minute to process. My Zeno was named after who? What now?

Blake held her cards in one square-fingered hand, facedown against her thigh. The fingers of her free hand tapped her leg as she spoke, but not in rhythm with the words. It made her seem more nervous than me. I wasn't going to turn out to be the weakest member of this pack after all. Next to the crazy girl, the sort-of-crazy girl seems sane. I felt like a dick, both for thinking that and for how relaxed it made me feel.

She went on talking, "But I also picked Zeno because he discovered infinity for the Greeks. Even if they couldn't deal with it. I figured my character, Cypher, is about the number zero, about dividing by zero, teleporting through the zero point energy of the universe—and Zeno is about infinities."

A pause. Fingers tapping without a pattern. She said, "Maybe Zeno can turn into an infinite number of forms? Then it's super ironic but also makes a point."

The basis for my character was infinity? And Cypher was zero? I liked these ideas. I saw them overlapping in the space of my mind, like the shapes of a sketch coming together to make the first draft of an illustration.

"You'd have to put a lot of limitations on that or it wouldn't make good conflict," I said. Caught up, thinking out loud. "Changing shape has to cost her physically or emotionally. Maybe it messes with Zeno's head, not ever knowing what her real shape is. Maybe she can take any form, but she doesn't want to, she simply wants to be herself but she doesn't know how."

I sketched a shape in the air with my hands: indistinct boundaries.

"I like that," Blake said, burning darkly. Staring at me over the smashed rainbow of the cards. "Zeno is everything but she's afraid she's nothing."

The words "she's afraid she's nothing" fell into me like stones dropped in a well, sending ripples through my body. I *was* afraid of nothing, afraid of becoming nothing.

"Zeno the infinite," I said, trying to laugh. The words came out flat. I was cold from the inside.

Blake gazed over my shoulder, across the room, then down at her cards.

Kordell said, "You bring together limits, zero and infinity and you've basically got calculus."

Blake grinned sidelong at him. "You're making it sound *less* cool."

He rolled his eyes at her theatrically. She leaned toward him and shoved her palm against his shoulder.

"Play your stupid card," Roy said, frowning at his cards in an effort to not watch them.

Blake threw a card down on top of the three in front of him. He groaned and swept his three cards to one side.

"How's that for a stupid card?" she asked.

I went into Sierra's room to get a heavier flannel because I was freezing. I wanted to get into the tub and warm up, but I'd never taken a bath in a house with strangers. Usually when I was in the tub at home I was alone, and I mean alone in the whole house.

Blake couldn't have seen me like that, couldn't have known how close to the truth she was. She was all about the ideas. No one saw me. That was the trouble with being so much nothing. They didn't look at me. They hadn't for so long that I was used to it. Being looked at felt like too much fire under a skin wrapped around ice.

I left my Pepsi on the dresser and went into the kitchen to find a hot cocoa packet and stall until Sierra got back.

CHAPTER NINE

Sierra returned while they were trying to teach me the card game, "Mystics & Mutants." Each deck included a hero with magic spells and an army. You fought each other until the last person standing won. I lost miserably in the first game because every card had so many different ways it could be played, especially with the mutations. I kept getting distracted by the art and missing possible attacks.

Sierra came into the living room through the front door, accompanied by a copper-haired guy with a skinny, curved body like a longbow. I recognized him from the Halloween photos as the one in the Obi-Wan robe, so he had to be Dustin. They were carrying pizza boxes and paused halfway between the door and the dining room, giving off the smell of onions, dough, spicy sauce and pepperoni.

"I got you veggie," Sierra told me. "I hope that's okay."

"That's great."

I thought I should get up but nobody else was, so I stayed in the middle of the living room, twisted around to see Sierra. She had on her cool black overcoat with the metal. Her eyes were outlined darkly and swept up with caramel eyeshadow.

"Lauren doesn't eat pork," she announced to the room, with a trace of pride that I found weird but charming.

Kordell asked, "Halal, kosher, or vegetarian?"

"Kosher-lite," I said.

He chuckled and started picking up his cards. "I like that. Can I steal it?"

"Be my guest," I said and pushed my cards into a pile. I didn't mind that the second game was over before it had gotten going. I was glad to see Sierra.

"Where are you ever going to use it?" Blake asked him.

"There are black Jews," he replied.

"There are a lot of things. But you've been going on about being a proud atheist all year."

He sighed in defeat as he put decks back into the box.

Sierra and Dustin the longbow carried the pizzas through the house to the kitchen. Everyone but me followed. There wasn't that much room in the kitchen. I'd wait until everyone else had theirs.

I picked up Roy's cards, put them in their box, and pulled the coffee table into the middle of the room again. It was too narrow for playing cards, but it would fit plates fine.

Dustin came back with Sierra right behind. He was an inch shorter than me with a long, gaunt-cheeked face, high-crowned head, and skin like freckle-infested cornsilk. His few boyish curls were the only round element to him. He wore ash-colored jeans tucked into earthy workboots and a fawn mock turtleneck sweater that even I could tell was the wrong shade for his skin tone.

"This is Lauren," Sierra told him. "Lauren, Dustin."

"It's good to put a face to a name," he said.

"Thanks, same," I responded, though I remained annoyed that he existed, that Sierra was dating him.

Sierra dropped into the middle of one couch and Dustin lowered himself next to her. She patted the empty space on her other side.

"I need to get some pizza," I told her.

The others were coming out of the kitchen. Roy took the far side of the other couch facing Dustin. Kordell planted himself in the middle, right next to Roy, who gave him an irritated glare.

Blake carried two plates across the dining room and offered me one. It held two slices of veggie pizza with a napkin tucked under the plate. When I took it, she went to sit next to Kordell before I could say thanks.

Sierra watched as I settled beside her with my plate. I couldn't read the expression on her face but it wasn't happy. I hoped she was getting a sting of jealousy—and that it was for me and not that she was secretly into Blake.

That would be my luck. Someday she and Dustin would split up and it would turn out she was into Blake the whole time. We were both dark-haired, slender, not-ghostly-pale white girls. Blake's hair was more true black than mine and completely straight, cut in a messy shag to her shoulders, framing her face. My hair went past my shoulders in coffee-brown curls when I was lucky and a pyramidal mass of frizzy Jewfro when I wasn't. I was also a hand taller than Blake, but sitting you didn't see that. Maybe Sierra picked me out to be friends because I was a more accessible version of Blake. That would be so great.

Roy made it through a slice of pizza while everyone else was halfway into theirs. Dustin leaned around Sierra and asked, "What's your story, Lauren?"

"Apparently I'm an infinitely shape-shifting werewolf," I said.

"That's redundant," Roy protested, holding his second slice barely away from his face between bites. He had orange pizza grease on his chin. "And he means in real life."

"So does she," Sierra told him.

Roy opened and closed his mouth with no snappy retort forthcoming.

"Not much of a story," I said. "I go to school, I draw, sometimes I write stuff."

"Family?" Kordell asked.

He had one bright jade leg crossed over the other at the knee, like a girl. Roy was jammed into the corner of the couch, as far away as he could be. Was Roy kind of homophobic? Not that Kordell had to be queer for that to be the case—in my experience homophobia didn't care if you were really queer or not—if you did anything that even looked queer, you were in trouble.

Blake rested an elbow on the back of the couch, her arm behind Kordell, the tip of one finger visible over the rise of his shoulder.

She was rubbing lightly on his shoulder but he didn't seem to notice.

"I live with my father," I said. "My mom works in DC and my brother's in college."

"Dating?" Sierra asked. She sounded offhand about it, but my heart jumped like a fish and wriggled in the air before dropping back into my chest.

"Uh, not so much."

She raised an eyebrow at me.

"It's hard to find a girl to date in Duluth. There's like three other lesbians my age."

"You should date a bi girl," Kordell said.

"Haven't found any of those."

I stopped trying to eat my pizza until they were done asking me questions so I wouldn't have to worry about having stuff caught in my teeth.

"Do bisexuals actually exist? Or do people just say that?" Roy asked. He was done with his second slice and wiping his fingers on a tattered paper towel.

"I'm bisexual," Blake said.

"Me too," Kordell added.

Roy stared at them like they'd announced they were from another planet for real. "Oh right, sure you are. Have either of you even *kissed* someone of the same sex?"

Blake looked away.

"I have," Kordell said. He extended his arm along the back of the couch behind Roy, who immediately leaned forward, awkwardly bracing elbows on knees, oily pizza plate held in front of him.

I reappraised Kordell. He'd kissed a guy? I liked him even more than I already had. Despite his pretty face and the bright clothes, he didn't come across as feminine. He was built with some muscle but enough weight that there wasn't definition to it.

"Blake hasn't had the chance," Kordell said. "It's not as if our school is crawling with opportunities."

Blake snorted. "Ha! No kidding."

"You'd let her kiss a girl?" Roy asked.

"Let?" Blake glared at Roy.

He held up a hand. "Hey, sorry."

"What about the rest of you?" I asked.

I realized how that question sounded in context when Roy said, "I'm straight!"

"No," I added quickly. "I mean, your story or whatever. I know more about your characters than I do about you."

Sierra put her plate on the coffee table and crossed her legs. She was in faded blue jeans but the gesture reminded me of skirts anyway. And of her legs in skirts.

She said, "I used to go to the same school as Blake and Kordell. I met Dustin through Bear, who I know from Cyd, but that's kind of complicated. Roy came in from the story. Anyway, you know me. Dust, tell her your life story."

He cleared his throat and rested his pizza plate on his leg, one slice still on it. "I was sent away to be raised in anonymity so that I may someday be the rightful King of England. Oh, wait, that was someone else. I'm a programmer, I run the story site, I'm an Aquarius and I hate mushrooms."

"Taste or texture?" Blake asked.

"Texture, for certain. Your turn."

Blake shrugged. "Okay. I like math. I write poetry. I haven't figured out how to write poetry in mathematical formulas, but I'm working on it. Everything else you can figure out by hanging out with me; I'm open bookish."

She poked Kordell.

"Kordell Graves," he said. "Fifth kid of six. I like a lot of things: plays, games, more games, Blake, Shakespeare, African diaspora science fiction. You know, this is harder than I expected."

Roy took over. He leaned further toward me, elbows out at the edges of his thick, furry knees. "Okay, other than you I'm the newest person here so let me give you a heads-ups. I've been hanging out with these losers for the past few months and here's the deal: Kordell looks gay, but he isn't. Blake looks like she's going to have sex with you, but she isn't. Sierra looks like she's all that and she kind of is. Dustin's a lucky asshole. And I could beat all of them at Mystics if I tried but then they'd kick me out because they need a sucker."

"Not true," Blake said.

"Which part?" Roy shot back at her.

"The cards. I am so *never* going to have sex with you—that's gospel."

"Lucky Roy," Dustin said. "We finally get another girl in the group and she's a lesbian."

I had a pang of sympathy for Roy. "At least we can commiserate," I offered.

"With beer!" Roy suggested. "Did you guys stock the fridge?"

"Bring me one," Sierra said. Dustin also asked for a beer, but neither Kordell nor Blake did. They both had mugs of pop and I had my can of Pepsi.

Roy got back with the beers and handed them around. He settled into his spot and said, "I've got an idea about the story but I don't know if you guys are going to like it."

"Go on," Sierra told him.

I relaxed a little. This was a good topic, far away from my sexual orientation and who was or wasn't going to have sex with Roy.

"Well, I was hanging out with The Machine and Shaman Bill," Roy paused and glanced at me. "They're the guys who run the gaming side of the story. The Machine runs all the cyborgs and does the gamemastering and Shaman Bill is in charge of the cool magic. Bill's his real name so that's why...yeah, okay, that was kind of obvious."

"Kind of," Sierra said sarcastically.

Roy ignored her. "They're in the middle of a campaign where their strike team, the roleplaying guys, found a way into another universe."

"How?" Sierra asked.

"Um, something about a black hole."

Blake turned sideways and sat against the arm of the couch. She bent her knees and put the soles of her feet on Kordell's thigh so as not to overlap him and touch Roy. Kordell rested one hand on her shin.

Blake said, "They're using the bubble multiverse theory. It's this idea that we're in a universe that's one of many in a multiverse, like soap bubbles floating on water. Our universe is one soap bubble. Because black holes are thought to create new universes, you can theoretically go through one to get into another universe."

She glanced around the room and added, "It's a thing. I'm serious. It's a real theory. Of course we don't have the technology to test it, but still, wouldn't that be wild? All those universes?"

I was getting chilled again. Multiverses were on the list of space things that creeped me out and made me think about being nothing. Not multiverses specifically, but anything that enormous. How could you get your head around that? The one universe was big enough, but an infinite number of them? I could *not* deal.

Did a multiverse mean there were other versions of me? What were they doing? How many of them had gotten laid already? How many of them were sitting in a living room with strangers and new friends obsessing about multiverses and sex?

"The soap bubble model is my favorite kind of multiverse," Kordell said and beamed at Blake.

She grinned back at him. Envy speared my heart. I had no idea why his comment made her grin, but watching them it was super obvious that I had no one to grin at like that.

"Yeah," Roy said, waving a hand in Blake's direction. "The Machine said that thing about bubbles. So the strike team goes through the black hole and in this other universe, the laws of physics are the same, but the laws of magic are different. They have to figure out if their magic works and how. But Shaman Bill said: what if in this universe the High God's power doesn't work? What if there are universes where the High God has no power? He was wondering if the strike team can get into one of those universes and find a weapon that could nullify the High God."

"Maybe," Dustin mused. "I see the power of that. What happens if we get the High God's locus from the future and then the strike team finds that kind of weapon? Or vice versa? If they kill the High God and we get the locus, are we the new High God?"

"Sounds like a great idea," Sierra said. "Is the Machine okay with us writing about that? And Shaman Bill?"

She was leaning into Dustin and smiling, like she was trying to mirror Kordell's gesture but couldn't do it right because they were sitting side by side. The more she leaned into Dustin, the farther away she was from me.

"I can ask them," Dustin offered.

Roy said, "I was thinking there could be a second strike team put together by Lord Solar."

Lord Solar was his character and now this all made sense. He'd figured out a way to make his character a lot more important.

When no one protested, Roy kept talking. "And I thought it would be interesting if…I mean, there has to be a faster way to figure out which universes are the right ones, so you'd need someone who could do that. Like someone who's good with information." He turned toward Blake.

"Like an infomancer, a master of secrets," she said. "I get it. But can information travel through the multiverse? I don't know. I'll have to look that up. It depends on what the water is. You know, in the soap bubble metaphor. What are all the bubble universes resting in? What's the medium? Is it information? Oh wait, what if it's the zero point energy field? Oh oh yeah, because the empty set is in every set, so zero is the one thing that's in everything. It totally works!"

"Huh?" Roy said.

Blake shook her head at him in annoyance. "It works," she insisted.

"So Cypher can see into black holes?" Dustin asked.

"It's because of how Cypher teleports," Kordell said. "She becomes zero and moves through the zero point energy field to anywhere."

"Right, yes," Blake went on. "So the universes all have to have zero in them. They can't not. Because of the empty set. So Cypher *can* be tapped into another universe. She could know where the black holes go, because she feels the zero point energy."

I mostly followed what she was saying. The water in the bathtub that held all the bubbles, all the universes, had to include zero in it. Cypher could use that zero-ness to know what was in each bubble. But she'd missed a step.

Since I regularly freaked myself out obsessing about the universe, I'd read about black holes. In addition to keeping me up late and making me panic, they were pretty fascinating.

I asked, "Wouldn't Cypher at least have to go to each black hole individually to find out where it went?"

Everyone stared at me.

"Um, I mean, I don't know what zero point energy is, but can it carry information out of the black hole's event horizon?"

Roy looked like I'd started speaking Russian, Kordell had an eyebrow raised, and Blake's eyes were wide and curling up at the corners from the force of her grin. When she grinned like that, her face went from broad-nosed and plain to…I don't know what but it made me want to keep looking at her.

On my side of the room, Dustin was leaning forward around Sierra, watching me, and Sierra had a curious, amused expression on her face.

I tried to ignore everyone's eyes on me and clarify, "I'm just saying, even if Cypher could tell what kind of universe it is, she can't pull that information out of the black hole from far away, all at once. See, because the gravity is so strong, nothing can escape it. Not even information. So she can use the zero thing to teleport through it and know what that universe is like, but she's going to have to go to each one and go through it to find out which universe is the right one."

Blake turned toward me, leaning, almost to the point of falling off the couch. She was shining in a dark way, like an eclipse.

"I kind of love you right now," she said.

My brain went through a black hole.

On the other side was a universe exactly the same as the one I'd been in, but way more complicated.

That wasn't something you said. Nobody in my life threw around the word "love" as a casual compliment. It reverberated in my chest like a bell ringing. I wanted to press my palm to my breastbone and make it stop.

I was saved from sitting there with my mouth open for an awkwardly long time by Dustin.

"That's a great idea, lots of story applications," he said. "But Cypher is supposed to be figuring out the future…"

"That's where I come in," Roy announced. "What if Lord Solar kidnaps Cypher to make her go to the other universes to find the weapon?"

Sierra said, "That would infuriate the Queen of Rogues. And probably piss off The Machine because you'd be competing with his team."

"Great conflict," Dustin pointed.

I remembered how to operate my lips and tongue and suggested, "The Queen could send Zeno to steal Cypher back." I stared at the raggedy smokestack-blue carpet, worried that this made me sound too interested in Blake.

"We could all go," Dustin suggested.

"Are you okay being kidnapped?" Sierra asked Blake.

"If I get to teleport through black holes into other universes, yeah, I'm okay with that."

"All right, that's our storyline for spring and summer," Dustin said. "Good job, Roy."

"Thanks!"

Everyone got up to get more pizza and pop or whatever they were drinking and then they talked about the story while I focused on eating. When I got through my two slices I went into the kitchen and got a third.

It hadn't meant anything, what Blake said. That was just how she was, all wild exuberance one moment and silent the next, a crazy blend of fidgeting and stillness.

I should read up on multiverses and figure out more smart things to say. Considering how everyone's attention kept drifting back to Blake, maybe if she said enough nice things to me Sierra would stop leaning into Dustin and lean my way.

CHAPTER TEN

Sierra worked at a secondhand fashion boutique and gift shop most days. Plus she was taking a writing class at the University of Minnesota so she had schoolwork. We fell into a pattern where we'd get up and have breakfast, chatting about the story, or what she was reading. She'd head out and I'd work on the story or read.

Monday and Tuesday when Sierra got home, Dustin also stopped by and we all sat on the couch watching movies on his laptop. The house didn't have a television, and seeing the high def on his 17-inch screen, I got why they didn't need one. He put his arm around Sierra and she snuggled into him and I felt like a fifth wheel—until late Tuesday when she threw an arm around me and tugged me next to her.

Three of us on the couch: his arm around her, her arm around me. I didn't know how to feel. The weird overshadowed everything else.

Dustin didn't seem to care. He half patted my shoulder with his hand. I wanted to pull away but that would have moved me further from Sierra so I stayed put.

The next morning after Sierra went to work, I sat down with my cup of tea and breakfast burrito at the dining room table, where

Cyd had her acupuncture books spread out. She rubbed her hand across her forehead like she already had a headache and got up to get herself a fresh cup of coffee. Her long sweater was deep terracotta over black tights.

When she got back to the table, she slid into her chair like grace was something tall people had naturally. She'd probably never tripped over her left foot and then tripped again over her right while trying to catch her balance.

She blew on her coffee, fingers curled around her mug. "How's your visit going?" she asked.

"Great," I said. "Thanks for letting me stay here all week."

"You said thanks plenty when you did the dishes last night. It's great to have you, and I'm not saying that because of the dishes."

Her hazel eyes had a natural downward turn to their outer edges, like she was always on the brink of smiling. When she did smile, her cheekbones went from enviable to amazing. (Why don't cheekbones like that come standard on all tall girls? Serious design flaw.)

"What's the deal with Sierra and Dustin?" I asked.

Cyd sipped her coffee and pressed her lips together. She rolled the mug between her palms.

She said, "They hung out a few times last fall and about three months ago she decided she was madly in love with him. She does that at least twice a year."

"Oh."

"I can't figure him out," Cyd told me. "But, you know, they're going to be soulmates until they're not anymore."

I studied the few black beans that had fallen out of the end of the burrito and seemed ready to make a run for freedom. If Sierra had fallen that fast, and that often, did that mean she'd get over him that quickly too? Would it be the same with me? Would our flirting turn into something and end as abruptly?

"You know, Sierra's *not* the only girl in town," Cyd said.

"Are you offering to fix me up?" I asked, my voice light so she'd know I was kidding.

She smiled back at me but answered seriously, "I would if I could, but I don't know any single queer girls. My sister has a girlfriend."

"Oh cool."

This cinched my growing suspicion that everyone in the Cities was amazing and that I absolutely wanted to go to college here. Ideally at the Minneapolis College of Art and Design, but my father would never go for that. It wasn't on the corporate track.

I pulled my sketchpad over and scribbled around for a bit while Cyd studied.

* * *

Thursday everyone came over again. One moment Sierra was sweeping through the door from work, pulling off her mouth-wateringly fashionable knee-high boots, and the next moment the house filled with people. Blake and Kordell brought a mountain of chicken wings, breadsticks and sauces from the aptly named Wings-n-Things.

We sat in the same spots we had days before and aside from Sierra wearing a skirt instead of jeans, we were dressed about identical: me in a flannel shirt and jeans, Roy in cargo shorts, Blake all in black, Dustin a collection of noncolors and Kordell in four complimentary shades of blue from sneakers to sweater: royal, pacific, and alternating stripes of aqua and dark slate.

After the plates were cleared away and we got through trashing and praising the current shows, Kordell asked me, "You've only got a few more days with us, do you feel like you've gotten to know everyone?"

"Pretty much," I said. "I mean, I already know I'll never beat you at Mystics."

That got a general laugh.

"It's too bad we don't have an initiation," Dustin said. He snapped his fingers. "Got it! We should all play Truth or Dare Spin the Bottle. It's the one guaranteed way to get everyone's secrets out. I played it in college. It's like Truth or Dare but upgraded with an element of randomness. You spin the bottle and whoever it points at gets to pick truth or dare from you."

Sierra looked around the circle. When her gaze came to me, I nodded. I assumed the rules of relationships were suspended during the game. Maybe I'd get to kiss her.

Kordell shrugged and said, "Sure."

Roy was nodding enthusiastically, and Blake smirked, so that was it.

Sierra drained the last of the beer from her bottle and set it on the coffee table. Dustin and Kordell rose from their spots on the couches to sit at the short ends of coffee table, creating an even circle of people around the bottle.

Sierra spun it and it came to rest pointing at Dustin.

"Truth," he said.

She rubbed the tip of her index finger under her crimson lips and asked, "What's one thing you've always wanted to do in bed but haven't yet?"

"Do I have to answer out loud or can I whisper it to you?" he asked. "If you say the latter, you'll get a better answer."

"Oh, okay, whispering is fine."

He unfolded himself, leaned over to her and said a long sequence of words into her ear. She blushed a few shades shy of her lip gloss. I burned with jealousy and envy, smashed together as one big sucking emotion.

He spun the bottle and it pointed to Blake. Her inky wardrobe for the day included jeans and an oversized button-down shirt, sleeves rolled up to elbows, the dark curve of an undershirt showing at the neck. She'd tucked her feet up on the couch when Kordell went to sit on the floor and it made her seem smaller.

"Truth," she said, jutting her chin forward.

"Other than Kordell, who in this room are you most attracted to?" Dustin asked.

She considered each person in the circle and when she came to me, her eyes flicked away. Her hands folded and unfolded in her lap.

"Lauren," she said quietly as she leaned forward and pushed the bottle into motion.

I watched the bottle, but my name was humming in my ears, making my face warm. Was she only saying that because she'd been challenged about her bisexuality? Was it because I was new? Was it that thing I said about black holes and the event horizon? Was it simply that she wasn't into Roy and didn't want to pick from Sierra and Dustin, so that left me?

If I got to ask Sierra a question, would I have the guts to ask her the same and find out how she felt about me?

The bottle swung around and chose Roy.

"Dare," he said.

Blake turned to Kordell and a silent question passed between them. He shook his head.

"I dare you to show us what kind of underwear you're wearing," Blake said.

That was a brilliant choice because it let Roy bluster and fluster and make a big show of turning away and taking down his shorts—and then showing us how he was already half hard in his boxer briefs—but no one had to touch him or anything. He was still protesting as he spun the bottle.

It pointed at Sierra.

"Truth," she said.

"What's the weirdest place you've ever had sex?" he asked.

"A kids' playground in the middle of the night. I swear that horse-on-a-spring thing was staring at me the whole time—and it liked it!"

We all laughed, Roy, Kordell and Blake louder than me and Dustin. Maybe because we both knew it wasn't either of us in that playground. Sierra spun and this time the bottle picked me.

"Truth," I told her.

"What's the weirdest place *you've* ever had sex?" she asked me.

"I haven't," I said. As soon as the words were out of my mouth, I realized I could be the only virgin in the room and my face got blazingly hot.

"Ooh, a virgin," Roy said, and I felt sure I was *not* the only virgin in the room.

"Remember, Duluth." I pointed at the center of my chest. "There are three other girls who like girls, and I'm not into them. I haven't found the right person."

"You could hook up with a guy," Roy said.

"So could you," Blake told him. "But I don't see you lining up for that opportunity. Lauren, spin."

I did and the traitorous bottle picked Blake. She didn't look away from me.

"Truth," she said.

"What's one thing you don't want people to know about you?" I wondered if she'd talk about having bipolar disorder. She hadn't brought it up, even in the introductions, and I'd been thinking maybe Sierra shouldn't have told me.

Blake's gaze held mine for another breath and then dropped. In a low voice, she said, "How hard it gets when everything goes dark." She took a breath and continued, "I feel like I want to lie down forever. The world is covered in death, everyone is dying and crumbling away and they don't know it, but it's all I see. Everything is worthless and dead and hopeless and I'm supposed to keep breathing anyway but I can't remember why."

I wanted her to look at me again so I could see the flash of her eyes, but she wouldn't. She shoved the bottle hard and it spun for a long time before it settled on Dustin.

"Dare," he said.

"I dare you to kiss Roy," Blake said without hesitation. She peeked up, mouth twisting wryly, eyes like aquamarine shattered on granite.

"No way, man, don't do it!" Roy said, hands up between him and Dustin.

Dustin grabbed one of his hands, brought it to his lips and kissed the knuckles.

"You didn't specify *how* I had to kiss him," Dustin told Blake. She laughed, open-mouthed, too loud, but her shoulders were relaxing again.

Dustin's spin got Kordell.

"Dare," Kordell said.

The dares were becoming a good strategic choice as the "truth" questions got deeper. Dustin struggled to come up with something devious.

At last he said, "I dare you to do something with Blake that you wouldn't normally do in front of other people."

"Ha!" Kordell's laugh was short and sharp. He turned to Blake, "Well, dearest, are you ready?"

"Of course. Will we need props?"

"What've you got in your backpack?"

She pulled her backpack from the side of the couch and sat on the floor with it between them. Kordell opened the front pocket and rummaged around, coming up with a tube of lip gloss. Blake held still while he carefully applied flamingo color to her lips. He kissed her hard enough that he came away with half of the lip gloss on his mouth. He rubbed his lips together and made a kissing motion at Dustin.

"If that's not enough, she'll probably let me tidy up her eyebrows if anyone has a tweezer," Kordell offered.

Dustin rolled his eyes.

Roy said, "I don't know how you're not gay."

"The love of beauty and sexual orientation are different parts of the brain," Kordell told him.

Blake returned to her spot on the couch.

Kordell put his long fingers on the bottle and spun it. The bottle rotated, wobbled and stopped with its mouth pointing at me. I was more afraid of the questions he could come up with than the actions.

"Dare," I said.

"I dare you to kiss Blake," he announced. "On the lips, for more than ten seconds."

"What?!" Blake and I both said the word at the same time, but mine came out incredulous and hers was all surprise and laughter.

"Then Roy can't needle you about not having kissed a girl," Kordell told Blake. She shook her head at him but her smile didn't fade.

There was no way I'd admit that I hadn't kissed a girl either—and that Blake was *not* where I'd planned to start. I'd already admitted to not having sex. Saying I hadn't kissed anyone would wreck my official lesbian status.

"Here?" I asked.

Kordell shrugged. "I don't care. You guys want to go in the other room, fine with me."

Roy deflated at that, but neither he nor any of the other people around the circle protested. I wanted Sierra to step in and claim me as hers, to tell Kordell this wasn't cool, but she was watching me and Blake with interest, as curious as everyone else in the room.

I stood up and went into the kitchen, my chest stinging. The kitchen had to be a safe room to kiss someone in, not suggestive like a bedroom and not small like a bathroom.

Blake hesitated at the threshold, glancing at me and away, not smiling anymore. Framed by the doorway and wrapped in shades of ebony on obsidian, still small.

She stepped into the room and asked, "How do you want to do this?"

It wasn't fair that this was going to be my first kiss for forever—that it was part of some game, a casual request from her boyfriend. I'd never get to tell a "my first kiss" story that made me feel proud rather than ashamed. But it wasn't fair to Blake either if I was a jerk about it. Intensity had come over her again, as if she couldn't fit her energy into her body.

"Come here." I held out my hand.

Her skin was cold. Against my hand, her fingers were flawless honey with the greenish undertone that gave olive its name. In my palm the blood rushed unevenly under the surface, creating four or five shades of ruddy sienna. I looked like a sweaty human holding hands with a finely carved statue.

I was going to say something (the words had gathered behind my lips ready to babble out in a nervous stream), but she reached her other hand around the back of my head. Cool fingers pressed against the top of my neck as she pulled me down to her.

Her mouth was wider than mine. I opened my lips a fraction to fit better. She opened hers too, sending a rush of heat up the inside of my body.

My hands fit neatly on her hips: the hard ridge of bone under my palm, the edges of my thumbs just over the line of her jeans. I liked feeling the softness of her waist through the fabric of her shirt. But her hands shouldn't have been cold and she shouldn't have been vibrating with nervous energy. I was supposed to be kissing solid, confident Sierra.

I nearly pulled back but the tip of Blake's tongue touched my lips. Shivering, I touched it with mine. Her tongue was rough, like a cat's, and it made me dizzy.

Ten seconds? Was she counting? As her tongue moved across mine, I couldn't remember what numbers were. She tasted like barbecue sauce and citrus energy drink. I was hungry. I wanted my arms all the way around her, to feel her body against mine.

My brain rebelled, reminded me this was Blake.

I pushed the feelings away, straightened up and stepped back. That had to be ten seconds.

"Dare accomplished," I said, trying not to sound breathless.

"Yeah." She grinned at me, a broad flash of mischief, humor, and warmth. Turning away, she walked back into the living room like it was nothing.

Maybe it was nothing. Why would I complain? It was a pretty good first kiss. Nobody mashed into anybody else's teeth or took a nose to the eye. Too bad it was with the wrong person.

I gasped in as much air as I could and went after her so it wouldn't look like she'd knocked me off-balance or left me trying to catch my breath in the kitchen or any of that stupid crap. Blake was settling into her spot, feet tucked up under her. Kordell cocked his head to one side and she winked at him. He chuckled.

"Still bisexual?" Dustin asked her.

"Very," Blake said. She studied me as I got back to my seat and added, "Thanks."

"That's what I'm here for, driving around the state affirming girls' nonhetero sexualities."

Everyone laughed except me.

I wanted there to be a First Kiss Tribunal that I could appeal to—find out if it really counted if you got your first kiss as part of a Truth or Dare game. Could that kiss be disqualified? I'd go back to needing a first kiss and maybe Sierra would oblige. Not that I wanted to break up her and Dustin, but they'd only been together three months and they seemed more like friends who were hooking up. Sierra flirted with me. I'd read back over her emails a number of times (just short of fully obsessive) and there was clear flirting.

And Blake was playing around, but I wasn't a game. I didn't have a lot that was purely mine. Art, stories, being lesbian—that was it. Everything else belonged to the outside world. Everything else was a place I had to get it right. And now I was proving that when it mattered, I still couldn't get it right.

Kissing girls should be mine alone. Not for people to play with and talk about.

The game went back to truth questions and broke up shortly after that. I think Dustin was afraid that Kordell would ask him to kiss Roy again and everyone was starting to realize how much information we had that we didn't want to share.

CHAPTER ELEVEN

Friday night Sierra suggested going out to a movie. I assumed it was going to be the whole gang again, but it ended up being me and Sierra. I didn't know if the others had been invited and couldn't make it, or if Sierra hadn't even invited them. She put on a long-sleeved short dress with diagonal slashes of reds and pinks, plus the delicious knee-high boots, so I abjured my flannels for a sea-green V-neck sweater.

I drove us to the theater early and we ate at a little Mexican place across the parking lot. I ordered shrimp tacos and didn't bother making any unkosher jokes.

As we were waiting for our food, me with a Pepsi and her with a slender, pale beer, she asked, "What do you think of everyone?"

"They're cool. Thanks for having me come down," I said. I globbed salsa into a little dish and dragged a chip through it.

"Specifically what do you think?"

At least the week let me be around her enough that I could chew and swallow like a normal person now.

I said, "Oh, Roy's kind of a letch, but I think there's a decent guy in there somewhere."

Sierra gave her tight, don't-mess-the-lip-gloss laugh. She said, "That's spot-on. What else?"

"I like Kordell. He's mellow but you can see he's smart and he thinks about things. Blake…I don't know what do think about her."

"You don't want to kiss and tell?" she asked.

"Uh, the kiss was fine. But that was a game. She seems interesting but kind of, I don't know, emotional. Not like emo, but way more expressive than I'm used to."

"Lauren, are you used to any kind of expressive?"

"I guess not so much."

"But you're right, she's super variable, goes through a lot of different stuff."

That wasn't what I'd meant. Bipolar or whatever, she didn't seem highly changeable. I'd been trying to say that Blake was emotionally loud, that you always knew something about how she was feeling. And while that scared me some, it was weirdly easy to be around.

"Cyd's great," I said. "We talked some about her sister. That was awesome. It's cool to be around people who understand."

"You should be around people who understand all the time," Sierra said. "I'm so bummed you have to go home on Sunday."

"Yeah, me too."

"What do you think of Dustin?" she asked.

"He's nice. I might be a little jealous."

Her face brightened.

"Good," she said. She didn't elaborate.

Our food showed up and I concentrated on not dropping anything out of the back of a taco onto my sweater. After we ate for a bit, Sierra said, "Everyone likes you a lot. And Dustin thinks your drawing of the Queen and Zeno is fantastic."

"You showed him?" I tried to remember if I'd told her that was all right. I was fairly sure that I hadn't.

"Was that not okay?" Her expression was innocent and slightly pouting, as if she was ready to be upset with herself if I said it wasn't.

"No, I guess, if he liked it," I said.

We talked about the drawing and about the story and about her week in general. I paid the bill and we walked over to the movie.

Despite being billed as a "science fiction thriller," it was slow. But beautiful with epic scenery and wicked special effects. I spent the first hour wondering if there was any way I could drop or fumble myself into touching Sierra's hand, but I couldn't work it out.

Coming home, I went up the front steps of the house and moved to the side so Sierra could unlock the door. She stood two feet away, watching me in the weak yellow light from the porch bulb. It made her look like a vampire. A sexy, predatory vampire in her black leather jacket and sanguine dress.

She shoved the keys back into her jacket pocket. Before I could figure out why, she put her hands on the sides of my face and kissed me. I froze, but with my mouth open in shock, so it was kind of like I was kissing back. Except my lips were stiff, as were hers, so our mouths mashed together hard. By the time my brain kicked into gear, she'd pulled away.

I grabbed the front edge of her jacket and tugged. She kissed me again, messy, her mouth loose and open, some tongue. My lips felt clumsy on hers, off rhythm. When our tongues hit together it got better. I almost knew what I was doing.

I put my arms around her. I was kissing a girl! I was kissing the right girl and it was like in the movies: the heroes standing in a puddle of light, surrounded by night. The cool wind made the sides of my face feel even hotter than they were. I was finally *that* girl: the heroine, the one who wins the love of the compelling stranger, the fucking princess.

There should have been music.

We stopped and she unlocked the door. In the living room, she pulled me onto the closest couch and we kissed for a while. I kept moving away from her mouth to kiss the sides of her neck because I couldn't figure out if it was okay to kiss and breathe at the same time. But she seemed to like that; she rested her head back against the couch and held me tightly while I ran my lips along her neck and up to her ear.

That was better than the plain kissing and trying to get my lips to line up with hers or against hers in a way that felt less wet.

It was super late. She got up and said, "We should go to bed. Do you want to sleep in my bed?"

I had a million questions. What did this mean for us? What did it mean for her relationship with Dustin? What were we doing? Was this a relationship thing or was she fooling around?

But I couldn't ask them. I was afraid of the answers.

"Uh yeah," I said.

"Cool."

I brushed my teeth and got into my T-shirt and boxers. She was in the bed before me and I climbed in carefully, staying on my side because I wasn't sure what was kosher and what wasn't. She rolled toward me and threw an arm over me. I snuggled back into her, thinking that I'd never manage to fall asleep with her hot body pressing the length of mine, but I did.

* * *

In the morning, we woke up and kissed, made breakfast and kissed, got washed up and dressed, and kissed. I was getting the hang of breathing. I decided it was okay to breathe through my nose midkiss if it meant I could keep kissing, but I'd forget, and stop breathing, and have to break away to catch my breath.

The breaks were good, useful even. We were getting the beat of things. The kissing felt less smothering. I started paying attention to other parts of her body, like her collarbones and, yeah, her boobs. I wasn't sure what to do there. When I fooled around with myself I didn't bother with my breasts because that seemed kind of porny. Now I regretted the lack of practice.

"I'm so bummed you have to go tomorrow," she said in one of the pauses.

"I'll come back. As soon as I can," I promised.

"I miss you already."

"Me too!" I agreed. "I mean you. I don't miss me. I'm not even sure why you miss me."

She laughed. "We should write a sex scene between the Queen and Zeno."

"Totally. I'll work on that during class."

Her phone buzzed and she went to get it and came back a shade whiter than she'd been.

"Dustin's coming over," she said and I got what the paleness was about.

Cyd had said that Sierra fell in love quickly and often. That had to be a tough thing, if she wanted to be with me now and didn't know how to tell him. They'd only been together a few months. I didn't know if that made it easier or harder.

"I'm not going to tell him," I said. "It's up to you, whatever you want to do."

"For real? You're not upset?" she asked.

"Should I be?"

"No, no, of course not. I need time to figure this all out." She rubbed her hand across the back of her neck, a tousled fallen angel in sweatpants and a breast-clinging tank top.

"I have to drive home tomorrow anyway," I said. "There's plenty of time."

She came over and kissed me. It turned into a longer kiss than either of us expected so we didn't have a whole lot of time before Dustin was due to show up.

"Thank you," she told me as she dragged her torn jeans over her curvy legs. "You're wonderful, fantastic, amazing. I don't want this to end. I need time to talk to him."

"It's okay," I told her. Anything that led to more kissing Sierra would be okay.

CHAPTER TWELVE

By midday, everyone was back over at the house and I fiercely wanted to be alone with Sierra. First Dustin had showed up with a big box of doughnuts. He and Sierra and I sat around talking about the story, planning out the details of how Lord Solar (who was not known for his subtlety) could possibly kidnap Cypher from the Queen of Rogues.

It didn't bother me as much now to see Dustin's arm around Sierra. That was a passing thing. I knew from the way we'd kissed that she'd end it with him. I wouldn't see her for a month or more anyway, which felt like a million years.

Based on the kissing, I figured that she was lesbian too, but for whatever reason she hadn't been willing to go all the way there. Dustin was her last-ditch attempt to like guys. The way she sat with him, close but also fractionally away, made me think that she wanted to like him more than she did. I felt sorry for him. And I had the sneaking suspicion that I might be kind of a jerk.

Roy showed up with a bunch of DVDs in his backpack, insisting that we watch them immediately. Dustin started one on his laptop, but then he and Sierra disappeared into her room, leaving me and Roy to watch a SyFy channel series about people taking their clothes off and having sex—oh plus some magic and all that.

I pulsed with hope that Sierra was in her room breaking up with Dustin so she could date me. I convinced myself that was the deal, then unconvinced myself.

I was starting to feel shaky when Blake and Kordell came in the kitchen door. I hopped up and hugged them both because I was so relieved for the distraction.

"We should play Mystics," I said, meaning: *please save me!*

"We have a convert," Kordell announced. He got the box out of his bag and started setting out the decks.

Roy pouted about his show, but Kordell told him to shove the laptop over and we could all play and watch at the same time. Roy was even worse at cards while trying to watch a show, so it started to look like I had marginal skill at this game. I played defensively and managed to outlast Blake, but Kordell trounced me.

"I'm going to make more coffee," he said, stretching his arms up (ultramarine today). He picked up his mug and Blake's and headed for the kitchen.

I helped gather up the cards and set Kordell's pile at his spot while Blake shuffled hers.

"It's too bad you have to go back tomorrow," she said. "This is more fun with more people."

"Yeah," Roy agreed. "But what I don't get is how your dad let you drive down here for a week. Aren't you like sixteen?"

"Yep," I told him. "He knows I don't drink or use anything."

"Huh, cool," he said, getting up from his spot. "We need the doughnuts in here."

As he walked out of the room, Blake watched me with her kingfisher eyes. No judgment, no clear opinion, curiosity maybe.

"I don't," I told her.

"Sure," she said, no argument in her tone.

Silence settled over us. It didn't seem to bother her, but it made me itch under the skin of my shoulders. I thought some pretty uncharitable things about Blake: that if she was the crazy one, I could tell her whatever I wanted and if she repeated it I could deny it. Maybe nobody would believe her anyway or she'd forget what I'd said because she'd have her own shit to deal with.

"He's not there much," I told her. "But his latest girlfriend dumped him, so I bugged him a lot when he was home. He said he was sick of all my drama. As long as I come back before school starts, he doesn't care what I'm doing. He's probably glad I'm gone. I don't think he likes me being in the house."

She nodded. "Good choice," she said.

What choice? My father's or mine? She was turning over cards from her deck, peering at them, arranging them on the carpet.

"Coming here?" I asked.

"That too," she said, glancing up and lopsided smiling. Her gaze flicked back to her cards but she continued talking, "You get that you can tell me things. Anything. We're alike in some ways. It would be a shame to miss discovering that because you feel shy."

Eyes on mine again, upturn of her mouth breaking into a full grin, she said, "Cast caution to the four winds. Agreed?"

I wasn't in my real life anymore. The whole week wasn't my real life, but now I was so far removed from it that we could have been in another galaxy—the one from the story.

I saw us as our characters—as Zeno the confused shape-shifter and Cypher, Master of Secrets—sitting together in a loading dock on a giant space station. The two of us shooting the shit about being henchmen for the Queen of Rogues. The image made me laugh.

"Agreed," I said quickly so she wouldn't think I was laughing at her. "You can too. Tell me things. I won't tell anyone."

"You did me a great favor, you know," she said.

"What?" I couldn't figure it, we'd known each other for all of nine days.

"I always thought I'd be in a relationship with a girl someday, but I kept pushing those feelings aside because I wasn't sure. Now I know. I was right; I do like girls too. I got to bring that sense of myself all the way to the surface and make that a fully working part of me. So, thank you. Now maybe I'll see about seducing a female friend of mine…" she trailed off, looked in the direction of Sierra's room, glanced down, peeked sideways at me. She added, "No one you know."

"Kordell's okay with that?" I asked.

After a long pause, she said, "We're not dating or any kind of formally together. We let people think that because it works."

"What are you?"

"Friends who have sex," she said. "But there isn't romance and jealousy and all that."

I didn't understand how that was different from being boyfriend/ girlfriend. I wanted to ask but Roy came back from the kitchen with the doughnut box and half a roll of paper towels. Behind him, Kordell carried mugs of freshly brewed coffee for everyone.

Sierra and Dustin returned and the whole house got loud again. In my mind there remained an image of Zeno and Cypher sitting on the edge of a massive crate, combat boots dangling over the side, softly talking about everything.

CHAPTER THIRTEEN

Sierra texted and emailed me every day. She wasn't supposed to text during work hours, but there would be a message in the morning and another one around lunchtime. She called me "Baby" and talked about how much she missed me.

Except for her being so far away, it was exactly what I wanted—this cute, funny, confident girl sending me sweet messages or a pic of the bottom of her dress and her boots so I'd know what she was wearing that day.

I texted Isaac: *Figured it out! I think I have a girlfriend.*

He wrote: *gratz, La! What's she like?*

Super cute, I said. *She lives in the Cities, though, sucks.*

So, you have that car.

Permission, I told him.

Do what Dad wants and he'll let you do what you want, Isaac texted back, as if it was that simple. For Isaac it probably was. He didn't have to wear dresses.

Sierra also sent pics from her job of funny new products or clothing she was thinking about snagging with her awesome discount. Some nights I called her. Usually we got animated and laughing, so if my father was home and working, I'd have to cut the call short.

On the weekends Sierra had more time and we'd work on the story together. The group had decided that King Solar would hire Cypher to go assassinate someone, but it would be a setup.

When Cypher showed up to kill the guy: boom, ambush!

There was a lot of debate about whether Solar would have to torture Cypher to get her to agree to do what he wanted. It was kinky as hell coming from Roy. Did that bother Blake or—because she sometimes called Cypher "that silly wench"—was she not that invested in her character and willing to be used as the dramatic linchpin?

I wondered if Sierra didn't have a crush on Blake. Everyone seemed fascinated with her. Although Roy had said, "Blake looks like she's going to have sex with you, but she isn't," he watched her like he thought any moment she'd make a special exception for him. Sierra and Dustin both seemed unable to leave the character of Cypher alone.

Kordell was the one least preoccupied with her. Was that why they weren't dating? Was *he* the disinterested party?

The good part of Cypher being captured by Roy—I mean, Lord Solar—was that it upset the Queen of Rogues a lot. And in Zeno's efforts to comfort her, the two of them could fall into bed together. I had so many ideas for that scene, but I couldn't manage to write any of them down. I thought about it all the time. But I hadn't had sex with anyone so what if I screwed it up? What if Sierra read it and didn't like it?

In the middle of all that obsessing and trying to keep up with school and stay out of my father's way, I got great news. He was going to a litigation conference in Chicago for the middle weekend of May.

I texted Sierra right away and asked if she wanted me to drive down.

She replied: *He's leaving you home alone?*

Yeah, it's not like I'm 12.

I could catch the bus up. More privacy. ;)

Oh? I thought, *Oh! OH!!*

I wrote back: *Yes! Come up! I'll stock the fridge.*

I spent the first two weeks in May freaking out about having Sierra in my house. Was it too big? What would my bedroom look like to her? Omg, I was going to have a girl in my bedroom. Would I know what to do with a girl in my bedroom?

CHAPTER FOURTEEN

I tried to figure out at what point during Sierra's visit I was no longer a virgin. Not when we were making out on the huge couch two minutes after she arrived, even though we had our hands under each other's clothes. Not even when she took my hand and put it down her pants and everything was super wet and soft and I knew what to do because I'd been practicing on myself for years.

Maybe that moment when she came, when her back arched up and I felt like I'd won the whole world.

Or later when we were in my bed, pulling off each other's clothes: that first instant when our naked bodies pressed together and I thought I was going to pass out from the overload of all that bare skin on mine.

I for sure started losing my virginity there. And kept losing it through everything else from that full naked delirium to the point where—well it went on for a while, so I guess the point where we fell asleep.

In the morning, I snuck off to brush my teeth, and we had another round in the bed. This time I slid a finger into her and felt like I wanted to explode or do backflips or something else wholly impractical in a bedroom.

She lay back and let me play around, moving inside her, watching her reactions. Trying two fingers, feeling how she liked that. She didn't look at me, but her body was easy to read. It was better that way; I didn't feel so self-conscious.

Being inside her, I knew in my gut how turned on she was, how much she wanted me. Her muscles, involuntary, caressed me, whispered to me that I was needed, tugged at me. The molecules of my skin registered how my touch changed her.

I'd put fingers in myself before and it wasn't like that. By myself it was fun and good but always somewhat mechanical.

Being inside Sierra felt like when you read a book and the words are right and they settle over you like a cloak of light. Like when you see a piece of art, just so, and it changes how the world looks. Like when sunlight streams down from between the clouds as if God is high-fiving the world.

When we got hungry, we nuked frozen dinners, curled up on the big couch together and watched one of the *Underworld* movies (the third or fourth, I forget the order).

How strange it was being the one with my arm around a girl on the couch in the primo-seduction living room of the cabin-mansion. (With a hot vampire/werewolf romance on the TV, as if I was good at this.) It transformed the cold, airy house for me. From now on, I'd always see Sierra on this couch. I'd always have the memory of her in my bed.

* * *

Sunday evening, she didn't want to go. She offered to wait until we saw my father pull into the driveway at which point she'd duck out the back and run all the way to the bus stop.

"It's two miles away," I reminded her.

"I don't care. I want to be here with you as long as I can."

Her eyes were deep cobalt blue under her purple bangs and I thought the Renaissance masters should have painted angels more like this.

"I'll come down and visit," I said. "You can't be here when he gets home. Let me drive you to the bus station."

"Okay, but wait with me there."

"I can't. I have to be home when he gets home," I explained.

"Or what?"

I shrugged. "He'll wonder where I was."

"So?"

How to explain there was a fifty-fifty chance of him ignoring me or cross-examining me like a hostile witness? And in the latter case, I sucked at lying.

"I don't want to have to lie to him," I told her.

"I thought you were out to him."

"Yeah, but…it's one thing to tell him I'm a lesbian and another thing to prove it. And if he knows, maybe he'd say I couldn't come visit you."

"Oh gotcha. Good thinking."

I drove her to the bus station and we kissed in the car. I made her get on the bus and leave, even though I wanted her to stay in bed with me for weeks.

I got home a half hour before my father, which gave me time to walk around and tidy everything. I greeted him and listened to him talk about his trip. When enough time had elapsed that I could politely excuse myself, I went up to my room to see if Sierra had texted me from the bus.

She had: *Baby, I miss you so much already. When can you come down? I had such a great time. You're really an amazing kisser. It's like I can still feel you kissing me. I miss you!*

I read that a few times and went to work on the story. Now I could probably do the scene with Zeno and the Queen. How much of what happened should I put in there? I mean, people we knew were going to read this and I didn't want them in my sex life. Especially Roy. He had a bit of a stalker-in-training vibe going.

I was staring at the screen, but I was remembering having sex with Sierra and I could not stop grinning. I opened my journal and started writing it down so I'd have an excuse to go through it all again.

* * *

Writing the scene between Zeno and the Queen remained hard. I tried a few opening paragraphs but when I read it back, it didn't seem right. After a few days, I gave up and sketched it.

The Queen was very tall, unlike Sierra, her face elongated and graceful, with long pointed ears and small fangs. I drew Zeno ordinary looking, like me but with better cheekbones. But I didn't like that.

I made her face more lupine, then more human. I tried to draw her hand so that it dissolved into a cloud of nanites. (Okay technically since nanites are microscopic robots you couldn't see a cloud of nanites, but for the sake of art I decided bunches of them could clump together and be visible.) Blake had suggested Zeno be able to turn into any form and in the sci-fi setting the easiest way to do that was nanites. If Zeno was composed of tiny robots instead of living cells, the tiny robots could put themselves together into any form they wanted.

Cool idea, but the illustration came out disturbing. I didn't know how to show shape-shifting on paper.

Finally I drew Zeno with her back to the viewer, kissing the Queen. We could see a sliver of her face but much more of the Queen's. I scanned it and sent it to Sierra.

This is so beautiful, she texted. *No one's ever given me art like this before. I want to frame it.*

I beamed at the screen and wrote: *Let me make a more finished version if you're going to print it out.*

But this is perfect. We look so good together, she said.

Yeah, we do.

She wrote, *I'll work on the scene. I can write about us together. I'll make sure I include a moment like this.*

That would be amazing!

I miss you so much, she said. *I can't wait to see you again.*

Me too! Omg, I want to drive down right now, I replied.

You should!

I can't. Big test this week and I have a bunch of stuff to do around the house. And the stupid garden that I hate.

Why do you have it then? she asked.

My father thought that girls should know how to keep gardens. But I hated everything about it: dirt, bugs, thorns, sneezy pollen, hot sun, muggy clouds, and that morally superior way of looking at you that flowers have. They're all: hey, I'm happy with sunshine and some moisture, why can't you be?

Last fall when I told him I didn't want to take care of the garden anymore, he said I was being selfish and lazy and shortsighted. I protested that it was getting in the way of school. His compromise was to hire a guy to help me with the work, which left me having to supervise a stoner kid who didn't know shit about flowers either.

But telling all that to Sierra seemed pathetic.

I told her: *My father.*

Sierra wrote: *Bummer. I'll get working on our scene. Go read up on the story, did you see the latest twist? Lord Ocean is protesting the allegiance between me and Lord Stone. We might have to send you to steal blackmail materials from Ocean, to keep him in line.*

I wonder if he's got a stash of old god porn, I wrote back.

Hahaha! That's genius. You NEED to write that!

I'll get right on that, I said. *It'll give me something to do while I miss you.*

She said: *Hey, don't get TOO distracted from missing me!*

I couldn't if I wanted to and I don't want to! You're all I think about. You're amazing.

You are too. Get your dad to let you come down again soon, I can't wait to see you. I've got to go do reading for class, but now I'm all distracted thinking about that weekend at your house. I don't know how I'm going to focus.

She signed off and I happily swung my chair from side to side. I'd made someone that distracted. She'd been here, in my bed. Knowing that I'd had that much impact, that she couldn't wait to see me, felt powerful.

I went to read about the plot twist she mentioned and throw myself into the story because it was an extension of Sierra. It was the easiest way for me to be close to her while she was so far away.

* * *

I sent Isaac a pic of Sierra in one of her dresses-with-boots outfits with the caption: *girlfriend!!!!!!*

He texted back: *Cute! Way to go! Senior?*

First year of college, I replied.

Do we need to have the sex talk?

I grinned at my phone. Isaac had a strong disgusting-boy streak, but he was a champion of girl things when he had to be. He was the one who went out and bought me tampons when I first got my period and was dying of embarrassment.

He texted: *There's safe sex for girls together, right? You are going to wrap it.*

Yeah, I texted.

There'd been a lot of sex already with nothing wrapped. I wasn't a hundred percent sure what to wrap. (And with what?) Crap.

CHAPTER FIFTEEN

I coasted through the first week after Sierra's visit on the memory of her in my bed, on the couch, and leaning against the granite kitchen counter wearing nothing but one of my flannel shirts. The next week wasn't so easy; I needed to touch her again, but I had three more weeks until the end of the school year.

I texted Isaac: *I want to see my girlfriend!! How do I get him to let me drive down to the Cities? He's going to harp on me about school?*

Your grades okay? Isaac wrote back.

Don't even.

Hah. Have you tried the people angle? Like how you need more social time to be well-rounded?

You rock!

My father was coming home late and in a bad mood because his case was floundering (while I secretly cheered, since he represented some mining/processing company out to pollute the world).

I waited for an evening when he seemed less tense. He was on the couch with a drink and his endless piles of paper from his briefcase. I left my Pepsi glass in the kitchen and stood by the side of the couch. He'd taken off his tie and rolled up his shirtsleeves.

"All my homework's done," I said.

"Good."

"Can I go back down to the Cities this weekend or maybe next? We're in the middle of this big story project."

He rubbed the bridge of his nose and stared at me with iced mocha eyes. "You have finals coming up."

"I can study in the Cities. Sierra's in college for English and Blake's doing math way beyond where I am. They'll help."

He lowered his heavy eyebrows and I wanted to back away. "Do you think for a minute I believe you'll study if you go visit these kids?"

"It's an important part of the maturation process to have friends," I countered. "I need more time around people to be well-rounded. You should be glad I have a social life."

"There is no reason you can't have one here."

There were so many reasons I didn't know where to start.

"I just want to spend time with my friends," I said. Not adding: *you know, with people who get me, who like me, who want me around.*

He stood up and squared his shoulders, which showed how much broader than me he was. "Are all your grades B+ or higher?"

I contemplated my shoes. Was it better to run for it or push through?

"Most of them are As," I said.

"Except."

"I'm getting a C in American history. But I've got an A+ in AP Art History and As in the others."

He went into the kitchen and refilled his glass with ice and scotch. I heard him pour the last of the ice out of my Pepsi glass and jam it into the dishwasher, as if I'd carelessly left it there, as if I hadn't intended to refill it.

Coming back to the couch, but not sitting, he said, "The good architecture schools are not going to take a girl who can't apply herself at a level better than a C."

"I hate history. And that class is late in the day and the teacher is boring."

"High school history is a very simple subject: names and dates. Are you being lazy or stubborn? Or is this an attempt to sabotage your life?" he asked.

I couldn't answer that. He sat down, put his drink on the coffee table and bent forward to shuffle his papers.

"Do you think people care about all of your excuses?" he asked. "Do you think excuses will buy you anything in the real world?"

"They're not excuses," I protested. "You've talked to my friends in the Cities, you know it's cool for me to stay there. You don't want me here. Why can't I drive down for a few days? I'll get the history grade up, I promise."

"It is not 'cool,'" he said. "You're being dramatic, Lauren. These few weeks aren't that long in the grand scheme. You need to focus and not be so emotional. Learn to delay gratification. Friends come and go, but your grades determine your future. You may not want to do the work, but you need to start growing up."

He said a few more things after that, but I tuned out the words. I heard the message between them loud and clear: *Why can't you be like Isaac? Why are you interested in all these stupid, frivolous things? Why can't you go to school all day, do your homework, and keep the house and yard neat with a smile? That's what girls are supposed to do, after all. What's wrong with you?*

He ended with, "You don't know how lucky you are to have all this. We didn't have anything like this when I was your age. We shouldn't have spoiled you. You have no appreciation. No work ethic."

Maybe he was right. We had the cabin-mansion and I didn't know a lot of other kids with cars at sixteen. I could afford any college I wanted (that I could get into). I was never hungry. He never yelled or hit me.

There had to be something wrong with me that I couldn't appreciate all this. I was a fucked-up person, made wrong inside so that I couldn't be happy.

"Sorry," I muttered and slunk off while he turned back to the piles of paper.

I wanted to slam my bedroom door, but I eased it closed. (The last time I'd slammed it, my father took it off its hinges for a week to teach me that we don't fuck around with doors.)

I ignored the textbooks on my short bookcase. Volume nine of *What Did You Eat Yesterday?* was on my nightstand, but I couldn't get interested enough to pick it up. I went to the story. I had nothing to add.

Opening my big sketchbook to the illustration of Zeno and the Queen of Rogues, I ran my fingers along the side of the page, feeling the thickness of the paper. I wanted to be inside the image.

But it looked wrong to me now. The perspective was off, warping the side of Zeno's face.

I tore it out of the book, crumpled it and threw it across my room.

I jumped up and ran to get it. I smoothed it out on the surface of my drawing table. I wanted to make it right and I wanted to tear it up.

I felt like I was exploding inside. No, that I already had. I was a burned-out shell.

I found a scene with the Queen of Rogues in it and pressed my fingers against the screen. I wanted to touch Sierra, to feel her holding me. I could call her, but what if my father heard me talking to her? Would I get another lecture about how my friends didn't matter and how a spoiled girl like me had to learn to make it in the world?

Sierra wasn't online. It was getting late and she had to work in the morning. It wasn't fair to insist on her attention because I couldn't deal with my own drama.

Tiredness pressed behind my eyes. If I turned off the light and got into bed, the emptiness would come over me. I'd try to see what was outside the universe again. I'd start falling into nothingness and I'd freak out. I had to keep the lights on. I had to think about the story.

At midnight, I heard my father getting ready for bed and made myself turn off my light. I read in the illumination from the laptop screen. It was far enough from the door that he wouldn't notice the weak glow.

Around one a.m., Blake posted a new scene. I wanted to talk to her because she knew Sierra and I could feel connected to Sierra through her. Was that an okay thing to do?

I messaged her: *Hey.*

She replied right away: *Zeno! What's shaking?*

Catching up on the story. Did you see the scene Sierra wrote about the Queen and Zeno?

Yep, interesting. Is that going to make Zeno a target from Dustin's character?

He doesn't seem like the vengeful type, I wrote. I didn't want to talk about the story as much as I wanted to talk about real life, so I added: *Sierra came up to see me about two weeks ago. Did she tell you?*

I heard all about it, Blake said.

You did?

She won't stop talking about you. There was a pause and she added: *Not that anyone wants her to.*

What's she saying?

No worries, nothing too revealing. She said you're a great kisser. I said, I know.

Blake inserting herself. Maybe it wasn't that everyone was fascinated by her, maybe she drew attention to herself on purpose because she liked it.

You're cool with all that? I asked.

With how you kiss?

I could picture her impish expression as she wrote that.

No, with the fact that Sierra and I are together, I replied.

Yeah, why wouldn't I be? I know you're only a few days younger than me, but believe me, I lost my virginity way before you. I'm glad you've got someone.

I want to come down and visit again, I said. *But I probably can't before the end of the school year. My father's being tough about grades and finals.*

Did you tell him you have a girlfriend?

No!

I'd typed it without thinking. I shouldn't have said it. She'd think he was homophobic and that wasn't it—but I couldn't define what it was.

I didn't think he cared, she wrote.

He mostly ignores that I'm a lesbian, I told her. *But he'd probably say no, like I'm too young for sex. But also...*

I stared at the screen for a long time. So long that Blake's name got the "away" flag by it and I wondered if she'd gone to bed. This felt easier if I was talking into space rather than to a person.

I wrote: *When he knows what I like, he can use it against me. He'd tell me I can't visit so he has that leverage to make me do what he wants. He'd hold it hostage. Like I have to show up for events and dress nice and all that shit.*

Most of the time it's like he doesn't realize I'm here and then suddenly he wants to make sure I'm getting good grades and that I look right and I'm behaving right. I don't know if he forgets he's a parent or...

I paused again as the words formed in my mind. Did I want to say them? Blake said I could tell her anything. Did she already know what was going on? Did she know it better than I did? Because I couldn't figure it out.

I don't think my father likes me, I typed. *He adores my brother. He's always telling people what Isaac is doing. Isaac has this amazing internship now and he's meeting all these important people. And my father stares at me like I'm a train wreck and he can't figure out what went wrong. Or like I shouldn't be here. Like somebody dropped off a daughter when he wasn't paying attention and he hasn't figured out how that happened.*

I think he lets me live with him because that's what a successful lawyer with a family does. It's this picture in his mind. But in reality, I'm in his way. And I'm not doing my adoring daughter role right. I should be happy with everything I have but I feel like I'm crazy. I get so angry and there isn't any reason. Nothing bad is happening but I feel crazy all the time.

I read over the words and wanted to take them back. If my father saw me talk like that, he'd hate me even more.

It felt like his hatred could reach back through my body, through my history, and unmake me.

I was shaking, breathing fast and shallowly, simply from typing words on a screen. Clearly losing my mind. Definitely the dramatic mess.

Blake's status switched from "away" to "available" and she wrote: *It's okay that you feel crazy. Don't beat yourself up about how you feel.*

What?

Trust me. It's okay to feel what you feel, even if it seems crazy. Don't let other people belittle how you feel. You can lose a lot that way.

I think most of it's already gone, I said, realizing the truth of the words as I typed.

Then let's go find it.

My eyes burned. A hot tear pushed itself down my cheek and onto my shirt. I pressed my hands against my face, lowered my head and cried, hard and silently for a long time.

She made it sound so possible and I knew she believed it was. In my chest, a tight darkness like a dense walnut showed a hair-thin crack glimmering with light.

She was away again, but I typed anyway.

How do I find things when I don't even know what I've lost? I asked.

She came back and said: *I thought you were the greatest thief in the galaxy. You can figure out how to steal them back. Write it into the story. I'll come with you.*

That's brilliant.

All in a day's work, dear girl.

That made me smile. I wrote, *Hey, I should get to bed. Why are you up?*

Infinities, she replied.

You know they'll still be there in the morning. Thank you...for all of it.

Go to bed, Lauren.

You too. If you can't sleep, you can do what I do—work out more of the story in your head. Help me figure out how a thief steals herself back.

I sat for a few more minutes, but she didn't reply and her status went to "away" again. Maybe she'd gone back to the story. Or she took my advice. Or she thought I was a meddlesome jerk for telling her what to do.

I brushed my teeth and got into bed. I wanted to think about the Queen with Zeno, how they'd hook up and what it would be like. All that came to mind was a scene with Zeno and Cypher. Somewhere in the middle of working it out I fell asleep and dreamed it:

Zeno huddled between two crates, shivering and flickering like a bad hologram transmission. Cypher knelt in front of her. She watched Zeno for a moment, then glanced around the room, checking for cameras, assassins, guards, spies, anomalies. When her gaze returned to Zeno, she had relaxed a fraction. Zeno was almost as good at picking unseen, defended corners as she was.

She wished she could put her arms around Zeno and teleport her to someplace even safer, but she couldn't. Whatever magic gave Cypher her teleport ability, it could only move somewhat static things, like human bodies. She didn't think it could move a bunch of sentient nanites. What did Zeno call herself anyway? A colony?

"Hey, you're flickering," she said.

Zeno looked up, her eyes shifting color and shape. "Bomb," she said, the word shivering on her lips. "Blew me out. Trying to pull together. Lost some. Damaged."

Cypher nodded. "Can you walk?"

Zeno shook her head. "Time. Heals," she mumbled through clenched teeth.

Cypher laughed. "Not fast enough. Be right back."

She teleported down to the medlab, making one of the nurses scream and leap sideways to see Cypher fold out of the zero point energy. She took what she'd come for and then had to walk, sadly like a normal, out the door and down the hall to the elevator. The contents of the box were like Zeno: not in a form that could be teleported.

Zeno was still crammed into her three-walled space, looking as miserable as she had when Cypher left her.

Cypher set down the box of medical-grade nanites and opened it. The swarm rose up, seeking whatever human-type body they were supposed to heal. Zeno's eyes lit and she held up shaking hands. The nanites streamed into her.

Curious, Cypher put her palm along Zeno's cheek. The cool surface raced with electricity. Over the next seconds she felt the surface, the skin under her hand, turn warm and solid. Zeno was filling in like a hologram turning into the person it projected.

On a whim, Cypher asked, "How do you think of yourself?"

"You mean how do I remember my patterns?"

"No, in your own consciousness, what do you call yourself? Is it just like 'oh I'm a person' or something else?"

Zeno grinned at her. "We're a community," she said. "But it bugs people if we speak in the plural." She put her hand over Cypher's where it rested on her cheek. "Thank you, that was smart. Cut my reconstituting time by a lot."

"That looked like it hurt," Cypher said.

Zeno shook her head. "Not like physical hurt. But yes, it's very disturbing to get blown up and have trouble cohering again."

"What is your original form?" Cypher asked.

Zeno turned her face away. "We don't know," she said.

"What?"

"We don't know what our original form was supposed to be. We might have lost the pattern, or the information that tells us what the first pattern was. We don't know what we are."

Cypher put her other hand on the bare side of Zeno's face, as if she could hold her in place between her two palms.

"What about this form?" she asked.

Zeno shrugged. "We like it so we gave it first form status. It's our default now."

"I like it too," Cypher said and kissed her.

For a second, Zeno's lips shimmered under hers and solidified. That process sent a shock of recognition and desire through her. It wasn't the same as teleporting, as being nowhere all at once, but it was close. Closer to her magic than anyone else she'd ever met.

Zeno pulled back. "Does it bother you that you aren't kissing the real version of us? That we don't know what that is."

"Don't be silly. I am kissing the real you. This is all the real you."

CHAPTER SIXTEEN

I woke up muddled and heavy, half-remembering a dream about Zeno and a bomb blast. Cypher had been there and she kissed Zeno and it felt like Blake kissing me. I wrote down as much as I could and resolved to fill in the rest later.

School was school.

After fourth period I got a text from Blake: *You doing okay?*

Yeah, I'm fine. Thanks for talking.

Anytime.

There was also a message from Sierra, fan art of two women kissing from a sci-fi show I hadn't seen and the note: *miss you!*

Miss you too!!! I wrote back.

For a few bleak days, I forced myself to do American history. So many names I didn't give a crap about. Bunch of white guys with awful hair. I did sketch out Aaron Burr as a cyborg, but no way was I getting class credit for that.

I wanted to text Isaac and ask for advice but I couldn't. Girls we had in common. Our father, we did not.

With cyborg Aaron Burr in the trash and my final paper mostly done, I dove back into the story. Roy had posted many pages of rambling, badly punctuated scenes featuring his Sunslingers and Cypher. He stopped short of rape or mutilation, but it was disgusting nevertheless. I felt sick. It wasn't for him to do this. It wasn't right.

I needed to be inside the story, but all this didn't belong. I had to get Cypher out of there.

It was late, but I saw Sierra online and pounced on her.

Hey, I wrote, *I want to go get Cypher back from Solar. I mean, that Zeno should go steal her back.*

Why?

What Roy's writing is gross, I said.

Yeah, it is. I'll ask Dustin to talk to him and have him take some of it down, she replied and I let out my breath in relief.

I wrote: *That's great! But we should also go get Cypher back now, don't you think?*

No. It's too soon.

The "No" was a glowing absence on the stark white of the screen. Why would she say, "No?"

Lauren? she typed.

I'm here.

What's up? she asked.

I'm getting a C in American history and my father thinks that's the easiest subject ever. But it's boring as shit. I spent three days working on this paper and it still sucks.

Sierra wrote: *Is he grounding you? I'd be super pissed off. I want to see you, when can you come down?*

I'm not grounded but he said I can't come down until school ends. Maybe what's getting to me is that he acts like I did this on purpose and I didn't. I don't know, maybe I did it subconsciously. Maybe he's kind of right.

She replied: *Could be. I mean, he gave you a car and stuff. And he lets you come see me, I like that.*

Yeah, he's working a lot and he gets stressed out and I don't live up to his expectations.

Get your work done, I want to see you so much, she said.

Okay, I've got to go. I'll talk to you tomorrow.

I pushed my chair back from the drawing table and bent over, arms across my chest, shaking and feeling like I was going to puke. She didn't get it.

I didn't get it.

What was wrong with me? Blake said I wasn't crazy, but what did she know? I was shredding apart. I pulled my sketchbook into my lap, hunched over, and roughed in the shape of a body.

I drew Zeno naked, not quite hunched over, arms and legs bent as if she was trying to sit up. One hand covered half her face, the other was dissolving. Pressing so hard that the tip of the pencil tore the paper, I drew a spear through her throat.

I bent in and did details: the skin tearing away from the tip of the spear, blood running down the front of her neck and chest, a bubble of blood at her throat where she was trying to scream but couldn't.

I went from bent over in my chair to bent over my drawing table. I switched to another pencil when the pressure wore down the point on the first one. I slowly stopped shaking.

When I got up to use the bathroom it was one thirty a.m. I woke my laptop. I told myself that it was to see if Sierra had talked to Dustin and gotten most of Roy's writing removed. But that wasn't it.

Blake was there.

Hey, why are you up? I typed. *Infinity?*

Infinities, she replied. *But no. I heard there was torture porn with Cypher. I thought I'd check it out.*

It's gross, I warned her.

I noticed. Not my scene. What's up with you?

I don't know, I said. That wasn't right so I added, *My father's still unhappy with me and I'm freaking out.*

What kind of freaking out?

I didn't feel like fighting my way through the words. I snapped a photo of the sketch and sent it to her.

A nonbreathing stretch of time happened during which I was certain she'd want nothing more to do with me or, maybe worse, be weirdly fascinated.

She wrote back: *Lauren, that's beautiful. And I'm sorry you're hurt like that.*

I touched the word on the screen, "Hurt." That was right. That was the word I needed. I felt it in my throat, a tearing pain like the spear through Zeno. Hurt.

I wish we lived in the same city, I wrote. *I wish I could see you. I want to see you even more than Sierra right now, is that weird?*

A gust of wind blew against the house and I jumped. I turned off my desk lamp and listened for a minute in case my father woke up. The wind sounded again and my heart sped up.

It's not weird, Blake wrote. *I like it. I wish you were here too.*

The wind is blowing here and it's making me feel afraid, which is so strange. When I was trying to go to sleep, I was afraid of the sound of my father walking around the house. And now I'm afraid of everything.

She wrote, *Maybe not everything. Maybe you can't yet see what you're afraid of. In your drawing, there's no person holding the spear.*

I can't draw that, I told her. Where there should have been a person stabbing Zeno with the spear, I saw the nothingness, disintegration.

You don't have to. I just thought it was interesting. I don't know what else to tell you. If I give you advice, even good advice, it might not be right for you. That's my advice.

I like your advice, I said.

Are you safe? she asked.

I contemplated my closed bedroom door and felt the silence of the house around me. I was always safe. That's why I was crazy, because I could feel this awful for no reason. Because I was safe all the time and yet I was shredding apart and dissolving into nothingness over and over again.

I wrote back: *Yes. I'm safe. I'm…hurt and scared.*

I know, she said. *I have to go now. Get to sleep and all. But you can write me or draw me whatever you want. I'll see it in the morning.*

I think I'm going to bed too, I said. *But if I can't sleep, I will. Thank you.*

No need to thank me, dear girl, she said and logged off.

Why did I feel so much better? My father thought I was a spoiled, melodramatic disappointment. Sierra had told me I couldn't send Zeno to rescue Cypher. I'd sent Blake a horrible drawing that she somehow liked, proving we were both mad as hatters. But I felt better.

I got into bed, rolling onto my stomach so I couldn't stare through the ceiling into space. Someday, when I wasn't afraid, I needed to get Blake to explain how she could think about infinities without losing it.

CHAPTER SEVENTEEN

I couldn't stay in this dull city, in this dead house, in my stupid life. It was June, school was almost out, I had to get back to the Cities.

As soon as I was done with finals, I cleaned the whole house. I polished chrome, I brushed dirt out of the tile grout, I fixed a shelf that was starting to come loose. I cranked up Halestorm on my iPod and did the garden. I went over the whole ridiculous thing from the mean roses to the stupid little groundcover plants. I weeded and edged and pruned. I sat outside in a blue and green sundress and drank iced tea so when my father got home from work I matched his perfect picture of the perfect life.

On the evening of the sundress day, he came into the kitchen while I was nuking myself dinner.

"I know what you're doing," he said.

I watched the tray turn in the microwave.

He crossed his arms and continued. "I'm not hard on you so that you'll be some glorified maid. I'm hard on you because you need to be able to succeed in this world. I've seen failure and I've seen success and the second is far superior. You can do better. This fall you're going to have to work harder."

"I know," I said. "Maybe if I toured one or two colleges, it would help me think about where I wanted to go, make it real. Cyd's sister is going to Macalester. She'd show me around. It's a really good school."

"Are you lying to me?" he asked.

I kept my face blank, thinking: *gee, thanks, way to have a high opinion of your daughter.*

"No," I said. "You can call Cyd."

"Why do you want to go to the Cities so much?"

I couldn't use any argument with words like "creativity" or "story" or "girlfriend" in it.

"It's like practice for the real world," I said. "Cyd and Sierra are a few years older and hanging out with them, it gives me a better sense of what it's going to be like."

"How long do you plan to stay?"

"A week?" I asked.

"All right. I expect to hear about colleges when you get back. The same rules apply as last time."

"Thanks!"

For a crazy second I considered hugging him. Yeah, no. I got my dinner and ran upstairs to message Sierra and see when it was okay to show up.

* * *

Two days later, I got up at five thirty a.m. while my father was at the gym for his crack-of-dawn workout. I grabbed the packed suitcase I'd left by my door and was out of there.

Even stopping for breakfast, I got to Sierra's house around nine. She'd just woken up. When she dragged me into her bed, I could see the imprint where her body had been. Being naked with her, tracing patterns across her body, and seeing the reaction I evoked, brought back the feeling of liquid power I had the weekend we were together. That feeling swept away all the others.

By midday, I was starving and happy. I'd showered and put on jeans and a light blue and shamrock summer plaid. Sierra and I were sprawled together on the couch: her against the arm, me sitting between her legs, her arms around me. Cyd flopped down on the other couch.

"Where's Blake?" Cyd asked.

I felt Sierra shrug. "Probably doing something with Kordell."

"Aren't they usually here by now?"

"I told them not to come over too early," Sierra said and squeezed me.

Cyd typed into her phone. "Bear wanted to come by and show off some sketches, she'll be here in a few. I hope that doesn't cramp your style."

"We'll be okay," I said. "We should figure out what we're doing for lunch."

"Dustin was going to bring over an old laptop for me to borrow," Sierra said, her voice casual. "I can see if he'll pick up food."

I sat up, away from her. Bringing her a laptop sounded like kind of a big deal. People didn't just loan laptops to their friends, did they?

Sierra pushed up from the couch and walked into the kitchen, saying, "We have take-out menus."

I followed her.

"You broke up with him, right?"

It couldn't take two months to break up with someone.

In May when she was at my house, when she was in my bed, we hadn't talked about it. I'd assumed she had broken up with him weeks before. You wouldn't go have a weekend of sex with someone and say "I love you" and "I miss you" about a million times if you hadn't broken up with your boyfriend, right?

Sierra opened a drawer and shifted its contents until she could pull out a crumpled yellow sheet of paper. She spread it open on the counter and faced me. Her fingers smoothed the wrinkles on the page.

Her eyes were azure with the barest hint of green, like the sky in autumn when the contrast of the dying leaves makes the color deeper than usual. The playful purple in her hair and the vibrant color of her eyes made my breath catch.

"Of course I did," she said. She put her hands on my hips, bringing our bodies almost to touching. "You're what's important in my life now."

I kissed her and ran my hands up into her hair.

After a while, she moved a half-step back. She said, "You know, you're so far away a lot of the time."

"Yeah?"

"And Dustin doesn't care about the formalities of relationships. I mean, he respects ours, but he doesn't care if he's officially dating someone or not. So he offered that if I get lonely, you know, I can go see him."

She was staring at the menu on the counter as she talked, her fingers flexing and relaxing on my hips. I had my hands on her waist but I let go and pulled away from her.

"He...what?" I asked.

"Just to hook up, to take care of our needs," she said. She went back to smoothing out the menu.

Usually my mouth was behind my brain, but now my brain stuttered and shivered and tried to catch up to the questions and answers happening in front of me. Had she actually said that when she broke up with Dustin, he said it was okay to keep having sex and...? Was she still having sex with him? (I so should have wrapped something.)

I stammered, "Wait, what?"

"It's a merely biological thing. Don't be a child about it," she said. "I thought you'd understand."

"You're still having sex with Dustin? And he's coming over? To lend you a computer?"

"Those are two separate things. Honestly, Lauren, you know I love you. You're the one for me. Don't be so insecure. What do you want for lunch?"

"Cashew chicken," I said automatically.

She took out her phone and I wandered back into the living room. Blake had told me that she and Kordell were friends who had sex, so maybe this was a Cities thing. Was I that backward coming from Duluth? Had I missed a crucial memo about casual sex in major metropolitan areas?

Did I care if Sierra hooked up with Dustin while I was out of town? It was hard being apart most of the time. If I had someone in Duluth would I hook up with them?

I couldn't figure out how to answer that. I mean, my first answer was: *no I fucking would not.* But I worried that was the wrong answer. Maybe I was being immature and too emotional about all this.

Someone knocked on the front door and Cyd got up to open it. She hugged a shorter person, about as short as Sierra, with a stout but well-balanced body. I'd expected Bear to be a towering Viking. So not. Warm umber skin and dark hair pulled up and wrapped with a scarf; graceful, solid nose; long, laughing eyes. She was in a gray, ankle-length skirt and an olive-tan T-shirt, loose around her big chest and belly.

Cyd turned and said, "Bear, this is Lauren from up north, the one who took over Zeno."

"Hey," Bear said with a nod and a wide, toothy smile. She had a portfolio in one hand and crossed the living room to set it on the dining room table. "Great to meet you. Love that sketch of Zeno."

"Uh, yeah, hi," I managed.

Bear either expected me to be conversationally fumbling or was used to giving people a minute to get over how much not a Viking she was. To Cyd she said, "I want you to pose for me so I can use your face for the High God, is that cool?"

Cyd laughed. "Sure, what do I get to do?"

"Basically run everything," Bear told her.

"Sweet. Just like real life. How do we do this?"

"Sit on the couch and read, I need you to not move for a bit."

Bear unzipped the portfolio and pulled out a sketchpad.

I touched the edge of the portfolio. "Can I look at these?"

"Knock yourself out," Bear said.

She and Cyd went into the living room. Cyd took her usual spot with her legs stretched along the couch. Bear sat in the middle of the other couch with her sketchpad in her lap.

I opened the portfolio. The first few sheets were illustrations I'd already seen online: King of the Wilds with an actual bear; Dustin as Lord Stone standing beside Lord Ocean and Lady Death; an illustration of a giant suit of battle armor labeled "The Machine."

I bent down to examine the line weights she was using with her inks, the shadows. I loved the dimensionality of the machine pieces on the armor. I wanted to ask her how she got that effect, but the kitchen door opened.

"I picked up the Chinese food," Dustin announced loud enough to be heard in the living room. "Do you want it in the dining room?"

"Sure," Sierra said.

"Put it in the kitchen," I called to them. "The art's on the table out here."

Sierra stepped through the kitchen doorway and gave me an annoyed look. "So pick it up," she told me.

I folded the art back into the portfolio and closed it, set it against the wall, out of the way. Was she angry at me because I'd been weird about her and Dustin? Was I being insecure and disappointing her?

Less than an hour ago, I'd been in bed with her feeling like the ruler of the universe. Now it was all slipping away. I wanted to run out of the house and drive back to Duluth and sit in my room until this made sense.

I leaned in the doorway between the rooms and watched Bear draw. Blake and Kordell arrived through the kitchen. I heard them talking to Dustin and the clatter of plates. When they came into the living room, I went to get my plate.

Cyd had moved from her spot on the couch and Sierra was in the middle again with an empty space next to her that she patted, looking at me. This time when everyone settled around the living room, it felt claustrophobic. I shoved the chicken around and ate the cashews. Dustin sat on the other side of Sierra from me. They weren't touching but I felt like they were.

I got off the couch. "I need to move around," I said. "I'm going to take a walk."

Kordell pointed toward the dining room and kitchen. "If you go that way about six blocks there's a decent park, if you like parks."

"Thanks," I told him.

Sierra didn't say anything at all.

I went out through the kitchen door and got my shoulder bag from my car in the alley. I'd left it because I'd been so eager to see Sierra.

Slamming the car door, I stalked up the alley toward the street. Running boots sounded behind me, but I didn't turn around. If it wasn't Sierra, I didn't want to know.

Blake caught up to me. She was in black hipslung trousers and one black tank top over another. The bottom one had been through the wash too often and its cherry undertone was showing. We reached the mouth of the alley and turned toward the park.

"She's still sleeping with Dustin," I said, and then, "Not sleeping. You know what I mean. Is that a thing here in the Cities? Does everyone casually fuck each other?"

Blake said, "You should get what you want. It doesn't matter what everyone's doing."

"But you and Kordell…"

"We're not you and Sierra. If you need her to only be with you, why don't you tell her?"

"It's not that easy."

We walked a block in silence.

I didn't want to talk about me and Sierra, so I said, "She told me about you one of the first times we chatted, that you're bipolar. I didn't know if that was okay or not, that I know."

"I have bipolar disorder," she said and laughed a little. "What a silly word that is. Disorder. It implies I had order to begin with. I don't mind that she told you. I'm glad you know."

We continued on and she added, "They're thinking about changing my medication again to see if they can get my brain to settle down. I hope they get it right this time."

"What's it like?" I asked. "Is it okay to ask that?"

"I think we covered the 'say anything' nature of our friendship last visit," she told me.

After another long pause she said, "Sometimes it's like just having enough energy to lie in bed and think about death and cheery things like that. And then sometimes gravity can't touch me. I fly and everything makes sense. It fits together so beautifully and I try to write it all down. Oh and there's the anger. One time, I was seeing this therapist and he was going on about how I should 'act out my anger' and I kept trying to tell him the only way I could do that would be to hit him with the chair because he was the object of my anger."

"Did he stop asking you to act out your anger?"

"After I picked up the chair and held it over my head, he did."

I stopped, turned, stared at her.

Her smile was faint and lopsided, quirked up on the left. Eyes narrow and wary, but also crinkled at the edges and warm.

I could picture it: Blake, compact and intense, eyes blazing, holding one of those plastic, institutional-style chairs over her head by its metal legs. Raven hair wild, black shirt askew, mouth twisted in anger.

I was afraid of her and I wanted to put my arms around her. Standing next to her I wondered—if I felt a fraction of what she felt—how did she move around in the world without yelling and throwing chairs all the time?

"What happened?" I asked.

She started walking again. I moved to keep up with her, easy with longer legs.

"I decided it wasn't a good idea to injure him," she said. "So I dropped the chair and ran into the hall. He followed and I think we freaked out the clinic staff and most of the other patients."

"You didn't want to hurt him."

"No, of course not. I was just so angry. I ended up getting another therapist."

A million questions jostled in my brain but wouldn't settle into words. I'd seen her laughing and intense, joking and thoughtful, serious and annoyed, but never angry. What would it be like to feel that angry and be able to show it? I could never.

I said, "I think normal is overrated. It's what your parents always wanted you to be and other than that it doesn't exist."

"What does your dad want you to be?" she asked.

"An architect or some kind of corporate robot," I told her. "A good daughter, whatever that is. And someone who never feels things."

We'd reached the park. It was a block square, half fenced off for dogs. We sat on a bench. I watched a bunch of dogs running in a frantic, playful circle after a scruffy black-and-white mutt with a bright orange ball in its mouth.

"I can't imagine that," Blake said. "To be without feeling everything. Maybe I could do without the dark, but not if I had to give up the infinities. Sometimes with the medication I get so foggy, not thinking, not feeling, and that's almost worse than thinking about death all the time."

"How do you feel what you feel? I mean, literally. What is it like?"

She turned toward me and asked, "Can I touch you?"

"Um, sure." Weird question coming from someone who'd kissed me.

She put her fingertips on my chest, in the middle, under the line of my bra.

"You're not breathing very much," she said. "I heard in a group once that if you close off your breathing, it makes your brain freak out because it's not getting enough oxygen. Then your brain has to focus on that and not whatever you're feeling."

She lifted her hand away and tapped her own belly, down low, over where her belt was. "Breathe into here," she said.

I tried. It felt like when I'd sat for hours and stretched too suddenly. Muscles on the edge of cramping, wanting to curl in on themselves.

"I don't think I like that," I said.

"You have to practice."

"Do you?"

She grinned. "Needing to feel more of what I'm feeling isn't a thing for me. I pay attention to my moods, to stuff that clusters together. Like when I'm angrier is that the same as when I have a lot of ideas? Stuff like that."

The idea of having to track more than one feeling at a time was overwhelming. "But how do you deal with all that?"

"How do you not? We're all having feelings all the time, it's what humans do. Do you really not feel things?"

I watched the dogs running joyfully. One body-checked another and it snapped back with a growl. The first dog backed off. If only it was that easy.

"I guess," I said. "I just go to school and do my work and draw. Most of the time I don't need to feel anything. It's better if I don't."

"How do you know what to draw?" she asked. "When I'm foggy, I can't write poetry like I can any other time. I have to follow my feelings to know what to write."

I pulled my sketchbook out of my bag and handed it to her. She flipped through it, images of Sierra's face, my attempts to draw the Queen and Zeno. She reached the blank pages.

The middle was blank but in the back there was another set of drawings, nothing like the ones in the front. I put my fingers under the blank pages and turned to the back section and the other illustrations I was working on.

With one finger Blake traced the image of jagged skin on an arm where a blunt blade had torn through to the muscle. She turned the page slowly. Here a woman had run through a thicket of thorns, bloody lines curving around her torso and legs. She'd run until pain and exhaustion overwhelmed her. She was huddled under the jagged thorns, slumped on her side.

"This is amazing," Blake said. "It feels frightening, but I love looking at it. There's so much pain in it but also here, the way her leg is tensed, the strength, like she won't give up. It's beautiful."

"You know there's something seriously wrong with us, right?" I asked.

She laughed, her full head-back, open-mouthed laugh and put her hand on my shoulder.

"Will you draw me one of Cypher torn apart?" she asked.

"Eaten by birds?" I suggested.

"Sure."

"I was kidding."

But I could see it in my mind already and there was a crushing, awful wonder to the idea. I felt it in my gut, the way I felt all of these drawings, like they crawled out from inside me.

"I'm not," she told me. "But do whatever you want. This doesn't trouble me. I get this. And it doesn't mean you're crazy."

I didn't want to say it out loud, but that's exactly what it meant. Sitting next to the girl with the official diagnosis, having her say she got me, that didn't help with not feeling like a crazy person.

A woman in a saffron shirt called to the fast dog with the ball. It dashed across the park to drop the ball at her feet. She leashed the dog, picked up the ball, and they walked together out of the park.

We started back.

"What do I do about Sierra and Dustin?" I asked.

"Tell her you're angry and upset."

"I am?"

"You tell me," she said.

We walked most of the way back to the house. I tried breathing like Blake had showed me but it hurt all the way down my ribs. I stopped at the mouth of the alley.

"I am upset," I said in a whisper. "And fucking pissed off."

Blake put her hand on my arm near the elbow and squeezed.

"And draw more," she told me. "Anything you want. Anything at all."

When we went into the house, they were talking about Solar holding Cypher captive and when the torture scenes needed to end. It was like we hadn't been gone at all.

Blake dropped into her spot on the couch and said, "I think I'd like her to be eaten by birds."

"Like Prometheus?" Dustin asked. "He had an eagle eat his liver every day."

"Sure, whatever. Now, let's talk about Cypher's daring escape."

I went into the kitchen for a drink. Sierra met me in there, leaning against the door frame, curvy and sexy and troubled.

"I'm kind of upset about the Dustin thing, if that's okay," I said.

She crossed the room and put her arms around me. "Baby, I'm sorry. Let's go out to dinner tomorrow night, you and me. We'll go someplace nice."

"Okay, sure. Thanks."

She kissed me and breezed back out of the room. She hadn't said she'd stop having sex with him, but she apologized and that meant something, right? I could ask her about the sex part later. A hundred electric currents of hot and cold, sharp and buzzing, were mixing in my chest.

How did Blake live with all of this?

CHAPTER EIGHTEEN

Sierra was in the mood for seafood, so we went to Joe's Crab Shack and got giant pots of clams, mussels, crab and lobster claws. It made me miss the full summers I'd spent with Mom on the East Coast, before her travel schedule got too heavy.

Sierra told stories about her co-workers, especially the OCD one who couldn't stop fixing displays the minute a customer walked away. She admitted she sometimes messed up the displays right before that co-worker's shift.

Then home to fall into bed together. In the morning Sierra made eggs and toast. We ate sitting in bed.

"Are you here through next weekend?" Sierra asked. "There's a party at Bear's parents' place that's going to be great."

"Yeah, I can stay. Is that cool?"

"Of course it is."

It was time to say it, so I asked, "Are you going to keep sleeping with Dustin while I'm gone?"

"Not if it upsets you that much," she said. "He's just a friend. He knows that. He said that he thinks we're good together: you and me."

"He did? You talked to him about us?"

"To tell him that we were together. Don't get paranoid, baby. I only talk about you to brag about how lucky I am."

"You do?"

"All the time. The other students in my writing class got sick of hearing about you."

I beamed down at the sunny yolks of my eggs. "You should probably talk about something else."

"I don't want to," she said and wriggled closer to me. She wrapped one of my curls around her finger. "But I miss you so much and it's not the same with Dustin. You don't have to be jealous of him. We're used to each other and it's easy. I thought you were the kind of person who could understand that?"

"What kind of person is that?" I asked.

"Advanced," she said. "You don't buy into things having to appear a certain way."

I hated when my father said we had to look right or do things a specific way because that's what people expected. Was I doing to her what he did to me?

"I don't," I said quickly.

"And you understand that sometimes it's nice to have someone around, even if I don't care about him like I do about you."

"Yeah, I guess."

"But if it upsets you that much." She shrugged, wiping egg yolk off her plate with a half-eaten piece of toast.

"I guess I was upset because I thought it meant something," I said. I wanted to feel better, but I didn't.

"It means I missed you."

She put her empty plate on the nightstand and took mine out of my hands, setting it on top of hers. Then she started kissing me. Sex with her was still great. Not like we were huge sex freaks, but once we got started, she went along in whatever direction I wanted to go. (Nothing too out there. Mostly some oral in addition to every which way we could fit two bodies together.) I loved how her curvy body looked in the sheets, especially when she was responding to me, arching her back up or grabbing handfuls of blanket.

In the middle of sex that morning, I realized that I was breathing fully into my belly, like Blake had said, and I laughed a little. Sierra was too absorbed in the patterns I was tracing with my tongue to notice.

So I could feel one thing very clearly: lust. Or love. Maybe both. Two emotions. The two best ones. I wasn't sure I needed any others.

CHAPTER NINETEEN

Had I told Sierra she could go on having sex with Dustin? I kept replaying the conversation. I hadn't said "yes" exactly, but I hadn't said "no" either.

I didn't want to be the jerk who imposed external rules on our relationship based on what people would think. I worried that was the real reason I'd been upset.

But then I would feel something else that I couldn't name, a thickly moving emotion like a whale trapped in an oil slick, powerful and helpless. I couldn't figure it out and I couldn't figure out how to figure it out. I wanted Blake and Kordell to come over and play cards so I could ask her a thousand questions about emotions and life and everything.

I texted Blake: *Are you guys coming over this week?*

She wrote back: *Kordi's doing a family thing today. What's up?*

I don't know, I just wanted to talk. I don't know how you do this whole emotions thing. I can't figure it out.

Talk to me, she wrote.

It's the stupid thing with Sierra and Dustin again. I still feel weird about it and I don't know why. Like maybe…I'm worried I'm being an ass about it. But I also feel gross inside. Does gross count as an emotion?

Of course, she said.

But why? Sierra's been great all week but I feel empty. I mean, gross and empty. Is that a thing?

What kind of empty? Bleak? Tired? Numb? Lost?

I put my phone down and wandered around the house. I didn't know there was more than one kind of empty, let alone so many kinds that Blake could rattle off options like that.

I went to get more Pepsi and figured while I was in the kitchen I'd tidy it up. That turned into me taking everything out of the fridge (not that there was very much in it) and wiping down all the shelves. While I worked I'd try breathing a little and feel awkward and give it up and then try again. All I felt was a very present nothing. Like Novocain at the dentist.

I went back to my phone and texted Blake: *Mostly numb.*

What's under that? she asked.

I tried to peer under the feeling. First came the gross feeling, and then a big piece of granite that was the numbness. When I shoved that aside I got a flash of lava-hot rage and a black hole feeling edged with pain.

Blake was wrong; I *was* crazy.

I put my phone down and went to finish the fridge project. After a while Cyd showed up. She took me over to walk around the Macalester campus and have coffee with her sister. Cyd's sister looked exactly like you'd expect the lesbian version of Cyd to look: lean, angular, elegant and vaguely butch. I loved getting the inside scoop on queer college parties from her, but seriously, I could not handle one more tall girl with killer cheekbones and nonfrizzy hair.

* * *

Blake and Kordell came over the next afternoon. Outfitted in electric blue jeans and a butter T-shirt, Kordell paused in the doorway, held up a six-pack of energy drinks and a monstrous bag of chips, and declared, "We're going to teach you to dominate Mystics."

We settled into the living room, Kordell sitting against the wall, me and Blake on the floor against the couch. Blake was in another pair of inky, straight-leg trousers sitting low on her hips, plus a well-worn black grape T-shirt.

She didn't mention me texting her about the numbness, but I saw her watching me like she was making sure I was okay.

Kordell pulled the decks out of Blake's backpack and offered me one but Blake snatched it out of his hand. She said, "Kordi, don't give her that deck. Lauren, swap with me and reshuffle. That deck plays too slow. And remember, don't play in turn one unless you have something great."

They'd lectured me more than once about what the great cards were. It had to do with their cost to play compared to their attack and defense numbers. (I never knew math would be so useful in real life.)

I shuffled my new deck, drew the cards for my hand off the top and looked at them. Or, rather, ended up staring at the sweet illustration on the shadow sorcerer card.

"Hey, we finally got to infinities in math analysis class," Blake said. She raised her face enough to look out of the top of her eyes. Her closed lips twisted in a smirk as wide as a grin. The effect was all nefarious mischief. "Or, as Roy says, 'anal math.' I don't think they're going to do transfinite numbers, though. It makes me sad."

"You know the kids can't handle that shit," Kordell told her. He was examining his cards, but one hand reached over to rest on Blake's leg.

"Trans-what numbers?" I asked.

"Transfinite. The mathematics of infinities," Blake said. "See, there's more than one infinity."

"How is that possible?" I asked, half-distracted by the cards. "Isn't it all just infinity?"

"No," she said with such emphatic joy that I looked up. Her face was shining, transformed from the wry smirk of a minute ago. Eyes wide, mouth-open smile. She went on, "There's a smallest infinity. If you take all the counting numbers, like zero one two three and so on, that's the smallest infinity but there are orders of infinity beyond that."

Kordell moved his hand to her wrist. "Blake, let Lauren play her card."

She jerked away from him, a flash of anger narrowing her eyes. Then she nodded at me, saying to Kordell, "Sorry."

Blake had more expressions in ten minutes than I did in a whole day. Was that from being bipolar? Did her face give an accurate map of an inner landscape I couldn't even imagine?

I felt tired from trying to keep up, but I wanted to go on watching her. I wanted to see how many expressions she had, to know what each one meant.

We put down cards. Blake played aggressively while Kordell controlled and defended. I had more attacking cards than defending but I had to put up some defense so Blake wouldn't steamroll me with her mutating monsters.

After a few turns, I asked Blake, "Is your whole wardrobe black?" Quickly adding, "I'm sorry, that sounded rude."

"You have to work a lot harder than that to offend me," she said, back to grinning. This grin was less wicked than her previous, more relaxed around the mouth. "It's not. All black. I have a few blues and an orange. Just one. But mostly black."

That didn't make sense. She didn't strike me as somber, morose, emo, goth, whatever. Of everyone I'd met here, she laughed the most.

"Why?" I asked.

She shrugged. "Because it's easy and Einstein didn't wear socks. Because of everything, and secrets, and we're all going to die eventually."

As much as I wanted to ask about Einstein and socks and secrets, the part about death caught my whole attention. I thought about death much more than I ever wanted to. When I'd lie in bed at night and feel myself falling into the nothing of space, I'd think about the end of my life. I'd get sucked into thinking about the end of all things and drop into a bottomless pool of terror. What would it be like to walk around in all black, aware of death, maybe not so afraid of it?

"What do you think happens when we die?" I asked. A slippery line of sweat formed between my fingers and the cards in my hand.

Blake cocked her head and looked at me deeply, a darker silver in her blue-gray eyes. "I don't think we can understand it because it's orders of infinities. Kordi?"

He lay down two defensive cards and said, "Last year I was playing this online game with a friend of mine—sharing an account. I had this character that I liked a lot and got pretty far in the game with. My friend decided to go hardcore. He changed the password and took the account and I could never log that character in again. For all I know, he deleted her. That's what I think death is like."

He brushed his hand down the front of his chest and said, "This is my character. And someday I'm going to have to log out and go play another character."

"What logs out?" Blake asked. "A soul?"

He said, "Infinities, right? Maybe we're all souls logged into our characters or maybe we're one infinite Soul playing all the characters."

I contemplated his hand resting on the bright blue of his jeans and my hand holding my cards. Could the same Soul underlie both of us? If we were all one Soul, would I lose my individuality when I died? Or was the Soul behind all of us so vast that each person's uniqueness was preserved within it?

I didn't know how to ask any of that so I went with, "But all the suffering. Why?"

Kordell lifted the hand I'd been watching, palm up toward the ceiling. "Maybe this game is only fun if you forget what you are. And maybe to do that you have to implement free will as a game mechanic. I don't know. But I think when you're in the game of life, the important thing is how you play it."

That sounded like what I'd learned at temple. The Rabbi never said much about an afterlife, all the focus was on this life and taking care of the people who needed it. Jenny never believed me when I told her we didn't talk about an afterlife at temple. In her Christian worldview, it was incomprehensible that a whole group of people might not be obsessed with heaven and hell and belief. She couldn't get why the words "faith" and "religion" were not synonyms.

I said, "I wonder if part of the game is about repairing the world. If it's messed up so that we have a lot of chances to make it better."

"Play," Blake told me and her word hung in the air like the answer to everything: that if life is a game the answer is to play through it. Forget about college and corporate careers, about growing up and becoming someone I couldn't stand. Forget it all and play.

Then I realized she meant the cards I was clutching in my hand.

I put down one of the two best that I could afford to play and Kordell nodded. "Good one."

We set down cards in a deepening, peaceful silence. Maybe this life was a character in a game and someday I would log out into another, bigger experience. I loved that idea.

But what happened to that person I became when I logged out? To that Soul? Would she also die someday? What was outside of the larger reality? Where did it end and what happened when you got to the end?

I came in second place in the Mystics game because Blake threw down many seriously aggressive monsters and wiped out Kordell. Of course after he was gone, she chewed through my army in two turns, but they said I should have bragging rights anyway.

We were setting up a new game when the kitchen door slammed. Sierra crossed the dining room and threw herself onto the couch lengthwise behind me and Blake. (Torso by me, feet by Blake.) Her hair hung heavily at the sides of her face, damp with humidity, and I had a great view of the beads of sweat between her breasts. She was in another one of the sundresses, this one cut in a deep V with a skirt that flounced as she walked.

She said, "The stupidity of some people. You would not believe the customers we had this afternoon."

Blake put a hand palm-down on the floor and worried a rough fingernail between two of the tightly-woven carpet ridges.

"Really?" Kordell asked, glancing up from his cards and back down.

"This guy must have been like fifty and he was huge and kind of gross, and I swear he ran into a display rack on purpose so he could watch me have to bend down and pick it all up. He stood there and watched me for like fifteen minutes and didn't even help. Ugh, I feel like I need a shower."

But she didn't get up. We played the next few rounds of the game. When she wasn't drawing a card or putting one down, Blake dug a tiny trench in the carpet with her fingernail. Sierra sighed. Twice.

"You okay?" I asked.

"Would you get me a beer? I'm too hot to get up," she said.

I face-downed my cards and got her a beer from the now gloriously clean fridge. When I handed it to her, she caught my wrist and drew me down to kiss her. After a few seconds I pulled way. It's weird to kiss in front of other people.

I sat back in my spot and picked up my cards.

Sierra sighed again. "You're more into those cards than me," she said.

"No," I started but didn't know what to say because I did want to finish that game. It would have been obnoxious to sit around making out in front of Blake and Kordell who'd have to wait for me to play my card.

"Where do you want to go for dinner?" she asked.

"I don't know. We could stay here and get pizza."

"How long are you going to be playing?"

"Kordell said he'd teach me to win and I haven't yet," I told her. "Maybe one more game after this one?"

"What am I supposed to do?" she asked.

"We can deal you in," Kordell suggested.

Sierra flopped onto her back and stared at the ceiling. Her fingers played with the end of one of my curls.

Kordell set up an impenetrable blockade and in a few more rounds Blake and I were both defeated. They gathered up the decks and started shuffling.

Sierra sat up. "I need a shower," she said. "Lauren, come with me."

"I, uh, I could…but…" Showering with her was always fun but it seemed rude to do with Blake and Kordell there.

"It won't take that long," she said. "They can play a game without you."

Kordell nodded slightly.

Blake's face was turned down and with Sierra behind her, only Kordell and I could see her frowning. But the sound of her expression carried in her voice as she told Sierra, "You two are girlfriends, we get it. You don't have to monopolize Lauren every minute she's here."

"Bitchy much," Sierra said. She shoved off the couch and stalked into the bathroom.

"We should go," Kordell said.

"Thanks for coming over," I told them.

Blake shrugged and boxed her deck. Her expression was closed. Not blank, but hard and shuttered, narrowed eyes emphasizing the planes of her cheeks. "Text me," she said.

After they'd left I got into the shower with Sierra because I could, because she was naked and cute, because she stared up at the ceiling and let me try things we hadn't done standing up yet, because I didn't want to fight. I wanted the water, her hands, and the hot steam all pressing on my skin.

We ended up going out to dinner, to a cool sushi and robata place with wildly painted Munny figures on its walls and all the decor in red, black and bamboo. Sierra told me more about her day at work and the story about the guy knocking over the display again in detail. I nodded and laughed and wondered what I was feeling because I couldn't begin to name it.

Later, I lay awake in bed next to her staring at the darkened ceiling. The white glow of a streetlight filtered in around the blinds and sketched the contours of the room in charcoals. Would my life wash out someday like color at night? What did it feel like to be nothing?

Blake had said that Zeno the character was afraid of being nothing inside—so was I. Even now I felt myself shredding away, turning colorless and empty. I put my mind inside the idea of Zeno. As nanites, could she become anything at all? How did it feel to be made of nanites?

Maybe being Zeno felt like a small version of a great Soul inhabiting all the humans of the world. Maybe all her shapeshifting was an attempt to show the truth of Zeno—a truth that could never be static.

Thinking about Zeno held the emptiness at bay, but I knew it wasn't far off, lurking, waiting for me to let my guard down again.

CHAPTER TWENTY

Friday night was the party at Bear's parents' house. Her family lived near a lake where we could swim, so I got a black high-necked swimsuit that afternoon while Sierra was at work. I packed the suit into my shoulder bag with my sketchbook, iPod, pens, pencils and miscellany. When Sierra got home, I watched her trying to determine the right suit to bring, which involved a lot of nice undressing.

Then the house was full of people. Cyd was there with her new boyfriend, sitting at the dining room table. They were drinking wine and sharing a loaf of French bread that they tore into chunks and dipped in olive oil and balsamic vinegar. I wanted to sit with them but I'd be in the way.

Roy showed up in knee-length khaki-colored shorts that I hoped were his swimming attire and feared were not. (Naked men and leeches topped my list of unacceptable lake creatures.)

Blake wasn't there. Disappointment and relief wrestled inside me. Kordell wasn't there either. Were they together? If so, what were they doing? What was it like with Blake in bed? She probably directed everything, but who knows, maybe Kordell was less reserved once you got his clothes off.

I rubbed my fingers over my eyelids to brush away those thoughts and went to sit next to Sierra. Dustin was there as usual, but he sat on the other couch and had a new girl with him: short, blond and heavy, with pink porcelain skin and a pretty mouth.

"Lauren, this is Gabby. You're not the new girl anymore," he said. "She joined the story this week. She mostly writes music, so she's going to compose the native songs of the Illudani." To Gabby, he added, "Lauren is Sierra's girlfriend."

I still loved how that sounded: girlfriend. That's right.

Gabby showed me the kind of shaky smile you give when you're surrounded by weirdos and starting to suspect you're one of them.

"Welcome and all that," I said. "It's a fun group."

"Rule number one: don't believe a thing Roy says," Sierra remarked with a sharp laugh.

Roy made a huff of protest. He was sitting on the other side of Gabby and she tried to shift away from him without looking like she was. That put her closer to Dustin, who failed to suppress a smile.

"Sierra tells me you want Zeno to rescue Cypher," Dustin said to me.

I marshaled my arguments and presented them. "I think we're going to need the other half of that artifact. We need Cypher to figure out where it is. If we have the whole artifact, the one that makes matter take its true form, we can use that on the High God, along with the weapon from the other universe. I think we're going to need both so the High God can't turn immune."

I held my breath.

Dustin nodded. "That makes a lot of sense."

"I don't think Solar's going to make it easy for us," Sierra said. "Are you, Roy? Or maybe Cypher will team up with Solar and go get the weapon."

"Not after he tortured her like that," I said.

"She might be into that," Sierra replied.

I remembered Blake saying it was gross, but I didn't want to repeat that here. Blake and I had agreed we could tell each other anything and I felt like that put a blanket of confidentiality over all our conversations.

"We should ask Blake," Roy suggested. "Is she coming over?"

Sierra answered, "She's meeting us at the party. She's staying the night at Bear's so she doesn't have to bus home late."

Roy said, "We should go. When are we going over?"

"Should head over around eight," Dustin told him. "Swimming isn't until near dusk. I've got to run by the liquor store and pick up some things."

"Lauren can take us over," Sierra offered.

"Sure," I said. "But if we're not going for a while, I have another question about the rescue. If Zeno's the best thief in the galaxy, can't she go steal Cypher?"

"How's she going to get out with Cypher's body?" Sierra asked. "She's in pretty bad shape."

"Well, Zeno's a colony of nanites, right? So she could fly in there, copy Cypher's body, take her place, send Cypher out in a disguise or even hide her somewhere while she recovers, and when Cypher's out safe, Zeno could change forms again and leave."

"That's pretty good," Dustin said. "Roy, you have a counter to that?"

"What if I put a chip in Cypher to track her?" Roy suggested.

"Can't I cut it out and absorb it into my copy of her body?" I asked.

"Put it in her brain," Sierra said.

I turned sideways so I could see Sierra's face. It was set in a doll-like half pout. She did not like the idea of Zeno rescuing Cypher.

"Don't you think Cypher's been through enough already?" I asked.

"Let's skip the brain idea," Dustin said. "If Zeno is going to cut a microchip out of Cypher and duplicate her, that's a pretty good scene. I'm for it unless I hear better."

"You think that's better than Cypher turning on us and going with Solar to get the weapon?" Sierra asked. "I don't. It's more dramatic the other way."

It was like Sierra was determined to pit Cypher against the Queen.

"She could pretend to turn on us," I suggested. "But plan to get the weapon and bring it to us."

So strange all of us arguing about Blake's character and she wasn't even there to say what she would do.

Dustin said, "Let's do both. Zeno goes to steal Cypher, does the stuff with the chip and all that, but Cypher tells Zeno to leave because Cypher's going to join forces with Solar."

Which she would never do, I thought. No way was I leaving Blake's character to team up with Roy. I said, "That could still be a trick. She has to lie to Zeno. There might be recording devices in the room so she has to convince Zeno that she's becoming a traitor for real, even if that's not her end plan."

"That's brutal," Roy said. "I like it."

Sierra shifted on the couch next to me and made a half-puff of air sigh, quiet enough that I was the only one to hear it.

"The Queen won't like being betrayed by Cypher. Even if it comes out later that she was lying," Sierra said.

"Good drama all around," Dustin declared. "Lauren, can you start writing that this week?"

"Sure," I said. "If Blake's okay with it."

Sierra's tone was cool as she said, "She will be. She doesn't care about the story that much. She'll go along with it."

When she got up to refill her drink, I followed Sierra into the kitchen.

"Are you mad at Blake?" I asked.

"She's not talking to me," Sierra said. "It's not me. Maybe she's depressed or whatever. She's supposed to be my best friend but we were at the same party weekend before last and every time I walked into a room she was leaving. She didn't even say hi. And she was all bitchy to me when you guys were playing cards. I don't know what her deal is."

"Maybe she does care about the story. Maybe she doesn't like Cypher being kidnapped."

Sierra shook her head. "Who knows? Dustin seemed to like your ideas a lot."

She seemed sad and I wanted to make her smile, so I said, "Well I didn't tell him the other ideas I have, about the Queen and Zeno."

"Oh really?"

"Yeah, but I think I'm going to need to do some research. I'll need you to help me out."

That went over very well, but it left me wondering why it was so easy to talk about the story and about sex, but not about how I felt.

CHAPTER TWENTY-ONE

The beach near Bear's parents' house was open until ten p.m. Sunset was at nine, so everyone planned for a sunset swim and hanging out in the backyard. When we got there, Bear showed us around the house: the upstairs was off limits except for the bathroom. The basement held a pool table, two guest rooms, and a shower we could use after swimming because lakes are gross.

A ton of food was set out along the kitchen counters next to a big, beautifully written sign that said, "No booze or pot in the house!" There were a bunch of people crammed into the kitchen eating and more in the backyard.

"Did you make all this?" I asked Bear.

"No, my mom did when she asked me to house-sit." At my questioning look she added, "And some of it was leftovers. They have parties here every other weekend practically. She figures my friends are safer over here than anyplace else. My uncle lives down the street."

That almost made sense. We got plates of food. Sierra saw people she knew from the university in the yard so she went to talk to them and I wandered back through the house.

I wasn't inclined to go around sticking my nose into groups of strangers. I got out my iPod and sketchbook and curled into an armchair in the corner of the dining room. It was a long formal dining room and no one attending the party spent time in there, so I got to draw and listen to music alone for a while.

A shadow fell over me and I glanced up. Blake was in black jeans and a black T-shirt. The shirt had a triangle on it with a moose walking up the long side. Written on the animal's body was the word "hypotemoose."

"What's the regular word for that?" I asked, pointing at her shirt.

"Hypotenuse."

"That's terrible," I said, but I thought it was wonderful. Who else showed up to a party wearing a math pun and making it look cool?

The shirt hung loosely past her waist and I wanted to slide my hand up under it, put my palm on the warm skin of her stomach or the rise of her hip. I mentally kicked myself.

"Thanks," Blake said with her midrange grin, her everything's-good grin. Not her making-trouble grin or her wild-flight-of-thought grin.

"What are you listening to?" she asked.

I pulled out an earbud and offered it to her. She dragged a chair over from the dining room table and sat close enough to slip the round plastic into her ear. She listened for a while, face lit with a thoughtful enthusiasm.

She had at least a dozen kinds of grins and more than that in smiles. I wanted to draw all of them. I wanted to draw this expression right now, eyes half-lidded and unfocused, her mouth barely open, upturned more on the left than the right. The squareness of her cheeks and the heavy, broad base of her nose.

"I didn't expect that," she said as she handed the earbud back to me.

"What did you think I listen to? Classical?"

"Hey, I listen to classical. It's elegant. I don't know. Alternative, sure, but not that hard...or loud. Who is that?"

"Halestorm," I told her.

"I did not picture you listening to metal. I like it. I mean, that you listen to it. I don't know that I could all the time."

"I don't all the time either," I admitted. "Mainly when stuff's going on and I'm trying to concentrate."

She peered around the empty room in the midst of the party, like the eye of a hurricane, and laughed.

I said, "Sierra thinks you're mad at her."

"I'm not in the mood for her," Blake replied. "You going swimming?"

The loose edge of her shirt. The memory of my fingers on her hips the night we kissed. My heart lurched and sputtered into a flurry of beating. It said: *swimming with you? Heck yes.*

I told my heart to cut it the fuck out.

I said, "In a bit. I'm working on an illustration of Zeno trying to rescue Cypher."

That got a broad, open grin. I wasn't sure what to call that grin, maybe enthusiasm-for-your-art? She said, "Sweet. Can I sit here while you draw or does that bug you?"

"You can sit here," I said, pleased that she'd asked first. "You want to keep sharing the iPod or is it too metal?"

She held out her hand and I put the earbud back in it, fingers brushing palm. She moved her chair closer.

"Is Kordell not here?" I asked.

"No, he had to go do another family thing. They left this morning."

"Do you miss him?"

"Of course," she said. She settled next to me and put the earbud in her delicate ear. "Bring on the metal."

Sierra came in while we were listening together and I was drawing. She looked at me strangely. I couldn't understand her face. It wasn't anger, it was cold.

After Blake hopped up and gave her a hug, she softened.

"Are we swimming?" she asked.

"Yeah, let me get into my suit," I said. "How far's this beach?"

"Half a block."

Running down the street in my suit with a towel wrapped around me was weird, but there were about ten other people with us and more already at the beach. The setting sun smeared the horizon with melting orange popsicle. It was a close, warm night, perfect since in June lakes can be chilly. I swam around (by which I mean dog-paddled lamely). Sierra pulled me into an alcove made by a tree hanging over the water and we made out, chest deep in the lake, hands roaming over each other.

She seemed not as much there as usual, not as responsive to me, but maybe that was the effect of the cool water. Or maybe it was me. I didn't feel right. Mostly numb and not from the chill lake.

Was it numb? Or tired? Or some kind of angry? I didn't like how she'd been about the character of Cypher. I didn't like how she reacted to Dustin showing up with Gabby. I didn't like how she'd pushed Blake and Kordell out the other day when we were playing cards. The way she'd called Blake "bitchy." The most Blake ever said against Sierra was that she wasn't in the mood for her.

But I liked how Sierra's body felt under my hands. I liked how my body reacted to hers, at least on the surface, but under my skin ran waves of heat cut through with queasiness. Numb was easier, especially with her tongue in my mouth and her breast filling my hand.

We fumbled around for a while and she said, "Let's go to the bonfire. I'm getting cold."

"Me too," I agreed.

We hurried to the house and slipped through the open gate to the backyard where a fire burned in the ornate fire pit. Bear came through telling people to keep the volume down. There were about a dozen people in the backyard, most of them stoners. They cut the volume by half after her warning.

"Do you care if I go smoke with them?" Sierra asked.

"No, go for it."

She went over to the far corner of the yard and I sat watching the fire burn down. I didn't know how to bridge the distance between us. I wanted to go over with the utterly cool right words and get her to come away with me, maybe go home and get into bed. But I also didn't.

Maybe I didn't want to work that hard. A month ago, two months ago, I'd been wild for her, wanted to drive to the Cities and spend every waking moment with her. Now all we did was have sex and eat dinners out and sit around her house talking about sex and eating.

Maybe I was a lot worse at relationships than I'd ever expected.

Blake came back from the lake while I was staring at the embers of the fire and trying to figure out what to do. She'd wrapped a huge beach towel around her shoulders like a cloak, and in the darkness the color of it had turned from dark blue to nearly black. I almost laughed—of course Blake would find a way to make even her swim towel black.

"I've got smoke in my hair," she said, gazing into the glowing coals. "I'm going to shower."

She went toward the house but stopped, turned around and looked at me.

I said, "Yeah, good idea, me too."

I followed her inside.

The basement had this big rec room space and two little guest rooms. Blake was spending the night in one of those rooms. Too bad she had a guest room to herself and no Kordell to share it with.

"There's a shower in the basement," she said.

"Are you saying I should…" I trailed off.

I remembered her leaning forward from the couch at Sierra's during my first visit, when I'd said the thing about black holes. She'd said, "I kind of love you right now." I felt like that too. All random and happy around her, but I thought that was more like a sister thing. Not that I'd know.

And I loved Sierra, right? When I was in town, we had sex almost every night and she cuddled me and she was always emailing and calling me "baby" and stuff. I wanted to spend the whole summer with her. Or at least I had until I actually got to the Cities this time.

Halfway down the stairs, Blake turned to look at me again. Like she was checking to make sure I was coming with her.

"I've got to get my clothes," I told her. I'd left them behind the chair in the dining room after I put my swimsuit on, so I gathered them up and went down the stairs.

The main room in the basement was dim, two people making out in one corner on the far side of a Ping-Pong table. Everyone else was in the yard or in the big, bright living room on the first floor. I went down the short hall to the open door with light spilling out. The larger of the two guest rooms had an attached bathroom, big enough for a shower, toilet and sink. I dropped my clothes on the foot of the bed.

Blake stood in the open sliding door to the shower, her hand under the spray. She got in with her swimsuit on. Her suit was a light tangerine with teal piping that made her skin warm and luminous.

She'd left the shower door open, like an invitation, so I got in. We washed our hair and chatted about school like we weren't standing in a shower together.

"I'm thinking about taking a math class at the university next year," she was saying while she rubbed shampoo into her hair. "I can take calculus II at my high school, or there's Intro to Advanced Mathematics at the U. I'd have to bus over there a bunch, but it sounds really cool."

She switched places with me so I could dip my hair under the water.

"I thought all math was advanced," I said, trying to sound casual and, if possible, nonstupid.

I couldn't stop thinking about the fact that we were a foot apart and it's not like bathing suits are the most covering garments. Blake favored loose tops or layers. In her swimsuit, she was stocky and slender, with smaller breasts than mine. Because she was shorter than me, I couldn't help but be staring down into her cleavage.

She went on talking blithely. "It's got probability theory, which would be amazing. Matrices, multivariable differentiation and integration. But I could take honors calculus II."

"It's like you stopped speaking English," I told her.

"Hey, do you know why they don't serve beer at math parties?" she asked, voice light.

"Why?"

"So people won't drink and derive."

I laughed, even though I didn't know why that was funny. Her laughter made me want to join in.

I ran the soap over my arms and glared at my bathing suit. My skin was wrinkling under the wet fabric. A lake plant had wedged itself into my suit and was sliming my back. It wasn't like anything was going to happen between me and Blake.

"This is stupid," I said. I set the soap on its ledge and pulled the straps down on my suit. "I have lake grossness on me. Sorry."

"No, it's cool," she replied. She turned half away and took her suit off too.

I squeezed the water out of mine and threw it over the top of the shower door and she did the same. For a moment I managed not to look. But my gaze wouldn't stop wandering over to her body.

She had that same beautiful olive color all over and it gave her skin a smooth and flawless quality. Her breasts hung lower than mine, making her seem more than a few days older than me, and I thought about resting the weight of them in my hands. I couldn't help it. Her nipples were dark brown and there was the softness of her belly and below that I saw, with a shock, that she was shaved.

Was that from having sex with guys? Did Kordell like that? Or did she like it herself? Did I like it?

I turned away, picked up the soap again. We rinsed off, carefully not touching. Switching places was even trickier with nothing covering our breasts as we moved by each other. I felt like the steam from the shower was collecting in my lungs, heavy and dense, making it hard to breathe.

She got out first and went into the guest room, giving me enough space in the bathroom to towel off. I wrapped the towel around my body and stepped into the room.

Blake was sitting in a chair by the mirrored dresser, brushing out her hair, still naked.

I had not a single clue about what we were doing here. Was she mostly straight and this was one of those surreal moments when a straightish girl doesn't realize you don't sit around naked with your lesbian friends? Or was she very bi, like she said, completely and totally bi and interested in me?

Did it matter? I was with Sierra.

I figured the safe bet was to do what Blake was doing. Pulling off my towel, I rubbed it across my arms and legs, then draped it over the foot of the bed. My clothes were there, folded in a neat pile, but Blake wasn't getting dressed. She'd started rubbing lotion on her arms and held the bottle out to me.

I took it and sat on the edge of the bed a few feet from her. She was talking about her math class and I listened enough to say "uh-huh" in the right places. I kept lotioning my legs and trying not to look at her too much while so much wanting to look at her.

She had her legs crossed but her arms open, like she wasn't trying to hide how naked she was. One hand rested on her thigh, fingers spread. I remembered those fingers on the back of my neck when we kissed, surprisingly strong. Her body was compact, hips broader than you'd notice in her everyday clothes, but broad shoulders too, slender but not skinny.

What do you say to a girl who's sitting naked in a chair talking about mathematics like this is all completely reasonable? Searching for something safe to comment about, I looked around. A massive daddy long legs spider was crawling up the edge of the mirror behind her.

I yelped (okay, screamed) and scrambled backward. Slipping off the foot of the bed, I fell onto the floor and kept moving back until I hit the wall.

The side of my arm pressed hard against the foot of the bed. The bed was level with my shoulder, so I could see Blake staring at me while the horrible creature blithely crawled along a few feet from her.

"Spider!" I managed to say. "On the mirror."

Blake's wide-eyed expression of alarm transformed into a grin. (I guess the naked-girl-freaked-out-by-spider-is-cracking-me-up grin.) She examined the edge of the mirror until she saw the spider making his creepy way up the wooden border.

"Hey, little guy," she said. "Let's get you out of here before Lauren has a heart attack."

She put one hand in front of the creature and tapped him. He scooted into her palm and she closed her fingers around him. Or her. Could've been a girl spider. Blake wasn't screaming in pain from being bitten, so maybe it was a girl spider and they had some sisterhood thing going.

I squeezed my eyes shut and pressed back into my safe corner bordered by wall and bed. I heard Blake get up and the creak of a window opening. Another creak and click as it closed, followed by the sound of her crossing the room. Water burbled from the bathroom as she washed her hands.

I needed to get up and put clothes on. Being naked and freaking out was so much worse than freaking out while dressed. If it hadn't been disgusting, Blake picking up the spider would have been amazingly cool. But right now I wanted clothes and to get out of this room and away from this spidery house. I needed to draw and think and listen to metal and figure all this out.

When I opened my eyes, Blake was standing in the bathroom doorway staring down at me. Still naked.

Still.

Naked.

When you're going to be looking at a naked person, especially a cute naked person, up from the floor is not the angle to pick. That is if you don't want to feel like a ten ton weight dropped onto your chest. Maybe if I'd been off her left shoulder and a hundred miles away…

Looking up at her, I wasn't numb anymore. I could see a million places I wanted to touch with my fingers and my tongue and my fingers again. I was white-hot, burning with a fire that didn't consume but spilled light through every cell of me.

"You okay?" she asked.

"Oh yeah, I do this all the time," I said.

I pushed to my feet and grabbed my shirt.

Turning to fully face Blake, I asked, "Why *are* we naked?" The words came out harsher than I'd planned because if all that fire wasn't going into lust, it had to go toward anger.

As she heard my question, the slowest, widest grin spread across her mouth and up to her eyes. Those eyes narrowed, grew wicked and joyful. I felt her delight that we were naked together and her desire. The hair on my arms rose. The impact of her grin hit my throat and my gut. It disintegrated the world around us.

"Oh," I breathed out the sound. I couldn't form words, but the rest of the sentence in my head was: *you* do *want me*.

My fingers dropped the shirt on the way to her.

Her lips met mine already open and I felt her tongue right away, still rough like a cat's, perplexing, fascinating. I drank in the feeling. I inhaled it. I wanted to compress my whole self into her mouth and feel nothing but her tongue. My hands on her back barely registered her skin because I was so into her mouth and kissing her.

Blake made a small sound and her knees bent. We went down in a tangle, half-sitting, half in the bathroom doorway so we couldn't lie down. Kissing her, I got to my knees and moved back a few feet into the bedroom, trying to figure out how to navigate with four legs and four arms. Her lips were neat and agile, her tongue playing in the joined space of our mouths.

She pushed against me, pressing me back from kneeling to sitting. Every time the movement of our bodies pulled our lips apart, she found my mouth again. Somehow with our lips together and her hands on me, she climbed into my lap.

Our breasts touched and a wave of vertigo hit me. My legs were out in front of me and she settled in my lap, facing me, wrapping her legs around my waist. Our hips rocked together. I couldn't tell who started the motion; it was like the rocking arose first and we followed like boats on a wave.

I wanted to touch her all over but I couldn't stop kissing her. She ground down against me and I rocked up into the heat and wet between her legs. She broke our kiss, panting near my ear as I kissed her neck, her chin, the side of her face. She smelled like shampoo, bright and commercial, but under that I got her real scent: maple-sweet and earthy, honeysuckle flowers and vibrant green moss.

Blake was holding onto my shoulders so hard I felt the edges of her short fingernails. She buried her face in the side of my neck and shook. She was coming already. I held her tightly, pressed my lips to the curve of her jaw and inhaled while the tremors in her body expanded then quieted.

After a while she said, "We're on the floor."

I didn't want to move. I didn't want to let go of her and I couldn't figure out what that meant. I was supposed to be with Sierra. I loved Sierra and I'd never been completely sure what to think of Blake. But in this moment I couldn't imagine how I could take my hands off Blake. I ran my fingers down her spine to the small of her back and she wriggled against me.

"Lauren," her breath was hot in my ear. "Can we get on the bed?"

"On?" I asked.

Her question didn't sound like a person who was done and ready to get dressed, but my brain was spinning and I might not have heard right.

"Yeah, or in it," she said and brushed the tip of her thumb over my lips. "You know, like people do."

"Get in the bed?" I asked.

What I meant was: *you want me to get in the bed with you and keep going?* But as usual the gulf between my brain and my mouth swallowed most of the words. My tongue felt clumsy in my mouth without her tongue to balance against.

With Sierra, after she came we were usually done. Occasionally she'd reciprocate but more likely I'd take care of myself somewhere in the middle of things. Even if she did reciprocate, I wasn't a sure thing and sometimes would just end up more frustrated, so it was easier that way.

"Do you have a thing about beds?" Blake asked. "Or is it too close to where the spider was?"

Remembering the spider, I laughed, but not so hard that I couldn't say, "The bed. Yes. I like beds."

She got up and pulled back the blanket, got into the bed and I followed. We started kissing again, deliberately slow, luxuriously. The feeling of her and the cool sheets on my skin was maddening.

I kissed her neck and chest and all over her breasts, watching her nipples rise and tighten. I reached between her legs and felt the light prickle of stubble. She pressed her hips up, pushing into my fingers and I slid my hand down to feel how wet she was. I played around, finding my bearings and spreading the wetness everywhere.

She grabbed my wrist. "Too soon," she gasped. "Anyway, your turn."

"You don't have to..."

The words faltered because her eyes were so close to mine, an inch away, full of intense sky and storms and shadow. She put her mouth on mine and rolled on top of me.

Then she was moving down my body quickly, not kissing or teasing, on top one moment and between my legs the next. Her breast grazed my inner thigh and the protest I was going to make caught in my throat.

I meant to say, "I don't think I like..." or "I can take care of that..." but she looked up at me with her face bright.

I tried again to say that I wasn't sure I liked oral. I'd never done it on the receiving end. I was sensitive, too self-aware. The words didn't work themselves out for me. I thought about how she'd grabbed my wrist, how I could catch her shoulder the same way and pull her up again, but she was leaning on the inside of my thigh, touching me, and I didn't want her to stop.

Her fingers and her tongue weren't tentative. She pushed against me in ways that felt intense, on the edge of pain. Not fluttering and nervous. Not like I'd been the first time.

Had she learned that from having sex with guys? Was that what they liked? Was this what I liked?

The pressure of her mouth varied soft to hard and I squirmed under her—part trying to get away but more pushing closer. Some of it hurt. Some of it was light but irritating. Moments of jarring pleasure shot through me, laced with strokes that made me more frustrated.

I kept thinking I should tell her to stop. It wasn't going to work. I couldn't come this way and I'd taken too much time already, too much focus on me. I felt strange and exposed. We'd showered, but I was so wet—did I feel okay to her? How did I smell? What did I taste like? Was it bitter like Sierra? I hoped not.

Her mouth moved away. Maybe that was it, she was done. I glanced down. Her face was turned toward me and she grinned. Another grin to add to my collection. A variation on the yes-I-want-you grin. I relaxed a little; I guess if she wanted to be doing that, I wasn't going to argue.

Watching my face, she slid a finger inside me. I gasped because it was good and I wanted more, but I couldn't talk. With her between my legs, I was too vulnerable. She pulled away again and I closed my eyes, steeling myself to kiss a bit more and be content, but her fingers were back inside me, more of them. Her tongue was there too, around and above, driving spikes of dizzy fire.

My brain shut the hell up.

I didn't come and I didn't care. The rough surface of her tongue on any part of me was shocking and brilliant. I had no idea what she was doing with her hand but I wanted it to go on and on. Concentric circles of wonder spun out from her through my whole body.

When the intensity turned more painful than good, I reached down, grabbed her shoulder and tugged. Blake pushed up and rested on one arm, looking questions at me. I sat up to where I could kiss her, both of us hesitant for a heartbeat and then deep in each other's mouths again. She lay down on me, our bodies jammed against each other.

I shoved my hand between my thigh and her legs, slid around until my finger was over her clit and let the rocking do the rest. She came shaking, quivering and making a half-sobbed sound into my shoulder that I wanted to hear about a thousand more times. That, plus the pressure of her leg between mine, made me come too, the pleasure shrill and disorienting, gone too quickly.

I wanted to catch my breath and do it all again. I wanted to never leave this bed and at the same time, I wanted us to be together anywhere but here.

All the moving parts wouldn't fit back into my mind. I didn't know where to begin thinking about this and I didn't want to. I wanted to hold onto Blake and explore how I felt with her. I wanted time and space enough to feel everything.

There were steps on the floor above. Lots of them. Everyone else must be coming in from the fire. We held tightly together and listened. Her chest shook with silent laughter and I wondered what she was thinking. The spider or something else?

I wanted to ask, but I realized with a chill of fear that Sierra could come down here any second and find us naked, covered in cooling sweat, wrapped around each other. I needed another shower.

"I have to get dressed," I said. "What do I tell Sierra?"

Blake shook her head but rolled away so that I could disentangle myself and get out of the bed. (What did it all mean? I needed to know.) I looked at Blake lying there, her hair coal-black against the pale pillow, her slate-blue eyes looking at me with warm humor or lust or both.

I wanted enough time with her to separate out the strands of what I was feeling and examine each one and figure out what it meant.

"Tell her I saved you from a spider," Blake said.

"That won't make sense."

"What would?" she asked.

"Uh…ask me again when I can think."

She laughed, got up and kissed me roughly. Going to her pile of clothes, she shrugged into them. She went from a beautiful, lithe form back to a black-wrapped mystery.

"You're lovely," she said and walked out of the room.

I put on my clothes and sat in the chair by the mirror, thinking: *what the hell just happened?*

CHAPTER TWENTY-TWO

I didn't tell Sierra right away. I wanted to hold being with Blake inside of me and look at it again and again. I wanted to figure it out before I talked about it.

Sierra and I went home after the party. She fell asleep. I didn't, not for a long time. In the morning she asked if she could borrow my car for errands. I said yes and went back to bed. Later, in the silence of the house, I wrote everything in my journal and read through it and still didn't know what to make of it.

Blake would have words for all this. She knew four different kinds of numb. She'd know what to call these feelings. Inside I was like a box of crayons left in the sun, colors and textures running together until they could never be pulled apart into what they'd been.

When Sierra got back I was sitting on the couch with my journal in my lap, staring at the words on the page. I had to tell her because she came over and kissed me. It didn't feel right to be kissing her without having told her.

"Can we talk?" I asked and closed my journal.

She sat on the other end of the couch and crossed her arms. "About what?"

She hadn't gelled her hair that morning and the purple locks tousled together all messy. I wanted to run my fingers through it and settle it. Her mouth turned down, halfway between a frown and a pout.

"I kind of did something," I said.

I remembered the stinging jealousy I felt when she told me about Dustin. I didn't want to go on. Why had I done that to her? I wasn't that kind of person. And at the same time, weirdly, having sex with Blake didn't feel wrong—but hurting Sierra felt awful.

"Did something bad?" she asked.

I braced myself against the couch, let my breath out in a quick huff, and went for it.

"I had sex with Blake," I told her. "But it was just a thing, you know? I still love you and I'm still with you…" I wanted to keep talking and fill the space with words, but I ran out of points to make.

Her pale face went paler. "You? When?" she asked.

I ran a fingernail along the rolled edge of the couch cushion.

"Last night," I admitted. "At the party."

"When?" she asked again.

"After the lake. It was late, you were out back smoking. I went to take a shower."

Her eyes were crushed ice as she said, "And then you had sex with Blake? After the shower?"

"Um, yeah."

"Why?"

How could I explain it? We were naked and there was this gross spider and suddenly I was kissing Blake. There was no way to put those words together that made sense to a reasonable person. I could pretend that I would have stopped after the kiss, that it was Blake who pushed it, but that was a lie. Even thinking about it now brought back an echo of incandescence from touching Blake.

Fear mixed with longing, how did that even make sense as an emotion? With Sierra it was simple. Our relationship had about three emotions to it: love, anger and…what was the third? Lust? Numbness? Numb lust?

"I don't know," I said.

"Were you trying to hurt me?"

"No! You had sex with Dustin. I guess I thought it was okay. That we weren't exclusive."

That sounded stupid even to me, but it was better than agreeing that I was trying to get back at her. She could run with that for days.

"So you thought it was okay to fuck my best friend?" Her words were knife-edged.

"I…"

I hadn't been thinking. That was kind of the thing. Also not a point that I wanted to say out loud—that Blake gave me this beautiful, wicked smile and I'd stopped thinking. That at the time, I couldn't imagine doing anything but kissing her.

"I only hooked up with Dustin because you're so fucking far away," Sierra said. She got up from the couch and stalked around the room. "You *like* Blake."

"No I don't. I mean, yeah, I like her but not *like* like. Not like you. I love you."

"Well you have a weird way of showing it."

"I'm sorry," I said.

I wanted to curl up in a ball, put in my earbuds turned up as high as I could stand, and wait for her anger and hurt to pass. But I'd done this. I was responsible. I had to sit and get through it.

"Was that why she was talking to me again?" Sierra asked. "Because she was fucking you? Was she laughing at me?"

"No! That was before. I mean, she was already talking to you. We didn't plan this, it just happened."

She glared at me and walked out of the room. I heard her get in my car and drive away. If she fucked up that car, my father was going to kill me.

I couldn't settle down enough to draw or journal. I kept bouncing between rooms, trying to find something I could do until she got back. I texted her that I was sorry and that she should come back and talk, that I'd make it up to her. She didn't reply.

I walked to the park with the dogs. Sitting on the bench I'd shared with Blake, I put my palm on the bare wood where she'd been. I wanted to talk to her—but what I wanted to talk about was Blake. I couldn't call her up as a friend to talk about the girl I'd had sex with when she *was* that girl.

Had I lost her as a friend? She was the one person I could talk to. She was the only one who saw what I was drawing and got it.

My eyes burned and my chest was so tight I could hardly breathe, but I couldn't cry. I could never cry in front of people, not even strangers in a dog park watching their pets.

I walked back to the house. In the bedroom, I put in my earbuds, curled into one corner of the small couch, and let the metal tear through me.

After a while, the door opened and Sierra came in. She got on the couch, crouching in front of me, not sitting, and brushed her hand over the top of my head. I took out one of the earbuds.

"Lauren, it's going to be okay."

I turned off the music and took out the other earbud. She put her arms around me.

"We'll figure it out," she told me. "I get it. You were pissed off about Dustin and you wanted to make it even. Now we're even."

If that's what she had to think to make us okay again, I wasn't going to argue.

"Yeah, I guess I was," I said. "I'm so sorry."

She sat back on the couch, resting one hand on my leg.

"I can't say I'm not hurt. I am. Blake was avoiding me and suddenly she gets friendly again the same night she has sex with you. It's like I don't know who I can trust anymore."

"You can trust me," I said.

"I hope so. I love you, you know."

"I love you too."

She turned toward me and studied my face. I don't know what she was searching for, but she said, "You do, don't you?" It sounded more like an answer than a question.

I nodded, feeling tears behind my eyes. I pushed them back.

"Let's go out somewhere," she said. "Let's get all dressed up and go out and have a date. It'll be fun."

"Sure."

She went across the room to change clothes and I dug around in my suitcase for something clean to wear. Stepping into my jeans, I saw myself in the mirror on the back of her bedroom door and shook my head at the reflection. She seemed to be judging me, saying that my father was right, I was a reckless, undisciplined girl. All I'd wanted was a girlfriend and now that I had one, I was destroying my relationship.

Maybe I *was* sabotaging my whole life. That's what the grade in American history was about, that's why I was so dramatic, that's what was wrong with me.

Maybe, like Zeno, I was masquerading as human. But I wasn't elegant like a colony of nanites. Whatever my true form was, it was monstrous.

CHAPTER TWENTY-THREE

I wanted to go to dim sum, but Sierra wanted eggs benedict so we went to Wilde Roast down by the river. Afterward we strolled along the bank, watching all the dogs out walking their people. In the middle of the path, Sierra caught my hand, pulled me close and kissed me. I felt too conscious of the people and dogs looking at us, but also relieved. We were making up, it was going to be okay.

"Bookstore?" I asked when I figured it'd been long enough for a make-up kiss.

"Of course!" she said.

We drove over to the Book House and I picked out a couple of manga for her to read next. She wanted the next novel in her epic fantasy series so I got that for her too. We sat in a nearby coffee shop and read while sipping fancy coffee drinks.

I pulled my phone out of my pocket. I'd turned off the sound in the restaurant. There was one text from my father, asking what time I planned to be home that evening, and a few from Blake.

I held my breath and texted back that I wanted to stay another day, leave Monday morning. Then I peeked at the first text from Blake.

She wrote: *I decided on Calculus II.*

I bit down on my tongue and held my breath to freeze the laugh rising in my chest. It was so Blake to send me a text about calculus after everything. Was she making fun of herself? (Had to be.) My hands tingled with the memory of her.

I put the phone away so I wouldn't read the next text from her.

"Everything okay?" Sierra asked.

"I texted my father that I want to go back tomorrow," I said. "Is that cool to stay another day?"

"Of course."

"He's out of town next weekend for a client thing, do you want to come up?"

"I'd love to but I can't," she said with a long, dramatic sigh. "We're doing inventory at work, I have to be there all weekend."

A flash of relief went through me. I shook my head and muscled myself over into disappointment.

"That sucks," I said. "I'm going to be all alone."

"Maybe Blake wants to visit."

"That's not cool," I told her.

"I'm sorry, I guess I'm still hurt about it. I'll be okay. Why don't we go home."

"Yeah," I said.

We went back to her place and she pulled me into the bedroom. When she kissed me, I kissed back, but I didn't feel like having sex. She seemed into it, though, and it would help the whole repairing-the-relationship phase. I got out of my clothes and slipped into bed with her.

She ran her hands all over me, like she was claiming me. It was okay, ticklish in parts, and I squirmed in a way that I tried to make look sexy. After a few minutes, I pushed her down and started kissing her harder to take the focus off me. It worked. She lay back and let me play around with her until she came.

I gestured for her to roll on her side and spooned up behind her. I didn't want her to see my face. I was afraid the flat feeling inside me would show.

She snuggled back into me and pulled my arm around her tighter. I needed a subject to think about that wasn't her or Blake or me, so I thought about ways to draw Zeno that would make it clear she was nanites and not a person at all.

* * *

My father responded with a single word: *Fine*. I stayed over Sunday night. In the morning, Sierra went to work and I packed up my stuff. I wanted to go, but I didn't want to go. I wanted to leave this house, but I didn't want to go home.

I read the other texts from Blake.

On Sunday in the early afternoon, she'd written: *I got a thank-you card from the spider's family. How are you?*

I grinned at my phone and read her text from a few hours later: *Some of these Halestorm songs aren't bad. Maybe I like metal more than I thought.*

An hour after that: *Do you know why we'll never run out of mathematicians? They multiply.*

Late last night: *Working on the story, are you around?*

This morning: *Luv ya, kid. Stay safe.*

My chest went tight and painful. I tried to breathe deeply but only managed a stuttering series of short breaths. Pain? Guilt? I couldn't tell. How could there be so many ways to feel bad?

No wonder I'd learned to stop breathing. Who needed all this shit? Emotions made you do dumb things and then feel awful about it.

But whatever I felt, Blake shouldn't have to worry about me.

I texted back: *I'm okay. Sierra and I are working on things. Thanks for checking on me. How are you?*

Her reply came a minute later: *I'm good. You told her? How was she?*

Angry, hurt. She thinks you did it on purpose.

What? I had sex with you because of her?

Did you? I asked.

No!!!

She didn't send another text and I couldn't come up with what I wanted to say. The more time that went by, the more I couldn't find the words.

I dug the bucket of cleaning stuff out from under the sink. It didn't have a lot of options for cleansers and there was no mop, but with the sponges I did my best cleaning the kitchen and bathroom.

I vacuumed and straightened up the living room and dusted with one of my T-shirts.

Then I had to get on the road, so I left Sierra a sweet note with a doodled mini Queen of Rogues on it and left.

CHAPTER TWENTY-FOUR

Arriving home, I tossed my suitcase in my room, stripped and got in the shower. I put my fingers against the cold tile. Inside me was all pain: nauseous, guilty pain about Sierra; edged ice-pain that I was so far away; burning shame and desire.

I remembered Blake in the shower with me. Closing my eyes, I tried to push the image away but that made it worse. I wanted to touch her again. I wanted her limber, deft mouth on mine and her tongue—I'd thought French kissing was kind of gross until she kissed me.

I should have thought through this emotions business before I went around having relationships. Tears gridlocked my throat and I tried to cry but ended up coughing in the steam.

When I was out and dressed, my father showed up from work. I went downstairs and watched *12 Angry Men* with him so he'd feel like we were doing the right family stuff. In the middle, he paused it and asked how my visit was. I went on about seeing Macalester and St. Kate's with Cyd. He made happy my-loser-daughter-visited-colleges sounds.

Then he went into how we (meaning me) only had a month to get the garden in perfect shape for the Garden Tour. There would be journalists and maybe a photo in a magazine, so everything had to be right. He also reminded me that not long after the tour, I was due to fly out east to spend two weeks with Mom and Isaac.

When we planned that trip, I didn't know how I'd survive being so far away from Sierra for that long. Now it would be a relief to get farther away. I told him I was looking forward to it, forgetting that this would set him off on a rant about everything she'd done to us when she left her own family, her own children…and so on.

I got away by suggesting I warm up dinner. One thing in favor of my father is that he could dig into a prepared dinner with the same gusto as a five-star restaurant entree. For all that he went nuts about the garden, he didn't give a crap about whether or not I could cook.

I could make basic stuff, but it was never better than what the Stouffers folks turned out. We ate on the couch in front of the movie. He gave his full attention to the meal and downed it in five minutes.

"Want another one?" I asked. "There's a 'lite' one, it goes very well with the steak dinners."

"Thank you," he said.

I brought him the next dinner. I wanted to ask him about dating, about how many girlfriends he had before Mom. Then I realized that he'd had many more after Mom and I didn't want to hear about any of those.

He was kind of a player.

Gross. Was I?

More gross.

I got us slices of frozen chocolate cream pie and let the movie roll on.

* * *

Mornings I started the garden stuff early to get it out of the way. Stoner Guy would roll in around eleven a.m. as I was finishing up and I'd tell him what I needed done and get myself lunch. After that, I'd check to see how badly he was fucking things up and send him off to the store. That usually took him about three hours.

Since I was already disgusting, I'd go work out, wait for him, realize he wasn't going to be back for another hour, give in and take a shower, and end up standing out in the yard again later trying not to get dirty.

My father would get home eventually and walk through the garden pointing out a million screwed-up things I'd failed to notice. I'd be thinking: *I don't even like plants!*

But if I tried suggesting he hire an expert, I'd get a lecture about responsibility and blah blah bullshit. Things were kind of okay between us right now. I didn't want to screw with that.

I fell behind on my communications with Sierra. Her messages grew further apart too.

Lauren: *How's work? The roses have scratched my arms up and I'm allergic to everything out here. My eyes are going to run right off my face one of these days. Am I missing any good parties?*

Sierra: *I miss you!!! I didn't go to the parties, no fun without you. Work sucks as usual. At least you get to be outside a bunch—I bet you have a killer tan. Can't wait to see it. Send me a pic.*

Lauren (after giving up and sending her a pic of me in front of the awful rosebushes—after my shower that day, of course): *Stoner Guy is useless. He got loads of mulch and put it all in the wrong places so we've been carting mulch for the last two days. It makes my face itch. Not just on the outside but on the inside too. I itch inside my eyeballs.*

Sierra: *Get Stoner Guy to share with you. If there's extra, bring it down next time you visit. When are you coming down again? That pic is beautiful! You should take one of you in that blue-green dress, it would look amazing with your tan.*

Lauren: *Stoner Guy carried a dripping hose of weed killer the full length of the lawn and back again so there's a crisscross series of dead grass patterns like alien crop circles. I expected a dedicated stoner like him to know how not to kill grass.*

Asked my father if I could come down for a week before my trip to see Mom. He says I'm spending too much time running around wild with you all.

She replied: *Hah! I bet your dad would freak out if he knew we were having sex. Maybe I should come up there sometime and make out with you on that big couch just to freak him out. I miss you!!!*

That was never going to happen. I'd told her over and over that it wasn't okay with my father for people to be emotional in any way. Making out on the couch "to freak him out" was so far over that line, I didn't know how she'd even gotten there.

I went for distraction and wrote back: *I like your couch a lot better.*

Then I put my phone away. I was tired all the time. Allergies probably. Every day for the last two weeks my head and sinuses ached like I had a cold. I wasn't drawing.

* * *

Two weeks into the month of pre-Garden Show torture, I found a thick envelope on the edge of the countertop in my bathroom. I hadn't gotten the mail today, so my father must have brought it up for me. It was weird enough that he hadn't left it on the kitchen counter, but on top of that, it was from Blake.

I slid my finger under the edge of the flap and opened it gently. There was no letter, only a small book: *Springs of Persian Wisdom.* So quirky and perplexing. What was it supposed to mean if you had sex with someone and followed it up by sending them a book about wisdom?

Inside the front cover, she'd written in her skinny, elongated printing: "For Lauren, I think of you every day. Love, Blake."

She'd written, "love," but as the signature line, so what kind of love was that? Was it casual, like on cards from distant relatives? Or was it what you meant when you told someone, "I love you?"

What kind of love was *that* anyway? I'd said it to Sierra so many times and now everything with her had this glossy, plastic feel to it.

What was Blake thinking when she thought of me every day? "Oh that Lauren, she's all right," or "God, I want to jump Lauren again," or "Lauren's story ideas aren't half bad," or "I can't stop thinking about you. I need you. As crazy as you are, my life makes so much more sense with you in it?"

Probably not that last part. That was me. Though she should have been thinking it. At least the crazy part. Super assholey of me to have thought of her as crazy when I was way more so.

I turned to the first page of the book:

"Such are the ways of fate in this harsh world: Today you are lifted gently into the saddle, and tomorrow the saddle is placed on your shoulders.—Firdausi."

What

The hell

Did that mean?

Irrelevant? Not the reason she sent the book?

Next page: *"If a word burns on your tongue, let it burn."*

No help.

But then: *"Through Love all things become lighter which understanding thought too heavy."*

I turned to another page.

"It was a night like no other…You came, oh my beloved! You made the night into blessed day…"

Blushing hard, I closed the little book. I held it against my chest and remembered how her body felt on mine.

I wanted to hold her (and kiss her!). Do everything again and more. I wanted to slide my fingers inside her and see what that did to her eyes and her brightly dark face. I wanted her to keep looking at me, the way she had when she was between my legs, all keen attention and wonder.

Could I trust this desire? And if I acted on it, what would I have to deal with from Sierra?

Everything jumbled together in my head like broken glass. I wanted to sweep it away, not have to pick through the fragments with bleeding fingers to find out what was real.

If I could figure it out, would it matter? I lived hours away. If I wanted to see Blake, I couldn't stay at Sierra's place. Was I going to drive down and stay at a hotel in hopes that Blake meant "love" in somewhat of the same universe as the one I understood? If it turned out that I understood love at all.

I put the book on the dresser in my bedroom. There was space for it next to the pen and the infinity pin. I touched the pen.

Blake had given it to me at the end of my first visit there. She'd handed it to me casually, saying she'd won it in a math competition but her penmanship was awful and it should go to a good home. It was beyond nice: a Retro 51 Tornado rollerball with a black barrel covered in tiny white math equations. (Blake had said they were Einstein's.) Heavy with great ink flow, it was solid in my hand and moved easily across a page.

The infinity pin she'd sent me for Zeno. She said she'd get herself a zero symbol and we could hang out together being incomprehensibly cool. (Literally, because nobody would get the symbolism but us.)

On the other side of my dresser was a dried rose that Sierra picked up for me at a gas station on her way here that time she visited. And that was it: the one flower, long dead.

But I loved her.

Because?

Because I had sex with her?

That could *not* be it.

I wasn't that shallow. I had sex with Blake and that didn't make me love her.

I remembered Blake looking up at me. The image was frozen in time because I'd felt so exposed and self-conscious. Her eyes, the darkly burning kingfisher's wings, studied my face with complete attention.

Sierra never looked at me like that. Mostly during sex she never looked at me. She didn't send gifts. She wasn't curious about me. She would walk off in the middle of conversations that weren't about her.

Blake was the one I wanted to talk to. She was the one who offered help, who understood me, who listened.

I closed my hand around the dried bloom of the rose and ground it to powder. Brown ash filtered down to the burnished mahogany of my dresser top. I carried over the trash can from my desk and swept it away.

* * *

For two days I did routine stuff. I worked out, wandered through the garden, watched movies, drew a little, cleaned. Randomly, I'd find myself standing at the dresser holding the book of Persian wisdom and staring at it as if it was going to get less cryptic over time.

"But while the eternal one created me, he word by word spelt out my lesson, love, and seized my heart and from a fragment cut keys to the storehouse of reality.—Omar Kayyam."

There were keys? Where?

I gave up.

I had no clue what Blake meant me to get from this book.

I went to my computer to see if she was online and ask. She wasn't. For all I knew, at that very moment she could have been having sex with Kordell.

If I couldn't ask Blake what the book meant, maybe I could write a scene about Zeno and Cypher that would convey my confusion. Maybe she'd understand and answer.

Cypher was with Lord Solar's people, doing the black hole thing, so I had to write it as a flashback...

Zeno sat alone in her little spaceship that was set to autopilot alongside the Queen of Rogues' fleet. She had the first half of the Sigil of True Form. She needed the second half in order to know all of her true self, to steal back the parts of her identity she'd lost.

She also had a gem Cypher had given her that she said would lead Zeno to finding the second half of the Sigil. But Zeno had no idea how to understand the secrets held in the gem's fiery heart. She turned it in the light and watched it shimmer and burn inside. Nanites too small to be visible, but felt as part of herself, lifted off from the top layer of her fingers and buzzed around the gem. Its crystalline structure was too dense and they couldn't get into it to find out more.

Zeno remembered the last time she'd sent out part of herself to explore. It was when she had copied Cypher into her library of forms. Zeno and Cypher had been sitting on the high crates again, up near the ceiling of the largest loading dock. She went up there to think sometimes. She could turn into a cloud and fly up where the dockworkers couldn't see.

Cypher had seen her flying up one day and teleported to join her. They were the only two on the Queen's battlecruiser who could get up there, so it became their spot to talk about anything and everything.

That day, weeks ago, Cypher had asked Zeno, "You keep patterns of lots of forms, right? Can you do that with any living creature? Can you copy me?"

"We can, but should we?"

"Might come in handy," Cypher pointed out.

"You'll find it unsettling."

Cypher laughed. "Can't be the worst I've been through. Does it hurt?"

"It's painless, but it will be very strange to see us as you."

"I think I can handle it."

Zeno raised her hand and pointed her fingers at Cypher. The air around her fingertips seemed to shimmer, but Cypher wondered if that was the effect of her expectations. No one could see nanites, could they? Not unless the swarmed en masse.

"Do I need to do anything?" she asked.

"No, we're sending a few of us to ride through your body. It'll take minutes to measure everything, read your DNA and the epigenetic factors in play. When they come back to me, we'll have the pattern."

"How do they get back?" Cypher asked.

"They fly, same as they went."

"They'll probably be tired from all that work, maybe we should shorten the trip."

Zeno's eyebrows went up. Cypher leaned forward and kissed her. Zeno tasted like heat and exotic metal, like Cypher imagined tungsten tasted.

I pushed away from my computer. There was no way I could post that. I'd have to rewrite it, maybe keep the beginning part and make the conversation a lot more strategic. Maybe as an infomancer, Cypher had a notion that she was going to be kidnapped. Not the details, but a premonition, and so she asked Zeno to copy her.

I could rewrite it later. I didn't want to have to change the image of Cypher kissing Zeno just yet.

CHAPTER TWENTY-FIVE

I can't say little enough about the Garden Show. It happened. With flowers, and people, and photographers, and more people. Oh and dresses.

My father stood next to me, resting his hand on my shoulder in that classical "proud father" pose. We looked amazing and like utter, steaming bullshit.

I had to listen to him going on about how this was all my idea and my project and I'd put so much work into it. He built up this image of me for everyone: the dutiful, wonderful daughter who loved flowers and pretty things but who was also smart and capable and never in a bad mood. She'd outgrow her lesbian phase and be a great wife someday, and a pretty good corporate whatever in the time left over from having three children and caring for her super successful husband.

I'm queer, I said in my head as I plastered on a fake smile and shook hands. *I'm super queer. I have sex with girls. Girls plural; more than one girl. And I hate flowers, especially roses. And I don't want to be a corporate drone.*

But I couldn't say any of that. And this time I almost persuaded myself I didn't care. I just wanted to get away.

After the Garden Show, I had a couple of days of cleaning up but then I could finally drive down to the Cities. My father was busy with summer parties and events and back to not caring what I did. He'd apparently gotten his fill of me because he got to stand next to me while people flooded through the garden with compliments.

I planned ten days in the Cities in late July. After that I was flying out east to spend two-and-a-half weeks with Mom and Isaac in a rented house on the beach in southern Maine. I drove down and fell into bed with Sierra and tried to feel anything for her. I didn't.

On the surface, our relationship appeared normal. When we weren't kissing or having sex, there was pizza and cuddling on the couch and watching movies. But it wasn't the same. I was gray inside. Touching her felt good physically, but there was a gulf between us. Had I done that when I had sex with Blake?

Or had Blake done that when she gave me the pen, the infinity pin, and the book? When she listened to me and didn't give me advice? When she talked to me about feeling things and breathing? When she reacted to how I felt, not to some ideal in her head—not to what she wanted, but to me?

Thinking about seeing her was the only time any sensation pushed through the dullness inside me. Then I was burning, but I couldn't tell if that was warm affection, or embarrassment, or lust, or shame. How did she keep track of more than one feeling at a time? I wanted to ask her, but I was afraid.

Since I was staying at Sierra's place, I played it cool. But I had to see Blake.

CHAPTER TWENTY-SIX

Friday evening, a few days after I got to the Cities, Dustin invited us over for pizza at his place. Dustin's apartment was taupe and brown (with accent colors ranging from ash gray to pewter gray).

It did have a big living room that opened into a kitchen, kind of like the cabin-mansion but not nearly as well-constructed. The whole living room space could fit a dozen people easily, but there weren't that many there. He had a bunch of pizzas spread out on the island in the kitchen, plus pop, juice, vodka and rum.

There was a couch, tan leather and not very broken in. Dustin sat at one end, with Gabby in the middle and Roy on her other side. Bear was sitting on the floor, leaning against the wall opposite the couch.

Perpendicular to them was an armchair with Blake in it. Kordell sat on the floor, resting back against Blake's legs. She looked darkly luminous in her midnight jeans and black button-down shirt. Compared to her, Kordell seemed coated in matte finish.

My heart expanded out and crushed in on itself at the same time, like a star exploding and collapsing into a black hole. I stepped into the kitchen area and spent a long time with my back to Blake, getting pop and deciding which pizza to eat.

When I turned back to the living room, Sierra had dragged a chair over and was sitting next to Blake. Sierra caught my eye and patted the front of the chair. I went over and settled on the floor between her knees, next to Kordell. Sierra played with my curls but I wasn't going to remind her that this would only make my hair frizzier.

I glanced at Kordell and he shook his head at me with a smile. "Bitches be crazy," he deadpanned.

"You call me a bitch like it's a bad thing," Blake said and I almost glanced up at her but I stopped myself. I didn't want Sierra to see that Blake had my attention.

I focused on the pizza slice in my lap, but I was grinning and I hoped Blake could see the side of my face. What she'd said was the title of a Halestorm song. She wasn't kidding that she'd been listening to them.

Sierra's legs pressed on the outside of my arms, but couldn't block out the stronger sense of gravity pulling me toward Blake. I decided I was an ass for telling Sierra to be exclusive with me, to not hook up with Dustin, because I was starting to see that this could be way more complicated than I'd suspected.

"I bet you're wondering why I've called you all here tonight," Dustin said to the group at large. "I'm proposing that we put Gabby in as the Queen of Love and have her character break with Lady Death and Lord Ocean to join forces with me and the Queen of Rogues."

"Can she bust in as a queen like that?" Roy asked. "She's super new."

"You did as Lord Solar," Sierra told him.

"No, you made me kill the old Lord Solar, even though that wasn't a real person. It took a while, remember. But hey, if that's what you guys want."

Roy shrugged and put a huge bite of pizza in his mouth to keep himself from saying more. He was leaning into the corner of the couch so he could partly face Gabby and Dustin, and he had his legs too far open like guys do.

This had to be a sucky place to be single with three couples sitting around the room. (Though Bear seemed to not give a shit about her dating status.) Or two couples and whatever Blake and Kordell were. I leaned more into Sierra's legs and she rested her hand on my shoulder.

"Seems fine to me if Gabby wants to be the Queen of Love," Sierra said. "We can always use more people."

"I'm just here for the pizza," Kordell remarked.

Dustin looked around the room and must have gotten enough nods that he said, "Okay, that's done. Where are we with the Cypher rescue and she turns traitor plot line?"

Sierra said, "I think too many plot threads involve Cypher. She's supposed to find a universe with a weapon to destroy the High God, but she's also supposed to locate where in the future the High God's locus is hidden. Maybe someone else should do that."

"We could say that love transcends time," Bear suggested. "Gabby could search in the future for the thing. It's easier to be new if you have a job to do."

"Love transcends time?" Roy said to her, leering.

"I *will* kick you," she replied.

Dustin turned to Gabby. "Do you like that? Maybe the locus of the High God is in a time without love."

She said, "Oh that's neat. But I can't write. Will you write it for me?"

"Of course," he said, all gallant.

Kordell rolled his eyes, but since he was at floor level with me, most of the room didn't see it. Bear caught it and smirked. I half listened to the rest of it (maybe less than half). I worried about what I'd say if anyone brought up the party at Bear's parents' house. I didn't think Blake would gossip about hooking up with me, but Sierra might.

When Dustin ended the general story conversation, Kordell went to get himself and Blake more pizza. Bear went to refill her drink. Roy excused himself to the bathroom and Dustin went on talking intently to Gabby about the Queen of Love plot line. This side of the room held only me, Blake and Sierra.

Sierra turned to Blake. I held my breath.

"I'm not mad at you," Sierra said, her voice cool and light.

I twisted sideways to see them better. Sierra's upturned mouth and expressionless eyes were too composed. Blake's eyes were wide enough to show the full round circles of her irises, flint gray in this lighting.

"That's good," Blake said, the second word almost, not quite, a question.

"I know you can't help doing things you don't mean to," Sierra said.

Blake flinched back in her chair and crossed her arms high on her chest. "Don't."

"I know you hate to be reminded of your disorder in front of our friends, but I'm trying to tell you that I forgive you," Sierra said. "I know you didn't *mean* to do it. You couldn't help it."

"That's not...it's not like that," Blake said. She was looking from Sierra to me and back again, the flashing sense of wings moving in her gaze, the bird trapped, beating against the glassy surface of her eyes.

Sierra went on talking, her voice lower now and colder. "Do you want me to believe you had sex with my girlfriend *on purpose*? I know you don't like to admit how you are, but you need to face up to this. Have you told your therapist about it? You really need to tell him."

"No," Blake told her. "You don't get to tell me how I am. Back off."

Sierra held up her hands. "You're being so irritable. I'm simply trying to get everything back to normal."

Blake surged up from the chair and stood next to it, shifting from one foot to another, like she couldn't decide if she was going to walk away or not. If it hadn't been a heavy armchair, would Blake have lifted it over her head and threatened to hit Sierra with it? (Would I want her to?)

I stood up. Height isn't great for everything, but it sure helps when you're trying to stop people from getting into a fight. I was shaking inside.

I told Sierra, "It was me. I kissed her first. I started it."

Not entirely true. Blake sitting there naked definitely contributed, but Sierra didn't need to know that. She needed to stop picking on Blake.

Sierra rose to her feet, even though that left her a half-foot shorter than me. She opened her mouth, took in breath like she was going to let me have it, but then stalked out of the apartment, slamming the door behind her.

Addressing Sierra's empty chair, Blake said, "You don't get to say that about me…"

"Hey," I started but I didn't know what else to say or do. Would she want me to touch her? And if I did draw her into my arms, would that be the exact moment Sierra returned? (Of course it would.)

Kordell came back with pizza plates. Blake looked up at him, tears spilling out of her eyes. He put the plates down on the coffee table. She tucked herself into his arms, face pressed against his chest.

He caught my eye over her quivering shoulder and asked, "What did Sierra say?"

"Something about Blake doing stuff she doesn't mean to."

Blake pushed a half-step away from Kordell and brushed her sleeve across her face, smearing her tears more than wiping them away. Her eyes were wet, still crying.

Face half-turned to me but angled down, Blake said, "She was saying I had sex with you because I'm hypersexual and I can't control myself. Like I don't have my own mind. Like being bipolar turns me into some kind of stupid…stupid."

"Dearest, her bullshit does *not* have to be your bullshit," Kordell said. He had an arm around her and he hugged her close.

Blake pressed her face into the inner curve his shoulder. She was laughing darkly or crying harder or both.

"I'll talk to Sierra," I said. "I'll make sure she knows that's not cool."

Kordell said, "Oh, she knows. That's why she said it. She's pissed that you two hooked up. But you put out for her so she's not going to go after you."

The bluntness of his words struck me. "I don't—" I started to say but had no legit protest to make. Was that how it looked to Kordell?

Was that how it looked to me?

"Why aren't *you* upset?" I asked Kordell.

"It's not my thing," he said with a one-shouldered shrug.

Was he trying to be the cool boyfriend…or whatever they were? What if our roles were reversed? What if I was with Blake and she hooked up with someone else while I was out of town with my family?

But if she was totally upfront about it, like she was, and I'd agreed. I couldn't compare it to the situation with Sierra and Dustin.

Blake went into the bathroom, Kordell settled into the armchair with his pizza plate, and I took Sierra's chair. When Blake came back, she sat in his lap, leaning against the arm. Her legs extended over the other arm and her feet rested on my thigh so that she was sitting across both of our laps. Kordell didn't seem to care.

I didn't either. It made sense that she was in Kordell's lap though I wanted her to be more in mine.

When the doorknob turned, Blake drew her feet away and leaned more fully into Kordell. Sierra went into the kitchen. I went after her. I didn't want Sierra near Blake again.

"Maybe we should go," she said when I stepped through the doorway, even though she was pouring vodka into a half-glass of Izze Blueberry Soda.

"Yeah," I said.

"You don't have to stand up for her. She has Kordell. And I wasn't saying anything that bad. She does need to talk to her therapist. Being hypersexual is a sign that she could be going manic."

The words sounded reasonable, but they stirred a pool of disgust in my gut. The way Sierra used that information was deeply wrong. Like when my father would argue a case and say all the true things to paint a compelling picture that was, in essence, a lie.

I didn't know how to challenge it. I didn't know that much about bipolar. And around the sick feeling, I was shaky. I got that relationships weren't all smooth and you had fights and stuff—but not like this.

"Can we go home?" I asked.

Sierra brightened when I said the word "home." She put down the cup she'd filled, took my hand and drew me toward the door. We said our goodbyes on the way. I looked at Blake sitting in Kordell's lap, his arms around her protectively, her eyes shadowed and somehow still shining.

I let Sierra pull me away.

CHAPTER TWENTY-SEVEN

In the morning, Sierra left for an extra shift she'd picked up at work and I sat at the dining room table drinking coffee. I couldn't stop wondering if Sierra was partly right about Blake.

I went online and read stuff about bipolar disorder that made my thinking 100% worse. What if Blake did have sex with me because she was in a manic, hypersexual state? One study said, "Twice as many women as men reported sexual intensity as 'very much increased' during hypomania."

What the hell was hypomania? I was barely figuring out what mania was and I couldn't remember what the "hypo-" prefix meant: more or less? Could you be more manic? Or if you were less manic, was that better or worse?

I couldn't stop thinking about sex with Blake. About being on the floor together and how fast her first orgasm was—did that come from her disorder? What if it did and I was thinking it had to do with me? Like I thought she was profoundly into me, but all along it was this disorder?

I remembered how bold she was in bed. I'd liked that. Would it go away? What if the things I liked most in her were only there part of the time? Would she someday get depressed and decide she didn't even like me?

But she and Kordell had been hanging around together for almost two years. Sierra told me that when she was giving me the scoop on everyone. If Blake changed her mind with her moods like that, there's no way she'd be with same guy for two years. She'd said they weren't really together, but they acted like it. They seemed to like each other a lot. They were always laughing together and touching each other, pretty much like any boyfriend/girlfriend relationship I'd ever seen.

He'd been so quick to close his arms around her last night when she was crying. What was it like to be able to cry like that? She felt hurt and she cried as if it was so simple. I could never do that. Maybe the key was having someone who would put their arms around you. Even if I had that, I didn't think I could. It made me too weak.

I could've been thinking about it wrong, putting myself in Blake's place when in truth I was more like Kordell. (Minus the sense of style and ability to win at Mystics.)

I put on my iPod, more Halestorm at high volume, and went through the kitchen and bathroom tidying up. I got done well before Sierra was due back from work so I went to the grocery store to stock the fridge and pick up dinner. This was so different from picking up items on my father's list and feeling like a kid. I was choosing what I wanted to make for dinner for my girlfriend.

Sierra texted to say she had to run an errand and she'd be late. Did I want her to pick up food? I told her I had dinner and not to worry.

You're the best, she wrote. *What would I do without you!*

I wanted to feel happy, but I remembered Kordell saying: "You put out for her."

I heated up spaghetti sauce and sautéed hamburger to go in it.

Sierra texted again, *I've got a surprise for you.*

She came in minutes later with a large, flat white box, the kind sweaters come in. (I did *not* think she'd gotten me a sweater.) I said a brief and very silent prayer that it wasn't a dress as she set it on the dining room table and told me to open it.

I forced a smile and lifted the top half of the box. It wasn't a dress. And it sure wasn't a sweater.

It was a whole bunch of pale lace.

I found two straps and lifted. A lacy camisole? Or more like a lace corset-like nightie with matching panties. I put a palm under the top layer of the mostly-sheer panties and contemplated the white embroidered rose against my skin.

My head went thick with the density of the what-the-fuckness I was feeling.

"You're going to look so amazing in that," Sierra said.

My first clear thought was: *I hate roses.*

Followed by: *I hate dresses. And you got me a rose-embroidered lace bedroom dress? I'm sixteen, do you get that? Sixteen fucking years old, what do I need lingerie for?*

I unstuck my tongue from the roof of my mouth and said, "Wow, thanks."

"Try it on," she insisted.

"Let's eat dinner first. You know, in case we're busy afterward."

The words came so easily to my mouth but sounded so flat to my ears. Sierra grinned and followed me into the kitchen. I drained the spaghetti and poured the sauce into a big plastic bowl while she put plates and silverware on the table.

I wasn't in the habit of asking God for favors, but I said a quick prayer along the lines of: *seriously, you have to help me out here. I'll owe you. I promise.*

And yet, lightning did not strike the dining room table.

Sierra carried the spaghetti out, pushed the lingerie box to the far side of the table and started serving onto our plates. I picked up the sauce.

I'd like to say I planned it, but it was a bona fide miracle. My toes hit the mismatch between the kitchen linoleum and the dining room wood and twisted in. The trailing foot snagged against the leading foot and I went down.

The sauce went up.

Gravity happened—all across the end of the dining room table, one chair and part of the wall.

I was on my side on the floor, hands wrapped around my ankle, pain and shock bouncing along my nerves. A glop of red sauce, weighted by a piece of meat, dripped off the side of the table and splatted onto the floor. I almost laughed but the pain kept me somber. I'd twisted my ankle and smacked my knee landing. I couldn't tell how bad the damage was.

Sierra knelt in front of me. "Lauren, are you okay?"

"Ankle," I said. "Hurts. I don't know. Ice?"

She got a bag in the kitchen, filled it with ice and wrapped it in a dishtowel. I watched red sauce drip steadily from the edge of the table to the floor like a warm, soothing summer rain.

Sierra put the ice pack on the coffee table in the living room and came back to help me up. I was limping, but I could put light pressure on my foot already without searing pain so it wasn't serious, maybe not even a sprain. (I'd sprained my ankle already three times in my life due to my excessive grace.) This was more of a twist. It would be sore for a few days, maybe swell a little, but not turn half my foot purple.

I let Sierra fuss around propping me up with pillows and setting the ice pack just right. Then she had to go clean up the mess. I could see from where I sat that a good cup or more of sauce had landed on the lingerie. Sierra made sad noises and went to wash it in cold water and hang it up.

I wanted to take a pic and send it to Blake. Maybe I *was* a huge jerk, but I was a happy jerk.

CHAPTER TWENTY-EIGHT

Sierra and I spent Saturday night watching movies and icing my ankle. By Sunday it was puffy but walkable. The lingerie, however, did not recover. It was a ghastly orange in the places where it was supposed to be white. I offered to try it on anyway, knowing Sierra would say no.

Sunday evening Sierra wanted to go to a poetry reading and party with a few of the other students who'd been in her writing class last spring. Dustin was having people over again (probably as a way to see more of Gabby). Sierra said I should go to Dustin's without her. I wondered if she'd invented going to a poetry reading as a test. Like she wanted to send me off without her to a place where Blake would be and have Dustin report back. I hoped I was being paranoid.

When I got to Dustin's place, Gabby, Bear and Roy were there.

"Where's Sierra?" Bear asked.

"She had a party, some literary thing."

"Sounds riveting," Bear said. "Can I look at your sketches? I like what you've been uploading."

We spent about an hour with our heads bent over my sketchbook and hers. Roy looked for a few minutes before wandering off to join Gabby and Dustin. Bear thought my take on josei manga was awesome (turning the usual girl-oriented domestic manga style more sinister) and we swapped recommendations for what to read.

Blake and Kordell came in while we were talking. I nodded in their direction, but didn't get up. Bear and I were furiously discussing the many merits of Moyoco Anno's *In Clothes Called Fat.*

They got drinks and food. Kordell sat in the armchair with Blake on the end of the couch. For a long time they were talking quietly together. After they'd eaten, Blake started pacing around and behind Kordell. Even from across the room, I could hear her well enough.

"No, you can't add one to it," she was saying. "You can't. The natural numbers are already infinite, you can't make them more infinite. That's not how it works. There isn't more of infinity, there are orders of infinity. Orders. Don't you get it? The continuum of real numbers has the same cardinality as the power set of the integers."

"Blake," Kordell said. "Slow down, please."

She sighed and stepped away from the back of his chair to stand by the glass doors of Dustin's balcony, staring out into the night. Kordell came over to me. I felt a flash of fear, like he was going to ask me to do something and I didn't know what it would be. And it was fear for Blake...no, fear of her. She was different tonight, harder and faster than usual.

"Do you have spare paper and a pencil?" he asked.

"Oh sure."

I carefully ripped a few pages out of the middle of my sketchpad and gave them to him with a pencil. He took them over to Blake and handed them to her.

"Can you show me why I can't just add one?" he asked.

She followed him back to the couch. Bear was watching them too so we stopped pretending we were talking to each other.

Blake sat down, pencil moving on the page while she talked, "Okay so, you've got the natural numbers, one, two, three, etc. and they're infinite but they're countable. If you had infinite time or whatever, you could count them. So you can't add one, because whatever number that makes, you'd get to it eventually in your counting so it's already in that infinity. It's part of it. It's in the infinite set of those numbers. Infinity plus infinity is infinity. That's part of the mathematics of infinities."

The fear melted away as I listened to her. Hard and fast words, but Blake's words, her ideas, her voice. I crossed the room to lean over the back of the couch and see what she was writing. There were a bunch of numbers and circles inside of circles. It didn't make sense to me, but I wasn't a math geek.

"I have a question," I said.

Blake looked up at me. Her eyes were wild but still Blake, only brighter and faster than I was used to. I felt stupid for having been afraid. I'd let Sierra's shitty remarks get inside my head.

I grinned at her and she grinned back.

I said, "I don't understand what happens when you get to the end of infinity. I know infinity isn't supposed to have an end, but I keep thinking there has to be something outside of it. It kind of drives me nuts."

"Oh! That's awesome. I'll show you."

Her contagious excitement swept away the usual panic I had around this subject. Plus she thought she could answer it for me. I sat down on the other side of her from Kordell. Close enough to lean over the paper with her, but not so close that we were touching.

"First you need to imagine there's a hotel with infinitely many rooms," she said.

"I can't picture that," I told her. "But I'll *imagine* that I can imagine it. Does that work?"

She bumped my shoulder with hers and drew a rectangle on the side of the page with squares for windows. "Let's say this hotel stretches away to infinity in the back. And each room is full—but you want to spend your vacation there. What do you do?"

"Hook up with someone in a room?" I suggested.

She laughed. "Or you go to the guy at the front desk and you tell him: 'Hey, put the person in room one into room two, and the person in room two into room three and so on, and give me room one.'"

She wrote on the paper: *1, 2, 3, 4…*

And under that: *Lauren's room, 1, 2, 3…*

"That hurts my brain," I said.

"What you need to know is that it's countable. You can count anything you put into the rooms. And you can put different things into the rooms, but anything that can be put in rooms is countable. Countable infinity, get it?"

I said, "So there's more than one kind of number that you can put into rooms in the hotel. And every kind of number that can have rooms you could count if you had infinite time…and infinite patience and infinite caffeine."

She was still grinning, but I was scared again. Scared of the numbers, which felt idiotic. Just because you could count all the numbers if you had infinite time, that didn't help me. I needed to know what happened when you got to the end of them. Or if there was no end, how was there no end? What would happen to me if I got outside of the numbers?

"Hey, I'm going to head out," Bear said. "Lauren, thanks for the chat. Anyone need a ride?"

Kordell put his hand on Blake's knee. "Dearest, do you want to go?"

"No," she said, like that was a stupid question.

He leaned around her and caught my eye. "Can you drive her home later?"

"I can take the bus," Blake said crossly.

"Let me drive you," I offered. "We might need the extra time for you to explain all this infinity stuff to me."

"Sure. Thanks," she said and got up to give Kordell a hug and a kiss as he stood up. "Tell your mom her pie was ridiculous."

After Bear and Kordell left, Dustin asked if he could have the couch so he could watch a movie with Gabby (and Roy, but I doubt he was part of Dustin's plan). Blake and I moved to the nook. She stood, shifting in place, frowning.

"Can we go somewhere?" she asked.

"Where?"

"I don't care. I need to be moving. Is that cool?"

"Yeah, we can drive around. Maybe go around the lakes?"

"I love the lakes at night," she said.

We said our goodbyes and went down to my car. She pointed me in the direction of the lakes. We opened windows and Blake put her hand out to wiggle her fingers in the warm night air.

Even though the sun was down, the first lake was crowded with people walking. Following Blake's directions, I drove to the next one and the next, curling around the big, dark basins of water. The houses got more ornate, different styles, some lit up inside, some dark.

Seeing Blake's silhouette in the diffuse light, I wanted to kiss her again. I wanted to tell her about the spaghetti sauce but I didn't want to say Sierra's name and I certainly didn't want to bring up lingerie.

"Let's go somewhere and walk," Blake said. "There's a park up that way. Can we go?"

"Sure."

I followed her instructions and we ended up in a parking lot by a golf course.

"Huh," she said. "This isn't quite what I was going for, but I think I know where we are. Come on, there's supposed to be a gap in the fence back there. We can get through."

"Should we?"

She shrugged. "Do you want to stay here?"

She wasn't saying it rhetorically and meaning that I was a jerk if I stayed here, but honestly wondering if I wanted to stay in the car in the parking lot. The fact was, I did not. I wanted to follow her, to spend the whole night following her around wherever she wanted to go.

"Let's go," I told her.

We went around the back of the fence for half a block. We found the spot where the fencing was loose and could be pulled up enough for us to squeeze through. The whole place was ghostly silent. As we walked onto the green, the lights of the city streets faded away and the stars came out.

"You should come up to Duluth sometime," I told her. "We get the northern lights and they're amazing."

"I'd like that," she said.

I didn't have a word for what she was to me. "Friend" sounded so elementary school and yet this wasn't all that romantic; she hadn't touched me all night except to bump my shoulder. Whatever was between and around us felt deep, fathomless.

We got to the top of a short rise and Blake dropped down onto her back, staring up at the sky. I lowered myself next to her.

"You want to know what's out there?" she asked. Her voice was slower than it had been at the party. The night settled warm and heavy around us.

"I'm afraid of what's out there," I whispered.

"It's not like you think it is."

"How do you know what I think?"

"I don't," she admitted. "What do you think?"

I'd never tried to explain this before, but in the dark, not looking at her, I could say it. "I keep thinking about the end of everything. That it has to end somewhere and then there must be an outside and what is that outside? What would happen to me if I got to the end of it all? I'm afraid of not existing, that there's a point you can get to and there's nothing. Real nothing. And if I get there, I'll be nothing too."

I shuddered. Her fingers touched my elbow and moved away.

She said, "We talked about countable infinities, so the next question is whether there are infinities we can't count."

"Are there?"

"Yes," she said. She said some things about rational and irrational numbers, about what was and wasn't countable, but I was distracted by the sound of her "yes" in the deepening night.

When she paused, I asked, "Do you think I could I get a room at the infinite hotel?"

"Are you a rational number?" She sounded dubious.

"Probably not. What are my other choices?"

"Irrational, imaginary, transcendental, transfinite…"

"Which are you?" I asked.

"Transfinite for sure. I think you might be transcendental. Pi is transcendental and that's a pretty artsy number."

"Thanks for not calling me irrational," I said.

"Oh pi is also irrational."

Alerted by the rustle of grass, I peeked over to see her grinning at me. In the dark, this close, her eyes were bluegrass and charcoal. If I had infinite time to draw her, I would never be able to draw her just right, like this.

"Bitch," I said lightly. The word came out more breath than sound.

"Like that's a bad thing," she replied.

"You listened to Halestorm."

I almost reached out for her but I pulled a blade of grass out of the green instead and rubbed it between my finger and thumb.

"Are you trying to get me to stop talking about math?" she asked with a sigh, turning her face back up to the sky.

"No, go on. You were about to blow my mind."

"You don't know the half."

She was quiet for a bit. There wasn't any wind, but the air around us shifted as the night cooled a degree. The lazy, moving air brought me the smell of her shampoo and the earthy-sweet-maple scent that I knew was Blake.

I focused on the distant stars and tried not to think about how close her body was. I wanted to kiss her so much the roots of my teeth ached.

Blake held a hand up to the sky and made a circle with her thumb and forefinger.

"Let's say that this is the countable infinities," she said.

She circled the first circle of her fingers with the fingers of the other hand to indicate a circle inside of a circle.

"And you have a kind of uncountable infinity that comes from taking all the numbers in that first infinity and putting them into all their possible combinations. There's a more accurate way to say it, but if I start talking about power sets, you're going to change the subject, aren't you?"

"I am," I agreed. "But basically you're saying a bunch of uncountable stuff makes a super infinity, right?"

"Yeah," she chuckled. "Super infinity, they should have called it that. They didn't, though. The countable infinities are called aleph zero or aleph null."

"That's perfect," I interrupted her. "The aleph. It's the first letter in the name of the unnamable God."

"How do you know that? I mean, I read that somewhere but how do *you* know that?"

"Years of Hebrew school," I said.

She laughed. "Fantastic. The aleph is the symbol for an order of infinity. So aleph zero is the first infinity and then there's aleph one."

"Is that the super infinity?" I asked.

She pushed up on her elbow and looked down at me. Her hair was tangled and rough with a piece of grass sticking out of one side.

"That's the thing," she said. "We have no way of knowing if it is or isn't...That's the problem with your question about what's outside of infinity. Human minds can't even figure out aleph one and we can barely guess at the alephs beyond that, at the increasing orders of infinity."

She settled back on the grass and went on talking, "Some of the mathematicians who tried to study this went crazy. I mean, they didn't have the good meds of the twenty-first century, but some people think it was the study of infinities that did it. Of course, you could also argue that it's the crazy ones who can make the breakthroughs, who can understand these things and pull human thinking forward."

"Do you think that?" I asked.

"Haven't made up my mind about it yet," she said. "What do you think?"

I didn't know enough about craziness and genius to say anything remotely smart so I thought about her orders of infinity. I put my hands up and made a circle with my fingers and another circle around that.

I remembered the circles she'd drawn on the paper, one inside the other. I'd heard people say about the universe or about God "Oh, it's too big to understand" and that had always sounded like a cop-out. Why it would be too big? If God made us, why shouldn't we be able to understand everything?

But Blake made it make sense.

We couldn't even count the first infinity, only understand that it was countable. And then there were many more orders of infinity out from that, like maybe an infinite amount. So when I tried to perceive it all and came to that place of nothingness, what I'd reached was not the outside of infinity, like I'd thought. I'd simply hit the limit of my mind's ability to understand.

Maybe anyone who got to that point felt crazy, trying to think outside their own brain.

In my mind, I saw the circles drawn on paper shattering, breaking apart, raining down on me in bits of ink and broken curves. It reminded me of a story about how the universe was made.

"The jars are a metaphor," I said. "I can't believe I didn't get that before."

Blake shifted onto her side. I felt her watching me. She said, "Lauren, of the two of us, you're the one I expect to make sense. What jars?"

I rolled toward her, still picturing the simple ink circles shattering around me, our faces inches apart.

"In Kabbalah there's this teaching about how the universe was made," I explained. "It says that God withdrew from Godself to make a space. Because before that everything was God, so God had nowhere to make the universe. After withdrawing, God had a place to make the universe. But when God tried to pour infinite light into some jars to put into the universe, they couldn't contain it and they shattered."

"Infinities are like that. They shatter things," Blake said. She was grinning at me and I echoed her grin. If anyone saw us like this, they'd think we were completely out of our minds and I didn't care.

I told her, "The broken pieces of the jars and God's light, that's what this world is made out of. We have to fix it because the jars broke and it's all fucked up. But I got—listening to all that and the circles you drew—what if the breaking happened in our minds? What if the jars breaking is a metaphor about why people can't think their way through this stuff? Because you can't contain infinities in human brains."

She lay back on the grass so I did too. After a bit she said, "There *is* no outside. The jars have to be only in our minds because that's where you can have an idea of an outside. In the reality of the universe itself, there can never be jars. There is no outside reality. You can't contain it like that."

"Yeah," I breathed out the words. "I like that. Thanks."

She touched the edge of my palm. Her hand slid into mine, fingers interlacing, and she held tight. When she relaxed her grip, she didn't pull away.

Whatever Blake and I were, maybe that also wasn't a thing you could fit into jars or brains.

CHAPTER TWENTY-NINE

After we'd been quiet for a long time, when I got done feeling like I was drinking the stars and the warm, black night sky, I tried to pull together the courage to ask Blake about the night at Bear's parents' house. Could I ask why she had sex with me without sounding ridiculous?

Her breathing was deep and slow. I peeked over and saw her closed eyes. She was asleep or near to it. I wanted to lie there and watch her, but that made me feel like kissing her again.

A phone buzzed.

"Get that for me?" she mumbled and rolled onto her side, her hand pulling out of mine. Eyes closed, she flipped her phone out of her front pocket and dropped it onto the grass between us.

The screen said she had six new messages from "Dad." I picked up her phone and read a series of texts from him asking where she was and when she'd be home.

It was after midnight now. The last message said: *Tell me where you are. I'll come get you.*

I texted back: *This is Lauren, I'm with Blake. She fell asleep. I can drive her home, what's the address?*

The reply came a moment later, a house address and the words: *Thank you.*

I touched her shoulder. She didn't move so I pushed a few times gently and said, "Hey, I have to get you home."

"Tired," she mumbled. "Bedtime."

"Then let's go to bed."

A soft laugh. "I thought you'd never ask."

I wanted to kiss her so badly that it burned all up the inside of my spine. So not the right time with her dad worried about her and her all bleary. Plus, if I did, I'd have to deal with Sierra about it.

"Your dad's wondering where you are," I said.

"Told him," she muttered.

"You told him you were taking me to go sleep on a golf course?"

She levered up to sitting and rubbed a hand back and forth across her face. "Close enough. Told him friends."

"Are you okay?" I asked because she seemed more tired than I would have been after napping for a few minutes in damp grass.

"Yeah, yeah, just tired really sudden. Didn't sleep much last night, or the one before. Tried but couldn't."

"Math?" I asked.

"No, I was angry."

Standing up, she wavered but I steadied her and she threw an arm around my waist. I tucked her phone into her pocket. When we got to the fence, she went through first, her movements lithe and economical.

She fell asleep again in my car. I pulled into the driveway of her house and wondered if I should wake her.

The porch light was on and a brighter light came on in the front windows. A man opened the door. He was wide and stocky with thick, dark hair and a neatly trimmed beard. I got out of the car.

"Lauren?" he asked as he came to meet me by the passenger side door. He was barefoot in worn jeans and a faded blue T-shirt.

"Yes, hi, good to meet you. Blake kind of fell asleep again in the car."

He smiled and I could see the resonance of Blake's grin in the way his broad cheeks bunched up.

"I've got her," he said. He opened the door, crouched down and rolled her into his arms, then stood up like she weighed no more than a cat. "Can you get the front door for me?"

I went ahead and opened it, hearing Blake behind me mutter sleepily, "Hey Dad, how'd you get here?"

"I flew," he said. "And now I'm flying you home."

"Don't let Lauren see your wings," she murmured.

"I think she can handle it," he said.

"Yeah, she's cool."

He went sideways through the front door and into the living room. Crouching, he slid Blake onto the couch. She snared a throw pillow, bunched it under her head, mumbled words that sounded like "aleph one" and settled back to sleep.

"Do you want anything?" her dad asked me. "I think we have Dr. Pepper or root beer."

"Thank you, but I'm fine. I should get going."

"Where did you two go?" he asked.

He had Blake's nose, or I guess she had his, triangular and broad at the bottom. His skin was a few shades darker than hers, about the same as mine but with a cooler tone, olive tinged, very Blake. His eyes were a deep brown and warm, unlike my father's calculating gaze. I wanted him to know Blake was okay, that she'd been okay all night.

"We went to a golf course," I told him. "To look at the stars. And she was teaching me about infinities."

"Were you able to understand it?" he asked, worried lines on his forehead.

"I think so. It was pretty great. She lost me a few times around all the rational, irrational stuff and something about the power set. I'm not a math person. But the part about orders of infinity was amazing."

His shoulders lowered a fraction of an inch as he sighed.

"Good," he said. "Thank you. I worry, you know. It's what we do, parents. We worry."

I didn't think my father worried. Not about me. But I wasn't going to say that. I wondered what it was like to have a dad who would come out and carry you in from the car. To have a dad who wanted to know what you'd been doing and that you were all right. If I fell asleep in my car, my father would leave me there.

"I wouldn't let anything happen to her," I told him.

"Do you go to her school?" he asked.

"No, I'm from Duluth, visiting. We're in a story together. I mean, writing it and stuff."

I didn't know what else to say so I walked to the front door.

He said, "Thank you for bringing her home."

I got into my car and drove down the street, turned the corner, and pulled over. I didn't want to go back to Sierra's. I definitely didn't want to have to explain where I'd been. I wanted to go back to looking at the stars.

I pulled out my sketchbook and drew the circles the way I'd seen Blake do on the sheet of paper, one inside the other, with the distances between each getting bigger as they went further out.

That was important. I hadn't understood that before. The increasing distance between one circle and the next showed that there were orders of infinity. That it wasn't simply one thing and then another until you got to the outside. The spaces between the circles kept getting bigger until you could no longer draw them. You never got to the outside. There wasn't any outside. You could not put the universe in jars.

I wrote down:

Pi

Transcendental

& irrational

Transfinite? What's that?

Blake

CHAPTER THIRTY

I had to return to Sierra's eventually. The longer I waited the worse it was going to be. I considered driving to Duluth so that I could get out of the conversation we were going to have. But it didn't seem safe to drive back at one in the morning.

Parked in the alley behind Sierra's house I checked my phone. There were four texts from Sierra:

Hey baby, I'm on my way home.

Hey, I'm home, where are you?

Dustin says you went to take Blake home hours ago, where the hell are you?

Baby, I love you, don't do this to me.

I felt like crap about that last one.

Cyd had given me a spare key, so I let myself in through the kitchen door and didn't turn on any lights. There was enough glow from the streetlight in the alley and the moonlight coming in the east window that I could navigate through the kitchen and into the bathroom. I washed my hands and face, peed, brushed my teeth, and then I had to go deal with Sierra.

I cracked open the door to her room and saw the shape of her body under the sheet. As quietly as I could, I crossed to where my suitcase was and changed into a T-shirt. I crawled gingerly into the bed.

"Where were you?" she mumbled sleepily

"Driving around."

"With Blake?"

"Part of the time," I admitted. "I dropped her off at home and drove around more."

"Did you fuck?"

"No."

"Kiss?"

"No."

"Good," she said and rolled over again.

I stared at the ceiling and thought about the stars. Crazy as it was, I wanted to be back on that golf course with Blake staring up at the sky. That was the first time I could remember gazing up at the night sky and not feeling afraid. I wanted to sleep there with Blake's hand in mine.

My breathing was all crammed up in the top of my chest like Blake said I wasn't supposed to do. I tried to push it down, to breathe at least into the middle of my lungs but that hurt. No, I hurt.

Sierra had fallen back asleep but it was hard to lie still in the bed with her body next to me. She smelled salty and bitter. I didn't like her smell, but most of the time I didn't notice it under the hair products and lotions and whatnot that she wore. I did like the way her skin felt, but now I wondered if anyone's skin would feel that way.

How wrong was it to think about sex with Blake while lying in bed with Sierra? I did anyway. They were both soft. Blake a little warmer. My body liked both of their bodies—maybe my body liked a lot of women's bodies. That was the thing about being lesbian, right?

Sierra's face was prettier, her eyes a more dramatic shade. People looked at her when she walked by in her purple-streaked hair and swishing dress and big boots. If you put them side by side, everyone would pay attention to Sierra, until they started talking. Then all the attention would go to Blake. She became magnetic when she opened her mouth and the ideas came tumbling out over each other.

And when we were in bed together in that basement room, Blake had *looked* at me. When I'd shifted away from her, she'd stopped or changed what she was doing. She paid attention to me, which at points had been too much, too intense.

I didn't prefer being with Sierra. Those first times we were together, when she kissed me, when we had sex, I was lit up and happy. But before Blake I had nothing to compare it to. And with Blake...with Blake...

Now that I'd had sex with someone other than Sierra, I could see what was the same about both—which aspects of joy and pleasure and power were the same. Those parts had to be me since I was the common element.

I saw it like an equation (which definitely meant I'd been listening to Blake too much). If I remembered my algebra right, I should be able to remove myself from both sides of the equation. If I took out every feeling that was the same, what was left?

When I removed all of that from my relationship with Sierra, there wasn't much. There were dinners and cuddling and movies. There was her showing me off, especially when I wasn't in town, talking about how cute I was—and hooking up with Dustin anyway. There was me cleaning the house, buying her things, listening to her talk about her ideas and her day.

That couldn't be right. I was doing the relationship math wrong, or maybe you weren't supposed to use math on relationships. It was late, my eyes were heavy and sinking back into my head. In the morning it would make sense.

* * *

In the morning it didn't make any more sense. Over breakfast I tried to get Sierra to talk to me about any subject other than what a hassle work was going to be.

"Do you think there's an outside to the universe?" I asked.

"I liked the soap bubble thing," she said. "Isn't that what it's supposed to be like?"

"But what's around the soap bubbles?"

"A big cosmic bathtub?" she suggested, peering up from her phone and then back down at the screen where she was texting.

"Made of what?"

"Something people can't travel through," she said. "I've got to get to work. See you tonight."

Monday night she had to run errands and asked if I wanted to come. We ended up driving around picking up a few things and wandering through a mall window-shopping. When we got back to the house, I took a long bath and she got into bed. By the time I was done in the tub, she was asleep.

On Tuesday when she got back from work, she pulled me onto the couch for a makeout session, then suggested we go into her bedroom.

"Not yet," I said. "Let's talk. Tell me about your day."

She shrugged. "Work and the usual. Come on, you've been here almost a week and I feel like I barely see you."

"You're seeing me now," I said. "I want to feel like we're more connected before we go, you know, do stuff."

"We're not connected?" she asked.

"It's like there's this distance."

"What distance? Like the kind where you go hang out with Blake and suddenly our relationship isn't as important to you?"

"No! That's not it at all. We don't really talk."

"Maybe you're the one not talking to me," she said. "Have you thought of that? If you want to talk, we'll talk. You want something to drink?"

"Pepsi?" I asked.

"I don't think we have any, how about Mountain Dew?"

"Ugh, no. Just water."

She came back with her beer and a glass of water for me and sat very primly on the far end of the couch. "So what do you want to talk about?"

"Did anything cool happen at work?"

"Um, no. Nothing cool ever happens at work. Well, we did get this one customer who was wearing two different tie-dyes. I almost snapped a photo." She took a sip of her beer. "Is this the kind of talking you had in mind?"

"I guess," I said.

I waited for a bit. She sipped her beer and looked around the room.

"It looks nice in here," she said.

"Thanks. What do you think about the story and the whole love transcends time thing?" I asked. "I thought it was kind of schlocky."

"Yeah, not my favorite. But whatever, Dustin does what he wants sometimes. Were you doing a finished version of that drawing of the Queen of Rogues with Zeno? We should post that."

"It's mostly done," I said. I hadn't thought about it in weeks and I couldn't remember what state it was in, but I could probably finish it pretty quickly.

"You know, I know a much faster way to get connected," she said.

"Sierra…"

"What is going on with you?" she asked. "We used to have so much fun and now it's like every time you're around Blake you get cold to me. What did she say about me?"

"This has nothing to do with Blake."

"I can't believe that."

"You think I'm lying?" I asked.

"I think you don't know what's going on," she said.

I didn't have to be a genius to get that the rising heat in my body was anger, even before I heard it come out in my voice.

"Because I don't want to have sex all the time?" I asked.

"You're not here for very long," Sierra said. "And it's been days. I love you, I want to be with you. I don't understand why you're acting like this."

"I'm not your living sex toy," I said.

She jerked back. "How can you say that to me? I would never call you that."

"I feel like you just want me to get you off," I told her.

She shoved off the couch and stood in the archway between the living room and dining room. "Lauren, sometimes you're such a child."

She slammed into her bedroom with a flourish.

I felt sick and shaky so I got off the couch and went into the bathroom. Snot swelled the back of my nose, giving me a headache. A tear slimed its way down my cheek. I grabbed toilet paper off the roll and sat on the cold floor.

Sierra said she loved me, and I thought I loved her, but I didn't feel loved. I figured that was because I didn't feel a lot of stuff. But now I was breathing deep, feeling into my body, and it was all pain.

Lying on the golf course with Blake, listening to her explaining about infinities, I felt warm inside. There was no pain. There was endlessness and depth. Maybe that wasn't love either. Maybe I didn't have a clue what love was. But whatever that was, I didn't feel it with Sierra.

When I did feel something with Sierra, it came from what I was doing, not what she did. When had she done anything that made me feel good that wasn't sex or saying the words, "I love you?"

When I was upset, Sierra wasn't the one I wanted to talk to. The times I tried to tell her what was going on with me, she'd listen for a little while and move on to another topic. I didn't trust her enough to tell her what I was afraid of or what bothered me.

How could I have a girlfriend I didn't even trust?

How did I end up with a girlfriend I wasn't sure I liked?

Was Sierra right that talking to Blake had changed our relationship? It seemed like the only way Blake influenced me was that she listened and she showed me it could be different. There was a part of me still unsure about what I felt for Blake—or rather, I knew I liked her, but I was also afraid of her.

She could be so big inside herself, with her feelings and thoughts spilling out into the air around her. I couldn't be like that. Would she want me to?

CHAPTER THIRTY-ONE

A soft knock sounded on the bathroom door. Sierra coming to apologize or to fight more? I didn't know how long I'd been in there.

"One sec," I said.

I got up and washed my face. When I opened the door, it wasn't Sierra standing there, it was Cyd.

"You okay?" she asked.

I pointed at Sierra's door and shook my head.

"She left," Cyd told me. "When I got home a few minutes ago, she stormed out. I figured you had to be in here. You two have a fight?"

She moved out of the bathroom doorway into the dining room to stand by the table. I followed.

"I feel like she's using me. Am I crazy?"

"Oh thank God," Cyd said.

"What? That I've realized I'm crazy?"

Cyd lifted one of the dining room chairs a few inches and slid it under the table so it was lined up with the others. She said, "I've been trying to figure out how to talk to you about that relationship...Lauren, she's not good to you."

"How long have you thought that?" I asked.

The sun was setting and the only light in the room came from its long rays through the front window, mixing with the diffuse bathroom light. It made Cyd's skin deeper and cast long shadows on her face.

She said, "I've never liked how Sierra is with people, but Dustin could handle her. And anyway, he's older than she is, I don't worry about him. When you showed up, I hoped it would be different. You seemed so in love."

"But she's your roommate."

"She pays the rent," Cyd said. "Honestly, the longer I'm around her, the less I like her. She goes on and on about what you do for her, but she doesn't talk about you. Do you know, when you said you were coming down this week to visit, she asked *me* what kind of pop you drink."

"Did you tell her Mountain Dew?" I asked.

"No, you drink Pepsi. I wasn't going to screw with you to make a point. I told her to ask you. To suck it up and admit she was being a shit girlfriend who wasn't paying attention and start taking care of you or she was going to lose you."

"You said that?"

"She told me to suck it, but not that politely. And then she went out and got whatever was on sale. You deserve someone who at least knows what pop you like after four months. And I need to see if Bear wants to get a place together. Did you eat dinner?"

"Nope."

"How do you feel about waffles?" she asked.

"Love them."

"We'd better take your car," she said. "Sierra won't fuck with mine."

"You think she'd fuck with mine?" I asked as we crossed the backyard.

"Why chance it?"

"Yeah, good point."

We went to a 24-hour breakfast place. Cyd ordered a cappuccino with about a dozen shots of espresso in it. I got decaf and we both ordered waffles heaped with sugar-laden strawberries and whipped cream.

"I need to tell you something else," Cyd said.

"What?"

She put her fork down and wrapped her hands around the white ceramic vat of cappuccino.

"I think Sierra has been lining up her next girlfriend. I think she sensed that she was losing you, even before the stuff with Blake. Or maybe she habitually moves on, I don't know. It always seems like she thinks she's going to be with someone forever, but with Dustin, she was already talking about you two months into that."

"You know about me and Blake?" I asked.

Cyd sipped the cappuccino, changing the white and brown swirl pattern on top from a spiral to a peak.

"Bear told me," she said. "Blake told her. Bear asked me if there was any chance you were going to split up with Sierra and go for Blake. Plus you cleaned our whole house right after that party, so I would have figured something was going on."

"What do you think about it?" I asked, worried that she thought what we'd done was wrong.

Cyd moved my coffee mug away from the side of the table toward the middle. "I think a million of Sierra couldn't equal Blake. I think if you've got a shot with her, you should go for it. Blake's Einstein-smart, and funny, and she's got a huge heart."

"I don't...what? No. I mean. I don't know. Don't you think she's also kind of...unstable or whatever?"

Cyd shook her head. "Wouldn't you rather be with someone who knows what her crazy is and is dealing with it instead of someone who acts like it's her God-given right to use people?"

"Uh," I said. Brain vibrating with too much to think about—and with the bell-struck rightness ringing in Cyd's words. "Can we go back to that first thing? You think Sierra is interested in someone else?"

"I think she's hooking a new girl," Cyd said. "One she met at school. Tracy whatever. She had her over to the house a few weeks ago, to have dinner and study, of course, but it was flirty."

She stopped and took a few bites of her waffle. I dragged a syrup-laden strawberry through whipped cream and ate it.

Cyd said, "I was curious. I joined them for a bit. And I saw that Tracy had a bunch of LGBTQ buttons on her backpack, so I brought up my sister. I know, cheap ploy but she's okay with me talking about her like that. I got Tracy's whole coming out story and how she got dumped recently and she's single. It made me very suspicious."

"Yeah," I agreed grimly.

I pushed the melting whipped cream off my sodden waffle. I didn't want to believe it. Sierra was pretty social. She could have had this girl over to study for real. It wasn't conclusive…and yet.

"Not to be completely presumptuous, but are you going to ask Blake out?" Cyd asked.

"I have no idea. I don't understand what the deal is with her and Kordell."

"Nobody does."

"Are they truly not a couple?"

Cyd nodded. "Not sure why, but that's what they tell me." She paused for a bit, stared out the window, sipped her coffee. "Blake likes you," she said.

I tried not to grin ridiculously.

"You don't think it was just for fun? At Bear's parents'?"

"Oh honey, she's liked you since she met you. But you can cross that bridge when you're ready. Tell me what you're working on? What are you drawing?"

The edge of my breath caught in my throat as I realized Sierra hadn't asked me that simple question. I'd been staying with her for over a week and she'd never asked. Cyd let me be while I got myself back together under the pretense of being super interested in my coffee and waffle.

"Some story stuff," I told her. "Though I'm not into that Zeno and the Queen drawing. I was working on one of Cypher and Zeno, but I can't post that. And a bunch of figure studies. My perspective gets off when I'm doing shoulders and hips, the people come out warped, I'm trying to fix that."

I paused but she seemed interested so we talked about art and acupuncture, meridians and lines and bodies, until the waffles were gone and our mugs were empty.

When we got back to the house, Sierra's bedroom light was on and there was morose music coming from behind her door. I couldn't imagine how I was going to get back into Sierra's bed and sleep. But I also couldn't curl up on the couch knowing that at any point she could wake me up and start up the fight again. Even the idea that she could watch me sleeping felt weird.

I asked Cyd, "Can I sleep in your bed? If that's too weird…"

She gestured for me to follow her into her room. "Sure, honey. In the morning we can tell Sierra you turned me gay."

"Like she'd buy that. Aren't you the straightest person ever?"

"I'm nature's way of keeping the girl dating pool open for the rest of you," she said.

CHAPTER THIRTY-TWO

The next morning I hid in Cyd's room until Sierra left for work. Then I didn't know what to do so I ran to the grocery store. Even though I had only two days until my flight to Boston, I got a six-pack of Pepsi to make a point. And I picked up a few things for Cyd.

When Sierra got home, she gave me a hug and kiss.

"I'm glad you're feeling better," she said, like it was all me.

"I'm not," I told her.

"What's wrong?" she asked.

"Maybe when school starts we should…I don't know. It's a whole year and we're hardly going to get to see each other."

"What are you saying?" she asked with an edge coming into her voice.

The whole situation was unfair. Sitting at one end of the couch with her at the other, trying to say anything that made sense when it didn't make sense to me. This was my first relationship, I wasn't supposed to have to figure out what was wrong and what to do about it.

But I didn't want to fly to Boston pretending that everything was great. I didn't want a bunch of "baby, I miss you" texts from

Sierra when I wasn't going to feel the same way. I couldn't forget the way Cyd had described Sierra as someone who used people.

"Do I make you that unhappy?" Sierra asked.

"No, it's not you." The lies came out fluently. "It's everything. My father wants me to focus on my grades this year and I know he's going to be stricter about letting me come visit and you've said how hard it is to be far away from each other…"

"How can you be so calm about all of that?" she asked.

"I'm not," I said, but even I could hear the flatness in my voice.

And I knew that if Blake were there, she'd be asking what was under the numbness and listening to my answer.

"You could've fooled me," Sierra said. "Maybe you don't feel about me the way I feel about you. Or maybe you're trying to get rid of me so you can be with Blake. You don't get that she's using you."

Her eyes were chips of glaciers in a face gone pale and waxy.

She said, "If you're not going to make an effort, maybe we should end this now. It is hard with you being so far away, and if you're not even going to try. That's what you're telling me, isn't it? That this fall you're not going to fight for us, to make this work. You're so self-absorbed sometimes. I can't do all the fighting myself. If you're not going to work on our relationship, maybe we don't have one."

My head felt like it was being crushed from the inside, like at any moment the pressure between my brain and skull was going to make my eyeballs pop out.

I stood up from the couch and said, "Okay."

"Lauren, how can you be so cold? What did I do? Tell me one thing."

But it was everything she didn't do.

I went into the bedroom and threw things into my suitcase. Sierra followed me to the doorway.

"I knew you were too immature for this," she said. "You don't know what it takes to keep a relationship going. Do you think you're going to have a better shot with Blake, seriously? As screwed up as she is and as cold as you are? You don't know how good you have it with me."

She went back to the living room and threw herself on the couch weeping. I followed her, leaving my suitcase in the doorway to her room. Watching her cry, under the numbness, I felt sadness and even more guilt. And under that anger. The kind of anger that made me want to break things.

I carried my stuff to the car and left. I drove toward Duluth until I was out of the Cities and suburbs, then pulled over in a rest area and cried for a long time. I sobbed and made sounds I was profoundly glad no one could hear and got snot all over my shirt.

Not because she'd broken up with me or me with her, whatever, but because the whole thing was such a disaster. And because I was terrified that she could be a little bit right.

* * *

My father was glad I'd brought the car home rather than spending the money to park near the airport for two-and-a-half weeks. I had one full day at home and the following morning, he'd drop me off at the bus to ride down to the Minneapolis airport.

He said he was pleased I was showing sense about the value of money finally. He had no idea how shattered I was.

I wanted to talk to Blake but what would I say? It kept starting out in my head like: *hey, Sierra and I split up…um…do you…would you…*

I couldn't finish the sentence. Not even to myself.

I fell into bed early and slept until midmorning.

As soon as I got up, I went to the story. There was a new entry.

Blake:

Bound to the slab of metal, Cypher shivered with cold and hunger. King Solar's Sunslingers had used magic-enhanced metal for the cuffs on her wrists and ankles so she couldn't teleport. They'd proven their ruthlessness and willingness to torture her until she swore fealty to them. Then they left her.

The air in the room shifted. Turning her head, Cypher saw a stream of dust filter out of the air vent and form into the welcome shape of Zeno.

"We're here to rescue you," Zeno said.

She came to the side of the table and turned her fingers into lock picks so she could open the cuffs. She helped Cypher sit up and got her water from a nearby canteen.

"Solar put a microchip in me. He can track me," Cypher warned.

"We know," Zeno said. "We're going to have to cut it out."

Cypher held out her left wrist. "Be careful, it's close to the vein."

Zeno turned her fingertip into a micro-thin scalpel. Cypher braced for the pain but the blade was so thin it hardly caused any. Blood welled up and dripped down her arm as Zeno used her fingers like tweezers and carefully pulled the chip out from under Cypher's skin.

Then Zeno did something surprising. She used the scalpel on herself and cut across her palm. She grabbed Cypher's wrist, blood to blood.

"Are we sworn siblings now?" Cypher asked.

Zeno laughed. "We're updating our copy of you," she said. "This is the fastest way to cycle our nanites through your system. We want to make sure we're indistinguishable from you, even on a scan."

"Great party trick," Cypher said.

"It's how we're going to get you out of here. We'll take your place until you're safely away."

"Zeno, I'm not leaving."

"What?"

"I've decided to stay. Solar's right. We need to find this weapon and I'm the only one who can do it."

"They brainwashed you," Zeno argued. "You have to come with us. You're not safe here."

"I can't go. This is where I need to be. Get out while you can, before they find you."

Zeno took her hand off Cypher's wrist and examined her palm where their blood ran together. She seemed confused.

"Why did you have me cut out the chip if you're not going?" Zeno asked.

Cypher held out her hand for the chip. "I'm not going to stay as his pawn. I'm not his hunting dog. I'm doing this because it's the right thing to do."

Zeno dropped the bloody microchip into Cypher's palm. She closed her hand around it.

"Go," Cypher told her. "Run."

I hadn't imagined the microchip in her wrist in my drawings, but I liked this scene. It was great the way she used the blood connection for the nanites to update their copy of Cypher.

But the way it ended...she said, "Run." Did she mean that for real?

She'd posted the scene late last night, hours after Sierra and I split up. Was this a response to the breakup? Did she think I was the kind of person who screwed things up? If I stayed away from her, would that make her life easier?

I stared out the window at the steel-gray sky. I was pretty far away now. Physically at least.

But not really.

I felt a kinship with Zeno—a flash of understanding what it would be like to send part of yourself to copy someone so that forever after you had the knowledge of their body inside you. Blake was copied into me like that.

I could never forget what it felt like to kiss her, to hold her, to feel her laughing.

CHAPTER THIRTY-THREE

The next morning I took the bus down from Duluth to the Minneapolis airport and flew to Boston. Flying away from the Cities felt good. Flying away from Sierra, from that whole train wreck. Back when I'd decided to get a girlfriend, I assumed it would be a one- or two-year thing, maybe longer. I'd have someone to date my whole senior year of high school, after which we'd part weepily on the steps of one of our colleges.

I had not planned for my first relationship to last under four months and end with me slinking away disgusted and sad and pissed off. If there was a lesbian jury somewhere (all dressed in flannels and smartly tailored suits), they would convict me for reckless dating, multiple counts of failure to heed warnings, and gross girlfriend misconduct. I'd probably shamed the whole lesbian establishment.

By the time the plane landed, I was contemplating trashing the dating plan until college.

Except…Blake. If I could ever figure her out. If she wanted me at all. But if she didn't, I so couldn't handle that right now. I kept taking out my phone and looking at her name, not knowing what to say.

"Run," she'd said. So I was running.

My mom was waiting at the end of a row of blue airport seats with her laptop open in her lap and her phone on the seat next to her. She isn't tall like I am. She's got that classic Jewish mother look: big-chested, heavy in the middle, thick black hair, warm brown eyes. Even her hair is different from mine: more tightly curled and kept short, which doesn't entirely stop it from frizzing out by the end of the day, but it helps.

I bent down to hug her. She said, "Hi honey" and kissed my cheek. We collected luggage and the rental car.

On the drive to the vacation house she opened with, "How's school?"

"It's okay."

"Art?"

I usually had a ton to tell her on that subject, but all I could manage now was, "I've been doing this group storytelling project with art and stuff. One of the other girls is great with perspective, I'm trying to learn from her. But it's kind of falling apart."

She said, "I'm sorry. Is the other artist the girl you're dating? Isaac told me."

I hadn't even thought to text Isaac about the breakup. I told Mom, "Uh, no. She's straight I think, the artist. Anyway, what've you been up to?"

She half turned her head toward me but kept her eyes on the road, opened her mouth and closed it. Finally she said, "I was in Afghanistan until last week. It's amazing what women are doing there. I've been working to connect Afghan women with mentors in the U.S."

She paused so I nodded and said, "Yeah? Does that make things better over there?"

"Very much so. When you create economic opportunities, give people a chance to earn a living and support their families, it lessens the likelihood they'll put on an explosive vest and kill people. So this is how I get to contribute to making the world a little safer and making the lives of people who live with conflict a bit easier. I wish you could meet some of these women. They're…"

"Badass?" I suggested.

"Badass," she agreed.

She went on about the women-owned businesses in Afghanistan, places I'd expect, like hair salons and handmade goods, but also gyms, woodworking and furniture businesses. She told me about a woman in Kandahar, the epicenter of the Taliban, who ran a successful business selling pomegranates and jam.

I felt grossly selfish for wanting her to spend more time in the U.S. so I could live with her. How could I take her away from all the people she was helping? Not to mention how much she clearly loved this job.

The house she rented for us was a cute bungalow on a stretch of beach in Maine. The first evening we spent stocking the fridge, walking the beach, getting used to the house and surroundings.

In the morning, I read Blake's scene again but nothing new came out of it. She hadn't texted me or emailed. For all I knew she was going to mail me another cryptic book of wisdom. Or maybe she didn't want to talk to me.

There wasn't any email or text from Sierra either. That was a relief. And sad. Not sad that I'd lost her. Sad that the person I thought she was maybe didn't even exist.

I walked up and down the beach until my feet ached from trying to keep balance on the shifting sand. I cleaned the already clean kitchen to keep moving.

Mom told me I didn't have to clean, it was my vacation too, so I sat on the sunporch with my sketchbook and tried to draw. It came out all swirls and darkness, like drowning. I gave up and went into town with Mom to buy fresh fish for dinner and pick up Isaac from the train station.

He's two inches shorter than me and he has our father's strong brow and a thick, powerful body that I'm sure looked imposing in suits like my father's did.

Spending time with them was like being in a long, slow courtly dance. Everyone had specific positions to move through at the right times. My role was to make basic meals and clean up and appear happy to do it. Isaac's role was to work out and walk the beach and tease me, but never harshly, and go into town for a six-pack and a bottle of wine for Mom as needed. He got me Pepsi.

Mom read the newspaper and walked the beach with us and showed us photos from her countries. And we pretended we were a great family. Except I was afraid they weren't pretending. They might be happy.

I wasn't. I was going back to being nothing inside. A thing that didn't know what it was and couldn't quite turn into what it was supposed to be.

* * *

After that first day, I ignored my laptop. I drew and I walked a lot and tried not to think about Sierra. Part of me kept saying that I was being stupid, that Sierra did love me. Maybe it was hard to date me. I could have tried harder.

Another part of me was clear that the first part was a raging idiot. Cyd was right about Sierra and the stupidest thing I'd done was fail to see it sooner. And thinking that I loved her.

Maybe I was hopelessly bad at relationships. I should stay away from Blake, at least until I knew better.

After a few days, I opened my laptop hoping Blake had written more than the scene telling Zeno, telling me, to go. Hoping I could find some clue about what she thought.

Maybe I'd have the guts to email her and ask.

When I opened my email, a message from Dustin got my attention. He'd forwarded me an exchange between him and Sierra.

He put a note to me at the top: *Lauren, I thought you should see this. I'd appreciate it if you don't let Sierra know I shared it with you.*

I scrolled to the bottom so I could read the emails in the order they were written.

Sierra, seven days ago, on Wednesday:

Dust, I want to add a new character to my court. She's a friend of mine from the university, Tracy Wade. She should be a marquis in the Court of Rogues, higher in rank than the knights. Her name is going to be Veritie and her powers are that she can read minds and do mind control and she's also an infomancer.

"Veritie my ass," I said.

Sierra had taken the name from the Latin word for "truth." That was so transparent and disgusting that I wanted to puke. This must have been the girl Cyd mentioned over waffles—the one she thought Sierra was trying to "hook"—the one she thought Sierra was going to replace me with. Of course Sierra would think the new girl should be in the story and outrank me and Blake.

The date of the email was the morning after I'd tried to talk to Sierra. Two days after lying on the golf course with Blake and staring up at the stars. *Before* Sierra and I officially broke up.

I tried to remember Sierra's tone and expression as we talked. Was she planning this all along? Or did she automatically line people up so she always had a fallback plan? Was I the sucker who'd fallen into place when she decided she wasn't that into Dustin?

Those two months between when I gave her my email and when she used it—had she forgotten about me until she needed a new person in her life?

Feeling covered in slime, I read the next part of Sierra's email:

Also, I hope you'll be open to the next logical step in the story of Cypher turning traitor on the Queen of Rogues. Even if she's doing it for our alliance, for all we know, she's now against us. It's logical that we would send an assassin after her. The best that we have.

Dustin's reply back to her was sent Wednesday evening (the night I slept in Cyd's room):

Of course, it's great to have new people, the more the merrier. Does Tracy write? Will she be setting up an account?

As to your question about the Cypher plot, I admit that does make sense. I can't see the Queen of Rogues merely letting Cypher fly around the galaxy advertising her dissent. Do you have a specific plot in mind for the assassination attempt and how Cypher will avoid it? Have you talked to Blake about this?

Sierra, late Wednesday night:

Some things have happened, I'll explain later. I'll make an account for Tracy. Her psi powers can help the Queen track Cypher. I mean to kill her. Not just make the attempt.

Sierra again in a new email, Friday, late afternoon (after we broke up):

I don't know how much you know about all of this, but Blake and Lauren have been having an affair behind my back. I tried to put an end to it but I think it did irreparable damage to my relationship with Lauren. We've broken up. I know she's young and not ready for a real relationship, but I can't tell you how betrayed I feel.

My hands were shaking and I pressed them between my knees, but that made my whole body shake. Sierra's email went on:

I thought Lauren was more mature than that. She acts so knowledgeable. But I should have suspected Blake. She's been getting colder and colder to me these last few months. I now wonder if she was waiting for an opportunity to hurt me. I don't know what I ever did to her. Maybe nothing at all, or something she took as a slight that you know I didn't mean that way.

I was seriously missing her friendship and then this happened with Lauren. I don't know how they could do that to me. You know they even had sex at Bear's party while I was there! At the same party! And they snuck away together! While Lauren was a guest in my house. Now I hope you can understand why I no longer want their characters in the Court of Rogues. If they want to go join the Solar Court, fine, but you have to see that it's in keeping with the Queen of Rogues character to hunt down those who betrayed her.

Dustin's reply came on Saturday afternoon:

I'm sorry to read all that. I caution you not to do anything in your anger that you'll regret later, but I can't fault your logic. Write what you must, but please leave Blake and Lauren room to do their own storytelling.

I could barely read his reply. My eyes kept going back to what Sierra had written, especially where she said I was having an affair with Blake. "Affair" was a word I'd heard yelled a lot in the house when Mom was leaving my father. I wanted to crawl into myself and disappear.

What Sierra said wasn't what had happened. Except it was. After making a huge deal about Sierra having sex with Dustin, I'd done worse. I'd had sex with someone else at a party when Sierra was there. Seeing it on the page I got how immensely shitty that would feel—to be standing out in the yard, smoking, cracking jokes, only to learn later that the girl you loved was downstairs having sex with your best friend.

But Sierra twisted it. We didn't sneak away together. I for sure hadn't planned it. Had Blake?

Sierra had said that Blake was being cold to her, and then Blake hugged her in the dining room at Bear's house. What if Blake did plan to get me away from Sierra and the hug was to throw her off? How could I be sure that Sierra was using me but Blake wasn't? They'd been friends.

Was I the pawn in a battle between the two of them?

If I wasn't and Blake did like me, I should stay far away from her so I didn't screw that up like Sierra. And if she didn't, if it was a power play between her and Sierra, I should stay even further away. My only two choices were to destroy my relationship with Blake or be destroyed by it.

I was better off when I didn't feel anything at all. I closed my laptop and shoved it to the back of the desk.

CHAPTER THIRTY-FOUR

I drew a few sketches of Zeno dissolving into space. I walked the beach and stood in the cold Atlantic Ocean until my feet went numb. Maybe being dead inside like my father wasn't such a bad idea. He never seemed to feel anything but cold anger and a drive to win.

I liked anger a lot better than feeling like someone yanked my heart out and shredded it in front of me and then rubbed heart-confetti in my face. Anger was probably my favorite emotion… other than lust, but me and lust weren't on speaking terms anymore.

By the middle of the week, I'd used the anger to push away everything else. Mom came down the stairs and asked if I wanted to walk the beach. We walked to one end of the beach and turned around to walk to the other.

"What colleges are you applying to?" Mom asked.

"I thought I wanted to go to school in the Cities," I said. "But now I'm thinking maybe I want to come out east."

"There are a lot of great colleges here," she told me. "I think you could have your pick."

"My grades aren't that good. And I don't have a lot of extracurriculars."

She put her arm around me and squeezed. "Honey, you got that story published in that comic anthology. That counts for more than an extracurricular. And what's your GPA?"

"Three-point-five," I said. "Well, technically three-point-four-six."

"That's great."

"No, it isn't. To get into the great colleges I need more like a four-point-oh and a bunch of outside activities."

"Did your father tell you that?"

"Yeah."

"He's...peculiar. Tell me the schools you want and we'll look at what they're accepting in new students. I think with your art and a great essay and a three-point-five, you're going to have a lot of choices."

We reached the end of the beach and started back toward the house.

"I don't like living with him," I said.

She stopped and faced me. "Did he do something?"

"No. I mean, he didn't like that I got a C in American history, but that's a normal thing. He's not bad or anything. But I can't talk to him."

"About what, honey?"

"I don't know, stuff. Anything."

She started walking again and I shortened my steps to stay right next to her.

"My girlfriend, we broke up," I said. "I'd been seeing her since spring but...how do you know if you love someone?"

"That's a tough question. You feel good around them, you look forward to seeing them, they listen to you. When you fight, it's not impossible to resolve. They don't cheat on you. Did you love this girl?"

I'd been about to tell her everything, until she said the cheating bit. There was no way I could tell my mom a story about how I had sex with another girl at a party while my girlfriend was there. Especially not when my father had obviously done something similar to her.

"It's complicated," I told her. "I thought I loved her but now I don't think so."

"When did you break up?" she asked.

"A few days ago."

She nodded, like that was the part that made sense. "You know what we should do? Let's go into town and get four pints of gelato and sit on the couch and eat out of the containers and watch dumb movies. That's the best cure for a breakup."

"How dumb are these movies?" I asked.

"As dumb as you want, and if Isaac complains we'll tell him to get lost. Oh we should have popcorn too. And pizza."

"Sure, that'd be great," I said.

"You'll feel better," she told me. "Breakups feel awful for a little while but then you move on. You'll meet someone else."

I'd already…I didn't want…I shook my head and quickly turned it into a nod. It did sound like a fun evening. But the idea of gelato, pizza and movies did nothing to budge the heavy, sunken feeling in my chest and belly.

* * *

I had loved Sierra. It was easy to tell Mom I hadn't, but that was a lie. I could remember how excited I was when she came up to Duluth and how much I wanted to see her before that trip to the Cities in June.

How could I have loved someone so much and a few months later feel sick when I thought about her? Isaac found me pondering this, sitting at the top of the seawall, staring out over the gray waves. He sat next to me, legs hanging down, his shorter than mine but thicker in the thighs.

"Mom told me you broke up with that girl," he said.

"Yeah."

"She dump you or did you dump her?"

"I did," I said.

"That's my sis. Sometimes those pretty girls are too much work. You gotta move on."

I put my face in my hands and shook my head. He made it sound like I'd won a court case. His fingers brushed my shoulder and moved away. As kids, even though he'd taken care of me, other than my morning bus stop high-fives he didn't touch me. In my father's house, touching was alien.

"Give it time," Isaac said. "You'll get over it. Fish in the sea and all. You going to come out east for school?"

I raised my head and stared out at the water. Blue and gray like Blake's eyes. I wanted to throw myself into the waves. *Drama queen much?* the other part of my brain asked.

"I don't know," I told him. "I'm not staying in Duluth, I know that."

"No one does," he said.

"Do you like it out here?"

"Yeah, I love it."

"You don't talk about girlfriends," I said.

He shrugged. "Don't date much. Too busy."

Busy or broken? Was it learned or genetic? Maybe our whole family sucked at relationships.

"Our father..." I said and stopped. I forced myself through the question. "I don't remember because I was a kid but, did he ever say things to you about, like, being overly emotional or trying to sabotage your life?"

"No," he said after a long pause. "When did Dad say that to you?"

"Just sometimes."

"La, has he said that more than once?"

"Yeah."

"That's pretty weird," he said.

"I don't like living with him," I told Isaac. "I mean, he's usually working or out with whoever he's dating. And it's nice sometimes to have the house to myself. But I kind of wish...do you think I'm old enough that Mom would let me stay with her?"

"I don't think she can. It's illegal in most states to let sixteen-year-olds stay by themselves for weeks at a time," he said.

"How do you know that?"

"Researched it back when Dad had that one girlfriend and barely came home, remember?"

"Not so much. What's illegal about it?"

He said, "It's neglect. But I don't think Dad meant it that way. It was right after Mom left and I think he was, you know, working through things."

"Yeah, I guess," I said, not adding that I was still living that way.

I felt bad that I'd brought up the whole "overly emotional" thing. If our father did say things like that to Isaac, I figured he'd know how to respond. Since he didn't, maybe it was me. The feeling that I was wrong and monstrous crept back in to my gut.

"You know there are rules to living with Dad," Isaac said.

"Yeah. Do whatever he says."

He shook his head. "Nope. Do whatever you can to make him look good and he'll let you do what you want."

That sounded horrible and phony. But I wasn't going to say that to Isaac. And the more I thought about it, I got how practical it was. That was the reason for the garden show crap—getting photos in a magazine that he could show around to his colleagues. That's why I had to dress up and go to the stupid parties and shake hands while saying all the right things and listening and batting my eyes.

"I try," I said. "It's never quite right or it's never enough, I'm not sure."

"One more year. Then you can come out here and party. You'll like college."

One year. One year of shitty moments packed infinitely densely, like numbers on the number line. I laughed to myself. And I wanted to call Blake so much, but I couldn't. All that slime from Sierra's emails was burning through my skin from the inside. I was full of poison. I didn't want to get that on Blake.

CHAPTER THIRTY-FIVE

I flew back to the Cities. Walking from the baggage claim to the bus, I considered texting Blake just to see…but I didn't. Even thinking about her hurt. It was all connected to Sierra and that email to Dustin, to the word "affair," to the fear that I'd destroy whatever I touched, to the wrenching awfulness of being that person. How many people had Sierra told? How many people in this city thought of me as the horrible double-standard cheating girlfriend?

I caught the bus to Duluth to get away and hide.

School started and the weather was gray all the time, inside and out, in the sky and in my mind, gray and flat. I went to classes, I doodled in my notebook a sequence of evil flowers. My body moved around in space and time. I felt like an alien—a shape-shifting alien colony of nanites who'd taken on this girl's body in a hopeless effort to blend in.

* * *

In the second week of school, I returned to the story. I didn't want to. I kept telling myself it was insult to injury and all that, but I had to know what happened. Was Sierra enacting her bullshit plan to kill Cypher and Zeno?

I scanned through the new posts for the ones from Sierra. There was a bunch of flowery crap introducing Veritie (who of course as Sierra's new girl was a thousand times more amazing than Zeno). The story mentioned that Zeno had gone missing and they presumed she'd been blown up by Solar's Sunslingers. There was even a scientifically awful paragraph about how by using the harnessed power of a sun, they could melt Zeno's nanites.

"No body, no proof," I snarled at the screen.

I saw with a shiver that she'd already gone after Cypher too.

Sierra:

Many had forgotten, but before the Queen of Rogues rose to her current station, she was the best assassin in the galaxy. Her powers allowed her to weaken others and blind their sight so she could pass unnoticed.

Using her smallest, fastest stealth ship, she closed on the fleet of Lord Solar as it hopped from black hole to black hole on its fruitless quest for a weapon they would find too late. After she disposed of her enemies, the Queen and her allies would travel to the future to get the locus of the High God that they'd recently found and needed to possess to rule the Universe.

The Queen tucked her ship to the belly of Lord Solar's battlecruiser and cut through the bulkhead to slip unnoticed onto the ship. Veritie brought her the key information she needed. Veritie's powers as an infomancer were stronger even than Cypher's.

Veritie had seen the docking bay on the cruiser where Cypher's ship was. She'd given the Queen the code to the microchip Cypher carried so she could confirm that Cypher was on board the ship and staying in her smaller starship, the one she used to approach the black holes.

The Queen waited until the security shift change and made her silent way down to the docking bay. Veritie was even able to get her the security code for Cypher's private ship and she opened the door without trouble.

Cypher was sleeping. The queen slipped a grounding collar around her throat so she couldn't teleport away. Of course that woke Cypher but that was part of the plan. The Queen jerked on the collar, sending Cypher to her hands and knees next to the bed.

"No one betrays me and lives," the Queen said as she leveled her blaster at Cypher's head.

"I wasn't going to," Cypher said. "Please don't kill me. I'm loyal to you. I was going to bring you the weapon, really."

"I don't care," the Queen told her. "I know you've been working against me and these are lies upon lies. You and Zeno were going to try to take my throne once you had the weapon, but now Zeno is destroyed and you're next."

"Please, I'll do anything!" Cypher said.

The Queen fired her blaster once into the side of Cypher's head and her body slumped to the floor. She walked out of the ship without looking back.

"Cold," I said to my laptop screen. "And bullshit."

I cupped my body around my anger like hands around a spark, praying for a fire to ignite. Sierra could come after me. I was the one who'd had the "affair." I was the monster. But not Blake. No way did she deserve that.

"There's no fucking way I'm letting you end Cypher," I said out loud. It felt good to hear the words.

But I didn't know how to fix it. She'd used a blaster so Cypher's head was ruined. It wasn't like I could write a scene where Zeno showed up and healed Cypher from that. She was clearly dead.

There had to be a way.

CHAPTER THIRTY-SIX

I paced the house, trying to figure out what to do. Anger burned through the layers of numb and shame and fear. Who could help me? I wasn't going to email Dustin. I had no idea where he stood. Not Blake, not yet. She shouldn't have to brainstorm her own rescue. I didn't know Bear well enough.

I texted Cyd: *Hey, sorry if I'm bugging you, but have you kept up on what's going on in the story?*

She responded: *Hi, it's kind of crazy down here. I haven't.*

What's going on? I asked.

Sierra has Tracy over all the time and I'm so sick of both of them. I'm moving out end of Oct. How are you?

I smiled at the words. I hadn't thought about what Cyd would be doing the last few weeks. So cool that she wasn't going to be Sierra's roommate anymore.

I'm... I typed and erased it. How was I? That should have been an easy enough question, but it wasn't.

I was afraid and sick inside to show her the emails from Sierra, but I had to tell someone.

I wrote: *Did you see the emails Sierra sent Dustin?*

Nooo? What?

What's your email? I'll forward them.

She gave me her address and I sent her the one from Dustin with the whole, long, evil conversation from Sierra.

A while later my phone pinged again. Cyd wrote: *I'm sorry, Lauren. I should have talked to you sooner. I thought she wasn't going after you. That's seriously wrong.*

It's okay.

She wrote: *It's not. She has no right. You deserve much better.*

I felt like I was going to cry but the pressure in my head was a relief compared to all the gray.

I typed, *Sierra's trying to kill Cypher in the story. I have to fix it but I don't know how.*

What does Blake think? Cyd asked.

I haven't talked to her, I wrote back.

What? Since when?

Since I broke up with Sierra, I said.

That had been over a month ago. It was strange that so much time had passed. Trying to not feel anything made it seem like I'd slept through entire days, maybe weeks.

Cyd wrote: *LAUREN!*

Why are you yelling? I never know what's going on with her. I don't even know why she hooked up with me. What if she doesn't like me like that?

She likes you, Cyd wrote. *LIKE likes you.*

How do you know? I mean about her?

The way she talks to you, the way she LOOKS at you. The way she talks about you. And the times she doesn't talk about you but she's thinking about you, it's obvious.

What if I fuck that up like I fucked up things with Sierra? It was easier to ask by text, disconnected words out in space.

*OMG Lauren! That wasn't YOU! Sierra is an epic *^* * *!&@%. Don't buy into that shit from her.*

If Cyd was right about all of this, I wanted to know what Blake's face looked like when she was thinking about me and not saying anything. Was it one of her smiles? Was it a grin?

Blake hasn't emailed me or texted or anything, I wrote.

She's dealing with things, Cyd said.

I was an idiot. Anger could not be my favorite emotion if it made me blind to stupid-obvious things like the fact that Blake might have problems of her own to handle. She was the one at ground zero for Sierra's bullshit. Why hadn't I thought of that? I should have texted her or emailed or made a comment on the scene she'd posted—or something.

Is she okay? I asked.

She'd love to hear from you. Especially now.

I assumed that last was a reference to Sierra trying to kill Cypher in the story. But it could be anything. How much did I know about Blake's day-to-day? I hadn't even asked her what she was doing the rest of the summer.

The last time we'd talked was lying on the golf course together staring at the sky. I hadn't even considered what she might think it meant that I hadn't texted her. What if she thought I blew her off?

Does she know I broke up with Sierra? I asked.

The whole Twin Cities knows and most of the first ring of suburbs. Blake didn't tell you about any of this?

Blake hadn't told me anything, only posted that scene telling Zeno to run. Maybe she said that to protect me. Not because she wanted me to go away but because she knew what was coming. And I'd kept running because of what Sierra said, because of her words: affair and immature and self-absorbed. I'd been afraid I'd mess up anything I touched.

Had I been a bigger jerk to Blake by trying not to screw things up? If I was going to mess up no matter what I did, I wanted to be talking to Blake.

I typed to Cyd, *What happened???!!!*

There was a long pause. I walked up the stairs and into my room and stood by the dresser staring at the things Blake had given me.

Cyd's message came through: *All that shit Sierra said in the emails to Dustin, she's been saying to anyone who will listen. She still has friends at Blake's school. She's been saying that you and Blake hooked up a bunch, that you used Sierra for a place to stay and a lot of other crap about Blake lying and stuff. Do you really want to know all this?*

YES!

Cyd went on: *She's been spreading lies that Blake can't be trusted and will have sex with anyone. That she used you to get back at Sierra for some made-up shit.*

She outed Blake at school?

Yep. Blake says she doesn't care if those jackass kids call her dyke or whatever. She made a joke about it the other day: being bipolar and

bisexual is being bi-squared. But she can't stand that kids are harassing
Kordell.

How does that figure? I asked.

They assume that if she's gay then he is too. Like nobody can be bi or
anything. Though they'd probably harass him for that too.

What are they going to do?

Weather it out, last I heard. Most of the school doesn't care, only a
small group. She won't say it, but she's scared and pretty down. Talk to her.
Right now. Stop texting me and text her. And let me know how it goes.

I stood over my desk, holding my phone, staring at the glowing
screen of my laptop and Sierra's last, ridiculous email to Dustin.
She'd said those things to people at Blake's school?

I could picture it. Sierra had a way of talking about people.
Like when she'd said Blake had bipolar disorder so casually while
telling me about her. It would have been like that, at a party with
her standing in the group of kids smoking or maybe sitting in a
chair like a queen.

She'd have looked around at the curious and eager faces,
knowing they went to Blake's school. She would start it as a story
about something else, probably the online story. She'd quickly, off-
handedly, mention that she and I split up. She'd say that we had to
because of Blake. She'd say just enough to get someone to ask. And
then of course she'd have to tell them more of the story.

Cyd was right. I had to text Blake. But I couldn't figure out
what to say. I bounced around the house but there wasn't anything
else I remotely wanted to do. Finally with supreme articulacy, I
texted: *Hey. I just talked to Cyd. I'm sorry I haven't texted. I wanted to*
talk to you. How are you?

She wrote back minutes later, *Hey monkey, how was the journey*
to the east?

Seeing the words on my screen next to her name made me
smile in a ridiculous Cheshire hyena way. I wrote: *Beautiful, weird,*
the usual. Are you okay?

Her hasty reply said: *Somewhat okay, avoiding Sierra. Social scene*
is pretty bad. Story group imploding.

I considered the glowing screen and the dark words. I took a
deep breath, into my gut, and another. I tried to be some kind of
honest with myself.

I told her: *I'm so sorry I didn't text weeks ago. I wanted to. I*
misunderstood. I wouldn't have gone away like that. I got all messed up.

Yeah, she wrote.

After a too-long pause of minutes, a series of messages from her rose brightly to the surface of my phone:

I'm sorry.

That I didn't send more.

Or write.

Or call.

I meant to.

My brain is plastic-wrapped.

I paced across my bedroom, staring at my phone, hating that I was so far away from her. I said: *That sounds uncomfortable.*

I'm a dusty jar, she said.

Unbroken?

I can't remember if that's good or bad, she said. *I'm sorry.*

I don't know if it's either. Anyway, you can't put a jar around infinity.

She wrote: *I feel lost in a fog. Like no one cares about me.*

I hit the phone icon and held my breath through one and a half rings.

"Hey kid," Blake said.

Hearing her voice, I started grinning too hard to talk. Something flew open inside me, like a plant sped up in time, throwing wide all its tightly curled parts and lunging up toward the sun.

"Blake," I managed to say around the grin. "Hey. Cyd told me. About your school and stuff and Sierra. Can I do anything?"

"Just talk," she said. "Tell me what you're looking at."

"Why?"

"I want to see what you're seeing."

I told Blake, "I'm in my room. The walls are a pale cyan with a gray undertone, white trim. There's a pretty unremarkable bed, my drawing table and my desk, which is this dark oak situation, kind of out of place here. There's a photo I took at the beach of the sky and the sea. It's pretty. I could send you a copy."

"I don't want a photo. I want to hear you talk. Keep going."

"Oh. Um, well, there's a strip of sand at the bottom of the photo and it's yellow tan pale speckled with bits of brown and gray. There are a ton of shells and stones that got polished by the waves. I brought a few of them home and put them around the base of the photo so it's three-dimensional sort of. I could bring you one. A stone from the ocean."

I was babbling with relief. The confusion wasn't gone, but alongside it was the rightness of talking to Blake, hearing her voice. I didn't understand her, but I didn't have to. Inside I was easing out from under the weight of all the numbness I'd been holding onto.

"I'll trade you for a lake stone," she said.

"What color do you want?"

"Your choice. Bring me one that you like. Pocket-sized, though."

I told her, "The sky in the photo is super blue and the ocean is too. I love looking at the ocean. Part of the time I was out east it got stormy and rained. I took photos of that too. It's beautiful like that. It makes the ocean look serious."

"What does a serious ocean look like?" she asked. Her voice was quieter than I was used to and slow, as if she was pushing the words out one at a time.

"Choppy white waves and a thousand shades of gray and blue in the water, kind of like your eyes."

"My eyes have waves?" she asked.

"Wings," I said. "Not waves. Gray-blue wings. Your eyes make me think of a kingfisher, flashing blue and gray. That way they have where they can be still but they look like at any minute they're going to take off into the sky."

"Lauren," her voice was low, on the edge of sad or maybe so deep into it as to be on the far side. "Why aren't you here? Why don't I own a teleporter? Why isn't it set to your coordinates?"

"Why didn't you text or call? I would have helped. I would have done something." The words tumbled out after each other. "What did the scene mean where Cypher tells Zeno to run? Were you trying to protect me? You didn't have to. What does the book mean that you sent me? You sent me that book of sayings and I didn't know if I was supposed to be reading the one about the saddle or the other one?"

"There's one about a saddle?" she asked. "And you thought I meant *that one*?"

"Uh, no, I don't think. It's not like it sounds."

"Which one is 'the other one?'" she asked.

I crossed the room to the book and flipped to the page that was pretty well worn by now. "The one that starts 'it was a night like no other.'"

She quoted the end of the poem back to me: "... you said the words, primeval and holy, that I have never forgotten, and the evil night disappeared like smoke.'"

Hearing the words in her voice I saw us again on the golf course looking up at the sky. The evil of the poem wasn't the night itself, it wasn't any specific night, it was my fear of the night. It was like a promise she'd made me that she'd show me how to be less afraid.

"Oh," I said. "It's about the infinities. Did you know you were going to explain them to me?"

"It's poetry," she said. "It's about a lot of nights. Some of them are even metaphorical."

I wanted her hand in mine again. I wanted to kiss her and feel her head tucked against my shoulder.

"How are you for real?" I asked. "You said dusty and plastic wrap and fog. That sounds not good."

She sighed. "I'm okay. With everything, they upped my meds again. It feels like plastic wrap around my brain. Layers. Like if you made clothes out of plastic wrap. Which is not a bad idea, now that I think about it. But too much work. And I'm still minus-one."

"Is that a math thing?" I asked.

"No, it's the stupid mood chart I'm supposed to keep. It's a misuse of numbers. Columns and neat little rows and I'm supposed to fit into it and I hate it."

"Is minus-one bad?"

"Kind of bad," she said.

"How minus does it go?"

"To three. So I guess minus-one is about thirty-three percent bad."

"What's minus three?"

She was quiet. I could hear her breathing, a little ragged, getting further from the phone. I worried that I'd made her cry.

"I'm sorry," I said. "You don't have to answer that. You don't ever have to tell me anything you don't want to."

She came back closer to the phone, or held it near her mouth again, took a breath in and said, "When I was minus-three, I was so deep in hating myself that I thought if I killed myself it would solve everyone's problems. Everything was wrong, and death, and useless, and I was the worst of it. I tried, you know, twice. I almost..."

There was a long pause and I didn't know what I wanted to say. I couldn't imagine her hating herself like that. Not that I'd never had moments when I felt like I wanted to die, when I felt hopeless, but Blake was so bright and funny and lovable. How could she feel that way about herself?

How could she feel that way so much that she'd tried to kill herself?

"I got how selfish that was," she said in a small voice. "I got that it hurts other people. If I killed myself, it would cause so much pain. And with the medication, I don't feel that way. Lauren…if you don't want to…"

"What?" I said, trying to get over the bolt of panic I felt picturing a world without Blake.

She was definitely crying. The skin of my palms itched and burned from wanting to reach through the phone and touch her. I went back over what we'd said, trying to get my brain and my mouth to sync again.

"What are you saying?" I asked.

"It's silly," she said. "It's not like it could work with you there and me here and everything."

Words spilled out of my lips like they were kicking through the brain-mouth barrier: "Okay first, I'm extremely glad you didn't kill yourself because I'd be seriously fucked up now without you. Is that okay to say?"

"Yeah," she said the word fast and breathy.

"And second, are you *not* asking me out? Are you saying that we could—except that we couldn't, because you're not asking—but you would if you thought that we could?"

"Yeah," she repeated, even faster this time, more breath than sound.

"God, Blake, yes. Yes! I can't not go out with you."

She laughed and I could picture her with her mouth open and her laugh ringing in the room.

"But I didn't ask," she said.

"When you do, it's yes. And, um, is it also okay to say I think it's adorable that you're supposed to describe yourself with numbers?"

She said, "yeah," one more time.

"What's the best number?" I asked. "I mean, the one that means you're doing really well?"

She sniffled and told me, "Zero."

"Seriously?"

"No kidding. It means my mood is 'within normal limits.'"

"Zero," I said. "It's my new favorite number."

"It's been mine for a long time. It's why Cypher is named that, because it comes from the Arabic, Sifr, and people used to say 'cypher' when they meant zero. Do you know it messed up the Greeks that their math didn't have a zero in it?"

"You were saying that the day I met you," I told her. "I mean, before I walked into the room. I was in the kitchen and I heard you say that but you didn't say how. So tell me."

I sat for a long time listening to Blake tell me about the number zero while I watched the sky outside my bedroom window grow deep and peaceful.

At least I felt something that wasn't anger or dread. I wanted to shred myself apart and flow through the walls and into the sky and fly to Blake. I wanted to put my arms around her and hold onto her and feel myself materialize out of nothing into a real person again.

CHAPTER THIRTY-SEVEN

Talking to Blake again every day. Mostly about nothing but also everything. She'd text me about math class and I'd send her a pic of what I was drawing.

Some days she wouldn't send me anything and now I understood it was because the fog was bad that day. Or she was in the minuses, minus-one or even minus-two. Or stuff was going on at school and she didn't want to talk about it. I sent her jokes and cartoonish doodles. I sketched a hippo walking up the long side of a triangle and labeled it "hippotemuse."

Every time I saw her name on my phone I grinned, even though it hurt to read her words and feel her so far away from me. It was like spikes of color driving down through the ice of my life. Like when you've been out in the cold too long and your fingers are numb and you run a bath—that first moment when the hot water doesn't even burn, it jabs raw pain up through your nerves.

I felt more things for Blake in a week than I felt for Sierra in a month. I felt more for myself than I could ever remember.

I got impatient. I snapped back at my father when he'd ask why something wasn't cleaned or stocked in the pantry. I let him write words on the asinine white board and didn't look at them before I went shopping. I bought the frozen dinners I liked and skipped the ones he did. When he was home I went out of my way to avoid him, but he never seemed to notice.

I researched colleges in the Cities and out east and I was afraid of both options. Would I get down to the Cities almost a year from now to find that I'd lost Blake to someone else?

Mom called every week, sometimes twice. I think she was checking on me. Maybe Isaac had talked to her. I kept wanting to tell her that I needed her help, that I couldn't stay here all year again, but I didn't know how to say it in a way that didn't sound pathetic. I was nearly seventeen so, "Mommy, can I come stay with you?" was out. Plus she'd have to say no or leave her job and I didn't want that.

"Are you dating anyone?" she asked on a call in early October.

"There's this girl I like," I said, hoping this was my opening to the bigger topic of moving. "But she's in Minneapolis so we can't really date. I wish I could move down there."

"What's she like?"

"Smart and…living here sucks. I want to move to the Cities."

"I know it's hard being far away from someone you care about. You could invite her to join us for the holidays. Do you know what she's doing? Would she like D.C.?"

That was almost three months away. I managed to say, "Yeah, I'll ask her. Thanks."

I wanted to ask Mom to talk to my father, to get him to let me go visit a few times before the holidays, but they never talked to each other if they could avoid it. If she sent him an email like that, it would piss him off.

"How did you meet her?" Mom asked, all bright-voiced and trying super hard to be my cool, accepting parent.

"She was in the group writing the story together," I said. "The one I was doing illustrations for."

Talking about the story made me feel like crying. While I was trying to keep it together, Mom asked, "Did you ask her out or did she ask you?"

Brain melt: basement…spider…affair…cheating.

I made the world's longest, "Ummm" sound.

"Am I not supposed to ask that?"

"Uh, no, it's just not that clear. She said she'd ask me out if I lived closer to her and I said I'd say yes if she asked. So it's not official but it would be. I want to go visit her."

"I'm sorry, honey. Maybe you can go to the same college. Do you know where she's applying?"

Eleven months away—if we even got into the same school or wanted to. What colleges excelled at both math and art? That was a mom-appropriate question, so I asked her and got the conversation on that safe track.

After the call I sat staring around my room, trying to figure out what I could say to make her understand when I couldn't even describe my situation to myself. All I knew was that I felt miserable most of the time for no reason. The feeling of missing Blake was clear, but all these other sensations I didn't have names for. What did you call it when your father was being strict about school and mostly gone and somehow this was worse than if he'd been yelling all the time?

It was easier to focus on missing Blake. When I didn't, I dissolved again. Not in a fast, painless way, but slowly, from the inside out, aching.

* * *

At least all the missing Blake and remembering what it felt like being near her gave me a great brainstorm for how to save Cypher. I started writing it in a private document offline to see how it could go:

Cypher's body lay on the floor for hours, cooling, the blood congealing, and only a careful observer would have noticed the way the shreds of burnt flesh around the blast wound were slowly knitting together.

A slender form appeared out of the zero point energy and knelt by the body. She touched its hand gently.

"Zeno, she's definitely gone now," she said. "Hang tight, I'll get you more nanites. What a mess. I thought I'd look better dead."

The real Cypher went to the secret compartment under her ship's navigation console and pulled out the large crate of medical grade nanites she kept for Zeno. When she let them loose, they swarmed over the body. At first they tried to knit it together into Cypher's pattern, but then they shimmered and, as Cypher watched, the whole form melted and shifted.

She poured herself a glass of iced Solarian tea that she'd developed a taste for these last weeks and sat at the little reading table in her sleeping chambers, watching Zeno cohere.

When Zeno's mouth was whole enough to speak, she said, "Good thing we thought to have you give me the microchip. The Queen never suspected it was me instead of you. I had to beg a little for show. I hope you don't mind."

Cypher laughed. "That's what she'd expect. You know, even if she knew it was you, she'd have shot you."

"But not with a blaster. She knows I can recover from that. Not this fast usually. Thanks for those nanites."

"Did you take a lot of damage?" Cypher asked.

Zeno got to her feet, kind of unsteady, and glanced around the sleeping cabin of the ship. There were scorch marks on the wall and bits of nanites that had been her head, now reduced to inanimate dust. She held out her hand and a stream of nanites turned into micromachines to carry the dust away and return to her.

"Enough damage," she said. "I should probably lie down."

Cypher gestured to her bed. Zeno held out her hand for Cypher to come with her.

Cypher quirked an eyebrow, "You won't get any rest."

"I don't want rest," Zeno said. "I want you."

Cypher was in her arms in an instant, kissing her, hands roaming over Zeno's body as if to reassure herself that it was all back together, all familiar. Zeno had assembled herself with the basic clothing she included in her pattern and Cypher's fingers tugged at her shirt.

Weak from the blaster and weaker from the effect Cypher had on her, Zeno stumbled backward and fell onto the bed. Cypher laughed and climbed on top of her, sitting across Zeno's hips and pulling her shirt the rest of the way open. Because she'd copied an Illudani body, she had all the sexual responses of any Illudani or human. Her nipples rose toward Cypher, begging her touch, and Cypher put her hand on one breast and her mouth on the other.

Zeno arched her back, holding onto Cypher, aware of nothing but Cypher's hands and mouth on her.

That was definitely more than I wanted to say online. It had gotten away from me. But I liked where it was going. Of course in my mind it was me and Blake, but that was kind of the point.

I read it over and debated where I should cut it off. Should I stop it when Zeno said "I should probably lie down" because it was clear to the reader at that point that Cypher and Zeno were fine? Or should I go all the way to "I want you" or to Zeno holding out her hand?

"I want you" felt like too much to say where anyone could see it, but I liked the image of Zeno holding out her hand to Cypher. It was suggestive. And it would probably piss off Sierra in a highly deserved manner.

My bit of story didn't break any rules and it didn't do anything to a character that I'd need to get permission for, so I posted it.

I texted Blake: *Have you been following the story?*

She answered: *Hey you, I'm trying not to. Bear says Sierra killed Cypher.*

I fixed that, I said.

Ooh? I'm looking.

There was a long pause and I went down to the kitchen to refill my water glass. When I got back up there was an message from Blake that said: *Blaster to Cypher's head. That bitch.*

Did you read mine?

Reading now. Very clever!

After a few more minutes she wrote: *Where's the rest of it?*

I glanced from her words to the extra paragraphs and wondered how she knew that. Even thinking about the idea of sending it to her, of her reading it, made me feel hot and shaky.

I asked: *How do you know there's more?*

Because if there isn't now, there's going to be. You're going to write it for me, aren't you?

Um, yeah. I'm emailing you the next few paragraphs.

I copied her the part from Zeno holding out her hand to the very end of what I'd written. After I pressed send on the email, I had an attack of shyness.

The scene as much as said "I want you" to Blake.

What if she thought it was too much? I mean, we were in some nebulous stage of couldn't wouldn't but would if we could going out-ness. And that was great, but was it "I want you" level great?

What if I was pushing too hard?

Blake wrote: *Goose, do you know how much I love you?*

I stared at the text. I scrolled back through our thread to see if I'd missed a line or two, but no, I'd said I was sending her the next paragraphs and, if you counted those, I'd said, "I want you."

And her reply was "I love you?"

I didn't care if it made sense or not. I didn't know what to say. I mean, I did and it was "I love you too," but after all the times Sierra had said that to me, it didn't mean anything anymore. I wanted a better way to say it.

What was more than "I love you?" This was like the thing with the infinities—that you couldn't add one. There was no "I love you" plus one. Or was there?

While I was trying to figure that out, Blake called me.

"Hey, did I freak you out?" she asked.

"No," I said. "I mean…me too. With you. The love. It's just, are there orders of love? Can you add one to that? Oh God, my brain."

"Lauren," she was laughing. "I don't usually get to say this, but, slow down."

I took a deep breath and said, "Can I ask…what are we?"

"Human, probably," she said.

"You know what I mean. What is this between us? Is it, I mean, do you want to be in a relationship?"

"Ask me later," she said. "Ask me when you're here."

I didn't love that answer, but it seemed fair. I didn't know what to say to it, though so I went back to the story.

"You know, Sierra's going to try to kill Cypher and Zeno again," I said. "We should come up with a way to prevent that."

"I'm not sure I care right now. She can't touch us."

"Ha! So there is an us!"

Blake laughed. "When you're here," she said.

* * *

I told my father I wanted to go down to the Cities for the last weekend in October. Cyd was moving into a new place with Bear and I wanted to help. I pointed out that it was close to my birthday, so I'd be happy to take that as my present.

I had to see Blake. The days when she didn't answer my texts drove me crazy. I worried about her at school, about Kordell, about her plastic-wrapped brain.

And I needed to see her for me. So I could be real again.

But my father was back in strict mode when he was home. He said no. He'd already gotten me a nice gift for my birthday and I needed to focus on school.

"I need to see my friends," I told him, too loudly.

"You *need* to take your SAT and be filling out college applications," he said.

"I can do both. It's only for a weekend."

"Applications and SAT first, and show me your grades, then we'll talk about it."

"That's too long! I want to help Cyd move. Please."

He shook his head. "I've let you go too often already. You're being moody and obstinate. I thought we agreed that this year you're going to do your work. You might think it's funny to sabotage your future, but I don't and you won't either someday. My letting you run around undisciplined is helping no one, regardless of what either of us might want. It's my job to make sure you turn out successful and a contributing member of society, not some spoiled girl who's going to be a drain on everyone around her."

I remembered Isaac's total expression of disbelief as he asked if our father said things like this to me more than once. I wanted to call Isaac and hold the phone up so he could hear what I was hearing. I wanted to say: *When he decides to pay attention, I hear this every week, Isaac. Variations of how awful I am and why can't I be a success like you.*

But I couldn't do it. Later, in my room, I called Mom and got her voice mail and hung up.

While my father was at work that Friday, after school, I packed a bag, left a handwritten note on the counter, and drove down to the Cities anyway.

CHAPTER THIRTY-EIGHT

Blake said to come to her house. The move wasn't until the morning, Cyd would be busy packing and I didn't need to be in a place where I could run into Sierra. I figured I could stay until I wore out my welcome at Blake's and then get a hotel or sleep in the car. I didn't know if I could even get a hotel room by myself at sixteen-almost-seventeen.

In the daylight, I could see that Blake's house was a cute one-and-a-half story. It hadn't snowed yet this year, so the small but well-kept lawn was visible, along with a tiny, dormant vegetable garden. I rang the bell and her dad answered the door.

"Lauren," he said cheerfully. "Go on upstairs, but watch your head."

He pointed to an open door with stairs leading up. At the top of the steps, I got what he meant: the half story had a low ceiling, six feet high in the middle with sloping dormers. If I moved out of the middle of the room, I'd smack my head on the slanted parts of the ceiling.

There were clothes hanging near the top of the stairs in open closets, mostly black, and further into the room a dresser, a nook with a beanbag chair on the floor, and the bed at the far end. Blake was propped up in the bed with a book in her lap.

She looked roughly washed and tumbled dry, but she smiled when she saw me. She got up and walked around the bed, standing at the foot, in the middle of the room, seeming small. Under her black hoodie, she wore loose gray sleep pants and it was strange, almost sad, to see her not in all black.

I put my arms around her. She rested her head on my shoulder and held onto me.

All the way down, driving, I'd been thinking of things to say. Mostly arguments for us to date, for why it could work even long distance. Now I couldn't remember any of it. Didn't need to.

Standing with her was everything. Inhaling maple-earth, honeysuckle and green darkness, feeling like sunlight in deep water.

A few infinities later, she pulled away and grinned up at me. I wanted to kiss her, but I didn't know if that was okay, so I took the beach stone out of my pocket. She closed her fingers around it. Inside her fist, it fit perfectly. Opening her hand, she peered at its layers of gray and white granite.

"I love this," she said. "Thanks for bringing it for me."

I nodded, grinning back at her, trying not to grin so much, failing. She went to the bedside table and got a flat, gray stone with a dip in the middle. It fit comfortably in my fingers and I could rub my thumb along the dip.

Blake sat down against the headboard and patted the spot next to her. The bed was made, so it wasn't a provocative gesture. (Yeah, a little disappointed.) I sat down.

"Where are you staying?" she asked.

I shrugged.

"I'll ask my dad. I think you can stay here tonight. How long are you here for?"

"However long," I said. "My father didn't say I could come, so I guess I'll go back in time for school Monday and see how mad he is. I mean, what's he going to do? Ground me? There isn't anything I want to do up there anyway."

"I wish you didn't have to go back there," Blake said. "You sound so sad when you do."

"I...do?"

"You sound flat," she said. "But I think that's how you do sad."

Sudden tears burned in my eyes. I looked away, blinking hard, trying to find something in her room to comment on, except that I couldn't get my eyes to focus around the water in them.

"Yeah," I said roughly. "It is."

I wanted to say more. To tell her how much it hurt all the time there, trying to be someone else and always failing. How bad it was to be so far away from her. How I'd messed up trying to have a relationship with Sierra and I got if she didn't want to date me because I sucked at being a girlfriend. How fucked up everything was.

I got up, to move and not cry, but I forgot about the ceiling and smacked my head. I swore and sat down hard on the side of the bed. It made me laugh even as the pain blossomed through my forehead.

She pulled on my sleeve, tugging me toward her. I went slowly and she directed me until I was lying down, my head in her lap, facing up at her.

She said, "If you run away every time you feel things…you don't have to. I like you this way."

"How can you?" I asked. "I'm a mess."

She bent down and kissed me. My chatty brain remarked that this was probably the first time she'd kissed me with her mouth closed. Purely lips on lips, ultra-soft. She kissed my cheeks and my eyelids and a random part of my forehead and my mouth again. For a long time we were just tongues playing, lips translating a thousand small feelings back and forth, the shared space of our mouths its own universe.

She pulled away and smiled down at me. I traced the side of her face and her lips.

"I could kiss you forever," I said.

"An infinite amount of kissing?" she asked. "In infinite time?"

"Not even. Completely outside of time and space. Eternal, I think. Like a kiss that happens once but is, in some sense, happening all the time."

Her head jerked up, eyes wide, mouth opening in a flattened O. "That's so perfect."

"Don't be too impressed," I told her. "I stole that from something the Rabbi said. Well the idea of it anyway. It was about mythology, that myths didn't happen once, they're happening all the time."

"Eternal mythic kissing," she said and laughed and kissed me again.

In our next pause, I said, "I'm sorry I don't live here. That I'm not around for you. Is it still bad with Sierra and all that?"

"Medium bad. It was a big deal when school started. Scandal of the month and all. Stupid gossip and Kordell got shoved around. Some guys figured I'd been covering for him and he had to be gay. Assholes going after him and not me. I got in a fight. Now they're afraid of me. Dad had to go in a few times."

She shook her head, mouth tight.

"Bad fight?" I asked. "Did you get hurt?"

"Wounded pride mainly. If you have a rep for being crazy and you start yelling, people back away pretty fast."

"I'm sorry."

"Silly goose," she said. "They're the assholes. Kordell's got a girl he's into anyway, so when she gives in to his inevitable charm, that'll help things. About time he got a steady girlfriend."

"I thought..." I said. "You seem to like each other a lot."

"I adore that boy. But we don't click like that."

"That made no sense." I became super aware that I was lying with my head in her lap and she was talking about someone else she had sex with.

She sighed. "It's like I care about him and I like having sex with him but there's another part that's supposed to connect and it doesn't. Plus I'm not the most reliable. I mean, you should probably know, sometimes I'm totally into having sex and other times I don't even like being touched."

"Well you should know I'm very used to not touching. I grew up in a highly not touching family. Also there's a pretty good chance that I suck at relationships."

"You honestly think that?"

I didn't answer at first because that was too close to making me cry again. I nodded and swallowed a few times while she waited.

Finally I managed in a mostly steady voice to say, "Sierra said I was cold and distant and you say I'm flat."

"Don't combine those. Flat is what you do, it's not what you are."

"Oh." Before I could stop myself, I asked, "Did you hook up with me at Bear's parents' house because you were...?"

The sentence hung unfinished. I stared up at the sloping part of the ceiling. Was there any word I could use to end that sentence that didn't make me a huge jerk?

"Hypersexual?" she offered. "You're asking if Sierra was right?"

"Sierra's never right," I said.

She half-smiled but her eyes were wet. I was definitely the biggest asshole in the world for making her cry. She turned her head so I couldn't see her face.

"Kind of, yeah," she said.

"Blake?"

She looked down at me, tears on her cheeks. I reached up and brushed one away with my thumb.

"What did it mean?" I asked.

"That sometimes I really want sex. And if it's like that I'm probably hypomanic."

"No, not that. I looked up the bipolar stuff on the Internet. I even remember that 'hypo-' means 'under.'"

That got a faint smile.

"What did it mean with us? It's okay if it was a random thing," I told her, but I was lying.

"You know, you took your bathing suit off first," she said and paused. Her fingers played with the collar of my shirt. "All night I wanted to be around you. Not only that night. You'd been asking me about feelings and I wanted to reach inside you, put my hands through your skin, help you feel things. And then I just wanted you. And we were naked. Before that I thought we'd hang out more, talk. But once we were naked I didn't want to *not* be naked with you. Does that make sense?"

I nodded. "I was so confused. I couldn't figure out what you were doing."

She laughed. "Neither could I. And then you kissed me."

"You *looked* at me," I said. "You looked at me like you wanted to put your hands through me."

"But you kissed me," she repeated.

"I'm thinking about kissing you again," I told her.

"Me too. Great minds."

I gathered the front of her sweatshirt in my fingers and pulled her toward me, but she stopped me by pressing her palm over my heart.

"It doesn't mean I wouldn't have wanted you otherwise," she said. "You get that, right?"

"I get that now."

"I'm sorry I didn't tell you. Hypomanic is like the volume is turned way up but the song doesn't change."

"So you don't suddenly give up math for sky diving, you just want more math? Heavy metal math?" She nodded and I asked, "Does the song ever change?"

"Not with the meds."

I wanted to ask a bunch of questions but even more I didn't want to ask. Didn't want to make it into a big thing.

Her dad called up the stairs, "Blake, is Lauren staying for dinner?"

"Yeah," she yelled back down, and to me said, "Let me go ask him about you staying the night. He'll want you to sleep on a three-thousand-year-old air mattress in his workshop, but if you can brave that, it's totally okay."

While she went downstairs to ask, I got out my phone. My father probably hadn't come home yet and seen the note saying that I needed to go to the Cities and help my friends and I'd be back for school. He hadn't texted or called. Or if he had seen the note, he was in that silently pissed state.

Maybe I shouldn't go back. Except I'd left so much of my stuff there. Things I wanted, like my sketchbooks. I had to go back at least to get that, but when I did, he'd probably make sure I couldn't leave again. Or he'd try. I didn't think he could literally lock me in the house. He'd have to let me out for school.

If I left again and came down here—where would I stay? Would I be able to graduate? How badly would I screw up my life?

CHAPTER THIRTY-NINE

Dinner with Blake and her dad was fun and painful (and not merely because of the bad puns). Her dad persisted at being as great as he was the night he carried her in from the car. Watching him talk to her, watching him listen to her, made me ache like I was one big bruise all down my ribs.

Blake's dad started the dinner conversation by asking, "Guess why wind power is so popular these days?"

Blake shook her head at him like she knew what was coming.

"It's got so many fans," he told her and they both laughed.

He asked me, "What do you get if you step on a live wire with two bare feet?"

"Electrocuted?" I offered.

"A pair of shocks," he said.

"I should have warned you," Blake told me.

"Don't worry about it," I said. "Nothing could have prepared me for this."

My father and I used to have dinner together once every week or two. I talked about my week at school, he talked about whatever case he was working on. I could only tell him certain aspects of my week: the things I'd done right, good grades I got, compliments from my teachers. I could mention one element that I struggled with and ask for his advice. I couldn't say that I was bored or trapped or felt like I was drowning.

When Blake's dad asked how school was, he listened intently to her answer.

She said, "I'm not following the math lectures very well. I try but it's not coming together right. I can't see it all."

"Did you get the professor's notes?" he asked.

"Yep."

"You want me to go over them with you?"

"Can we do it Sunday evening?" she asked, adding, "and you have to do the impersonation."

He laughed and in a grumbling, badly German-accented voice, that I assumed was her math teacher, said, "Vat iz de trouble mit divizing by zero?"

"Infinity," Blake said and grinned at him.

I was glad after dinner to sit and watch a movie with Blake until it was time to get ready for bed. I needed space to uncompress my head. I got into a T-shirt and sweatpants, and tried to see if I could make the air mattress situation any more comfortable.

When Blake came in to say good night, I put my arms around her and buried my face in her hair. After a moment she pulled away.

"I can't stay," she said. "I wanted to say good night."

"Okay," I replied, confused because I hadn't asked her to stay. I didn't know what the house rules were. Her dad seemed cool and all, but I could get that he didn't want us sharing a bed.

"I mean, I have to sleep," she insisted.

"Okay?"

"No, I mean, I *really* want to kiss you again, but…"

My hands were on her hips, her hands on my shoulders, the air shimmering hot between us. If she felt anything like the pull I was feeling, the wrenching desire, she was having trouble letting go of me. That was almost better than getting to kiss her again.

I pushed her lightly. She took two steps back and stared at me, wide-eyed.

"I'll be here," I said. "Go to bed. It's bedtime, right?"

She grinned lopsidedly. "Yeah. Thanks."

She was out the door so fast I wondered if that meant I'd done something wrong. Crap. We already knew I sucked at relationships. I wanted to go after her, but I'd make all the stairs creak and wake up her dad and make everything worse. I settled onto the makeshift air mattress bed, which was like lying on an extra-thick rug.

I got up again.

I walked barefoot around the room, trying to be silent. There were shelves of drawers labeled with electrical-sounding names. And there was a shelf with photos in frames. I saw one of Blake as a little kid, beaming and mischievous. I picked it up and stared at it for a long time.

Finally I made myself get back into the shallow bed. I contemplated the ceiling and wondered what part of her room I was looking up into. One of the closets?

This was so different from being around Sierra, who after that first spring break week never only made out with me. Kissing was always a prelude to sex. That afternoon, being in Blake's bed, it was nice to kiss each other without feeling like it had to go anywhere. Way nicer that it was Blake I was kissing.

The problem with Sierra wasn't that we had lots of sex. I still liked sex a lot. It was that we didn't do much else. Having sex or writing scenes about sex or flirting was more than half the relationship. And the other half was going out to eat, walking around shopping, talking about the story, but never talking to each other.

In a super creepy way, it reminded me of living with my father: how he never wanted to know how I was or what I was interested in. That thought was so gross that I rolled over and resolutely focused on falling asleep.

CHAPTER FORTY

I heard Blake's dad moving around the house, the shutting of a door and his truck starting in the garage. The sun was up, but it was early. After a quick trip to the bathroom, I sat on the bed and read because I didn't feel okay rambling around the house by myself.

Blake stuck her head in the door and grinned at me. Her hair was damp, like she'd tried to wet down the bedhead effect but a few wisps on one side were still making a run for it. She wore a black tank top and faded blue and white striped loose pajama bottoms.

"Hey you're up," she said.

"And still here, as promised."

She dropped down onto the air mattress and kissed me. We made out until someone's stomach growled.

"Let's eat," Blake said.

"Can I make coffee?"

"Sure."

She showed me where the coffee was and I started a pot brewing while she contemplated the inside of the refrigerator.

"Last night's leftovers?" I asked, looking over her shoulder. "I can do dinner for breakfast."

She shook her head. "Sit down. I'm no cook, but I excel at reheating."

I watched her pull a bunch of stuff out of the fridge and freezer. In minutes she'd set out a spread of little brown pancakes, a tub of sour cream, smoked salmon, capers, red onions, chopped hard-boiled eggs and two flavors of jam.

"Blinis," she said, pointing to the pancakes. "From my grandmom. You can eat them savory or sweet or alternating. I like to go two savory, one sweet and repeat."

"What about one savory, one sweet, two savory, three sweet?" I asked.

Blake laughed. "But then you have to eat five savory. How long have you been planning that joke?"

"At least a month. I read about the Fibonacci sequence and figured I'd get a chance eventually."

"Are you planning ahead for Pi Day already?"

"You know I am," I told her. "We're going to eat three-point-one-four pieces of pie."

She took a blini and put sour cream and smoked salmon on it. I did the same, feeling deja vuish. (Or was that deja Jewish?) Replace the blinis with bagels and you had half the meals I ate when I was out east. Call me a stereotype, but I loved bagels and lox. The blini was dense and hearty and great with the salty fish.

When she'd had her first two blini, she got up and went to a cabinet, took down a prescription bottle.

"Can I see?" I asked. "Is that okay?"

She turned around, eyes wary, but held the bottle out. I examined the label with her name printed all in capital letters and the pills inside. The only person in my family who took prescription medication for anything was my grandpop for his heart. My father would say many deeply stupid words about weakness at this point—I could hear his voice in my head. I didn't want that to ever be my voice.

I handed the bottle back to Blake and said, "Thanks. Can I ask you stuff about it?"

"Yeah."

"When did you know?"

She raised an eyebrow at me. "How did I get diagnosed?"

I nodded, feeling awkward for not asking right.

She said, "My mother has it too. Dad was watching for signs of bipolar in me, in case. Genetically, it's likely." She took a pill from the bottle, downed it and put the bottle back in its place.

Sitting, she went on. "Mom and Dad split up a long time ago. I don't even remember. She wasn't…she couldn't stick around."

"Where does she live?"

"Wisconsin, I think. She moves a lot. Anyway, I remember things starting to change when I was eleven. I'd have these weeks where everything was amazing, I'd get all my school stuff done and extra projects and hang out with everybody and have a blast. I'd get tired for days but I thought that was because of all the partying and staying up reading. But the tiredness got dark. I'd wonder about it but then I'd feel good again. Except the dark times got darker and longer. And really bleak, like I was hollowed out inside except for pain and hopelessness."

I put together another blini while she talked, to do something and not stare at her.

"Did he find out because of the suicide attempts?" I asked. Hard to say the word, to even think about it, but I wanted to let her know it was all okay to say.

"You'd think," she said. "But no. I was lucky that the attempts didn't…work. Dad didn't know. Not until after I started therapy and I told him. He figured it out when I was manic. I got in a fight with him about electrical engineering. It sounds weird when I try to retell it, but I thought he was doing it wrong. I was fourteen and he has a PhD and I thought he was doing it wrong. I was in his workshop and I was convinced I knew how to make this amazing combination of circuits and stuff, I don't even know what it was, but it made total sense to me. It was going to revolutionize the world, a new kind of communication, but so much more than that. He came back from work and found me in the middle of this project he'd been working on, totally screwing it up, and I was trying to tell him how to make it right and I wasn't making any sense. So he took me to the hospital."

"Wow, for real?" It seemed like such a big move to make, from finding her messing around with his stuff to going to what I assumed was the psych ward.

She shook her head, got up from the table and walked a few steps away, looking into the living room.

"It's not like that, okay? I'm telling it wrong. I'd been awake for a few days and he came home and he kept trying to get me to stop, to leave the project alone, and I wouldn't. When he tried to carry me to bed, I started yelling at him and fighting him. I don't remember all of it now, but he did what he was supposed to do."

I said, "I'm sorry. I don't mean to be judgy. If you haven't noticed, I'm kind of a jerk sometimes."

That got a little laugh.

"I don't want to be a jerk to you," I told her. "Can you tell me how not to?"

"Don't assume things. Like mania…people say all kinds of dumb stuff about it, like, 'it must be nice to have all that energy.' But it's not fun. And it's not even like being out of control, because I didn't know that I wasn't making sense. I could see this whole design and it was perfect and it was genius and I had to do it, I couldn't stop, and I thought it was all me, the most natural, logical sequence in the world. When we got back from the hospital the mess was still there in Dad's workshop and it made no sense at all, to me or him or anyone. After that, for a long time, everything felt unreal. How do I know that what I'm thinking is what's real?"

"What do you do?"

"I ask people," she said. "I write numbers in annoying little boxes and report to my shrink. And I take my meds and try to do what I'm supposed to even when it sucks."

"What sucks?"

"Bedtime for one thing," she said.

"Last night?"

"Messing with my sleep is supposed to be bad. I mean, it is bad. But I hate it. Trying to sleep and maybe I can and maybe I can't but I have to be in bed for eight or nine hours and write it all down. I want to get up and do things or go out or kiss you and I'm supposed to go to bed like a little kid."

I put my arms around her. She turned to face me and wrapped her arms tightly around my body, shaking against me.

"What time is bedtime?" I asked, trying to remember when it was last night that she'd left the workshop/guest room.

She shook her head against my shoulder.

"I'm asking so I can make sure I get you into bed a couple hours before that," I said.

She was laughing, or crying, or both. She pulled away and went across the kitchen to get a tissue, then turned and faced me.

"How?" she asked.

"What?"

"How are you going to get me into bed at all when you live three hours away?"

"Two-and-a-half," I said by reflex.

She wiped her eyes with the tissue. "How can this even work?"

"I don't know, but it has to. Doesn't it?"

"Yeah," she said, but her voice was low and sad. "Maybe it's better this way."

"It can't be," I insisted. "It can't ever be better to be away from you."

"You won't see how messed up I am," she said.

"Yeah, that's a good point. If you're here and I'm there, you won't discover what a total moron I am in a relationship."

"You are not."

"Really? Have you dated me? Because if you ask Sierra…"

"Oh fuck her," Blake said.

She started around the table but I scooted away so I could keep talking and not get distracted.

"In addition, I'm told that I'm moody and a bit of a drama queen," I told her. "Plus I can't tell what I'm feeling most of the time."

She was lopsided grinning and moving more quickly around the corner of the table to catch me. I attempted to bolt into the hallway, but she caught my wrist and tugged me toward her.

"On top of that," I said. "Apparently I can be cold."

"No. You're just a little broken."

"Yeah. Or a lot."

"I don't want you to go back there. I hate it. You're going to shut down again."

"Can we not think about that? Can we pretend today is the first of lots of days like this?"

"No," she said. "I don't want to pretend."

I remembered what she'd said about not knowing what was real and what wasn't and nodded. "Okay. No pretending. Let's go help Cyd move."

I went to change into my grimy moving and cleaning clothes. As I was putting on my shoes, I heard Blake's dad get back. His voice and Blake's carried to me from the kitchen and I went to say hi.

When I got the doorway, Blake and her dad were standing in front of the refrigerator. He was putting a new carton of eggs on the shelf and asking, "Guess why I got out of the market so fast?"

"You used the eggs-press lane," Blake told him.

"Clearly I need some new material," he said.

Stepping back from the refrigerator, he slung an arm across her shoulders. She tucked in toward him and put her arms around his body. The fabric of his shirt wrinkled as she squeezed him tightly. He kissed the side of her head.

In profile, I saw the side of his smile and one eye unfocused, half-closed with joy.

I turned around and went back into the guest room. Standing in front of the family photos, I saw how often the two of them were touching. He'd have an arm around her or, when she was a little kid, be carrying her or holding her hand.

"You ready?" Blake asked from the doorway.

"Yeah."

She raised her eyebrows at me, questioning whatever expression my face had going on, but I shook my head.

"Let's go," I said.

CHAPTER FORTY-ONE

The moving effort was intense. Cyd only had the U-haul for a few hours. We began loading around noon. Bear was busy moving all of her stuff, but Roy showed up with a guy he introduced as Shaman Bill. Cyd's sister showed up with her partner—both of them tall and beautiful and completely enviable for a thousand reasons. We got all of Cyd's stuff into the truck in about two hours and drove to the new place where we unloaded it as quickly.

Cyd and Bear were moving into the bottom half of a duplex, like the place Cyd shared with Sierra, but this one was smaller and nicer. It had natural woodwork and wood floors instead of carpet, so it felt warm all through. The living room and dining room were open to each other, with a small kitchen in the back. Off the dining room were two bedrooms on either side of a bathroom.

Behind the kitchen, steps led down to a wide, low-ceilinged basement that looked like someone had wanted to finish it in their spare time but wandered off in the middle. There was one finished room, mostly wood paneling, and a much larger unfinished area that would be both the laundry zone and the new home to all of Bear's outdoor gear. She had camping packs and a tent and snowshoes and lots of boxes with labels like: Rain, Mild Cold, Heavy Cold, Heavy Snow, Summer, Boundary Waters, Climbing.

The side of the basement she'd picked to store the gear was gross. Every side of the basement was gross, but this was the grossest. When all the boxes were in, I started mopping. Blake was upstairs helping clean the kitchen and unpack things into it.

By the washing machine, dryer and utility sink, a household disaster had happened. It involved a cracked bottle of detergent, lint, dryer sheets and assorted bits of anything that drifted by. The detergent had all leaked out of the bottle months ago, pooled on the floor, attracted every tiny object it could and congealed into a dense, sticky mass.

I refilled the mop bucket and found a stiff-bristled brush. I was trying not to think about Blake's dad. Scrubbing hard on hands and knees was usually a good not-thinking activity, but it wasn't working. I kept seeing his sandstone-colored lips against the raven black of her hair, the tiny wrinkles that gathered in the corner of his eye from his smile.

I remembered the night I'd driven her home from the golf course when he said, "It's what we do, parents. We worry." I remembered the way he watched her, joked with her, made her laugh, made sure she was more than okay.

I pulled my mind back to the present and forced my eyes to focus on the navy blue detergent and gray lint. There was a penny, tarnished and old, stuck to the cement floor with blue gunk and I scrubbed at it until it came loose.

The mess was near the floor drain under the utility sink. I'd washed about a third of it down. Maybe the previous tenants had left it because they thought eventually it would all slip down the drain. But it wouldn't. It was a hardened, stuck mass that would never change no matter how long you left it alone.

I wasn't sure I had enough water and strength to scrub it all away.

From the wall behind the sink, a daddy long legs spider looked at me.

I yelped and scrambled backward until I hit the Boundary Waters gear box. The spider took a few steps up the wall and paused.

"Blake would carry you outside," I told it.

That was a better memory than thinking about her father blatantly caring about her—Blake sitting at the mirror, seeing the spider, her face softly laughing.

She'd been so careful with the little creature.

Tender. Like her father was with her. Like he'd been that morning in the kitchen, fingers cradling her shoulder. The blocky shape of his smiling cheek that was so like hers. The tenderness of his fingers curled around her shoulder like he wanted to protect her forever.

I slid sideways and back, crammed myself between Boundary Waters and Heavy Cold. Tears pressed behind my eyes, in my throat, but I heard someone coming down the stairs and forced the tears back.

"Lauren?" Blake called.

I couldn't talk.

She came around the corner, saw the bucket and brush, turned in a slow circle, saw me.

Crouching in front of me, she said, "You look sad."

I stared at my hands, curled uselessly in my lap. I wanted to shred apart like Zeno into a billion particles. A tear dropped onto the pad of my thumb.

I can't cry, I thought, *she'll think I'm weak and childish and dramatic.*

No. That was my father's voice. If I could turn into anything, I would never turn into him.

Tears slid down my face. I looked up at Blake.

She shoved Heavy Cold out of the way and pushed in next to me. With her arms around me, she tugged me toward her. I let her tip me sideways, my shoulders and head in her lap.

She curled around me.

Tears ran until they'd soaked my face and my hands. Blake sat with her arms around me, solid and warm.

After a long time, she asked, "Did something happen?"

"You hugged your dad," I said and started crying again. Sobbing like a little kid, embarrassed and too relieved to stop.

"Goose?"

"The refrigerator. Eggs-press lane. You hugged him and he kissed you like…like he loves you."

"Oh," she said. "Your dad."

"Father," I told her. "He doesn't get to be called 'dad.'"

Her arms held me harder.

I said, "I don't want to go back. I feel like I'm dying. Like I'm going crazy. I hurt all the time and I don't know why."

"You know why."

"Nobody gives a shit about me up there. Nobody cares. It's like I'm already out in space, already at the edge of everything looking into nothingness. The end of everything isn't far away. It's here. It's happening—I'm disintegrating."

Blake rubbed the side of my arm with her palm. She said, "It's not nothing out there. You don't get to the edge of everything and find nothing. Nothing is everywhere, already inside of everything. That edge where you are, that's the leap to a higher order of infinity."

That made me cry more.

My nose was running so much that I rolled out of her lap and got a handful of paper towels from on top of the dryer. I blew my nose, but I was still crying.

I wanted to get back into her lap but didn't know how to fold myself down again. I knelt, trying to figure it out. She took my hand and pulled me toward her. I kissed her, lips closed, but with pressure, trying to say how much I loved her. She kissed back harder and we were tangled up together again.

Blake pulled back, her cheeks wet from my tears. She brushed my cheeks with her thumbs, dried her own cheeks with the back of her hand.

"Higher order of infinity?" I asked, my voice catching on the last word.

"Zeno the infinite," she replied.

"You know we might have to start a new story. I have a bad feeling about Zeno and Cypher. I don't think Sierra's going to stop until they're dead."

Blake said, "Let me work on that."

"Oh yeah, because I have to work on this stupid real life plot," I said and thumped my chest. "Shit. I don't know what to do. You know the day I first met Sierra at my school there was this kid who climbed in through the window yelling and waving a hard drive. They had to call the cops. Maybe I should pull a stunt like that."

"I can't tell you what to do. But don't do that."

"I guess I'll call my mom again. Even if she said I could go live with her...she's in D.C. I don't want to go further away."

"I've never been to D.C.," Blake said, but now she looked like she was about to cry.

Blake might not want to pretend anything, but I did. I wanted to pretend I had hundreds of days with her all in a row ahead of me, not the one more day until I had to drive back north again.

CHAPTER FORTY-TWO

Movies and bedtime, making out in the morning, holding each other and talking, I had less than a day of it. Then I had to drive two-and-a-half hours of dread back to Duluth so I could go to school on Monday. When I got to the house, my father was calmly furious. He put down the pages he was reading and stood up from the couch, but didn't move toward me or away. That tender look on Blake's dad's face, I'd never seen a look like that on this man's face. I never would.

"No more car," he said.

"Fine," I told him.

"No more trips to the Cities."

"Try and stop me."

He walked around the couch and stood between me and the front door, as if I was going to bolt that instant. I took a deep breath and stood as straight as I could, making our eyes level. His eyes looked like frozen ground under a layer of frost.

"Give me the car keys," he said.

I took the fob off my key ring and dropped it in his hand.

"And your credit cards," he said. "Both of them."

I pulled out the card I used for shopping and the one I had for emergencies. He clenched them in his fist.

He said, "If you want to find out how hard the world is without money, without an education, be my guest. You might think you can run away to the Cities and hang out with your friends whenever you want, but they'll get sick of you. Trust me, I know. This is a give-and-take world. You can't keep taking and expect everything to come to you."

"I give," I spat the words at him. "I give all the time. I clean. I worked on that awful garden. I go to school and I get good grades and I don't know what more you want from me."

"I want a child I can be proud of. Not a daydreaming fool who spends her days with comic books and running off with people who will never matter at the end of the day."

"They do matter."

"Not to the rest of the world. Maybe to you, but you don't know what the world is like. You're wasting your time and your life. I am trying to teach you to be a winner. Do you want to be a loser all your life? Do you want to be a drain on others, laughed at, ignored, worthless? You let your emotions rule your life. You need to toughen up. That's how you win in life."

If those were the rules of life, I didn't want to win. Blake had said that the end of everything was the start of a higher order of infinity. My father had never seen that infinity. I might not have seen it either, but now I knew it was there. Maybe I could get there.

"I can't live here with you," I told him.

"You don't have a choice," he said. "You're not even seventeen until next week. If you leave, the police will bring you back."

"You'd call the police on me?"

"We don't need that kind of shame in this family. But you need to grow up."

I stared at my feet and the pristine tile of the kitchen floor. And something else Blake had said came to mind—about feeling like minus-three, deep black, like the world's problems would be solved if I weren't in it anymore. She'd said she was wrong to think that.

I closed myself around her words, like her fingers wrapping around the stone I'd given her.

"I'm trying to grow up," I said. "To turn into anything that isn't you."

"Do you hate me that much?"

The words stopped me. I stared at him, his dark eyes the same color as mine. A wave of fear went through me, and dread that the answer to his questions was "yes."

"No," I said almost in a whisper.

"Things have to change around here. Leave your phone in the kitchen and I'll be turning off the Wi-Fi in the evenings. You need to focus. You need to learn what real work is."

I walked to the far edge of the counter, where it swung out into an L-shape near the front foyer. I put my phone on the cold granite. I would set my alarm for 2 a.m. and come back for it.

"May I go to my room?" I asked.

He nodded so I went up to my room and shut the door. I had to think it through, figure out the best way to get out. I couldn't stay, but I didn't know how to leave.

No car. No money. I couldn't walk down to the Cities in the middle of winter. Hitchhike? Maybe.

I stood at the window. Outside was a bleak, dark gray sky and the dormant rose bushes. I wanted to lie down among them and let myself bleed away into the ground.

* * *

Somebody got through the next few days. Not me. Maybe Zeno shaped into a pattern that was hollow inside, lost, never knowing what we were truly meant to be.

I had my phone at school and texted Blake: *Father took car & money. Only have phone during school. No Internet at night. Trying to call Mom.*

She wrote: *You okay? Safe?*

I had to think about those questions for a long time. Safe from my father? That depended on what I was keeping safe—my body? Sure. All the rest of it? I didn't know.

Anybody else I would have told I was fine. But Blake had been further up than me and for sure further down and I could tell her the truth without freaking her out.

I replied: *Safe. Not okay.*

She wrote back: *Friend from therapy group says: only dread one day at a time.*

Hah, wise, I said.

I couldn't come up with anything else to say. She kept texting me a few times a day, bits of poetry, bits of math, awful puns.

She never said "I love you" in the texts and I felt oddly grateful. Like that wasn't a thing you said to make someone feel better, even though Sierra did that all the time. Sierra had said it to shut me up, to stop arguments, to get me to go along with her. I wanted to tell Blake how much it meant that she didn't say it. But I couldn't figure out how. My few texts back to her said "lol" or "haha" when she sent a funny or awful message.

I could have called her on the house phone, but an edgy paranoia haunted me. My father was coming home from work early now, like he was staking me out, like he knew I planned on leaving as soon as I could. I was afraid he'd pick up the phone extension and try to hear what I was saying to Blake.

I considered taking the car keys and going, but my father had hidden them. I went through my things to figure out what I could sell to get enough cash to rent a place in the Cities. There was some decent jewelry. I didn't even know how to go about selling it. And I didn't think you could rent an apartment if you were under eighteen.

Every plan I started trailed off into smoke.

I was getting up later, struggling to get to class, not doing homework, forgetting to eat and seeing my ribs in the mirror.

The sun went down at five p.m. and I went down with it. I thought about letting it all slip away and falling back into my father's world. Dying inside. Until Blake texted me to go look at the story and what she'd written. I logged in from one of the school computers during lunch…

"The Queen will never let us rest now that she knows she failed to kill us," Zeno said. "And if she gets the power of the High God, if their plan works, nowhere in the universe will be safe."

They were in Cypher's ship, on the landing deck of Lord Solar's cruiser. For the last few weeks, Zeno had been trying desperately to find a system they could hide in. They needed a place out of the range of the infomancers, of the Rogues, and of the High God's power.

She'd found no such place.

Cypher leaned over the universe map that Zeno had called up on the table top. Her hand covered whole galaxies.

"While you were standing in for me, waiting for the Queen to show up and shoot you, didn't you wonder where I'd been going when you were too polite to ask?"

"Too polite by half," Zeno said with a wink. "I don't like to intrude on you, except when you want me to."

"I always want you to," Cypher said. She leaned up and kissed Zeno very thoroughly until neither of them could breathe.

Cypher went across the cabin of her ship and got a familiar leather pack out from under a bulkhead.

"Remember the artifact you found? The first half of the Sigil of True Form?"

"Of course," Zeno said. "It showed me that I wasn't what I thought, that I could become so much more. But it wasn't enough to give me my true form."

"And I said I'd help you steal yourself back," Cypher went on. "Well, I found the other half."

She placed a second, smaller leather pack next to the first. Zeno stared at it.

She told Zeno, "Figure out how to fit them together while I fly us out of here."

"It won't matter where you go. The Queen almost has the locus of the High God's power. Once she does, she'll be able to find us anywhere in the universe. She'll come for us. Don't you want to spend our last days together focused on each other, not flying around in space?"

Cypher touched Zeno's cheek. "A few days isn't enough for me," she said. "I'm getting us out of here."

"There's nowhere we can go. She'll find us."

"Assemble the artifact," Cypher told her and went to program coordinates into the nav computer.

Zeno put the two pieces on the table and moved them around until they started to make sense to her. She felt the ship lift off the deck surface and fly free of the artificial gravity of the battlecruiser. The ship's own lighter gravity took over.

"I've got it," Zeno called forward to Cypher.

Cypher came to the doorway of the sleeping cabin.

"Do it," she said.

"Are you sure? What if I'm hideous?"

"You couldn't be," Cypher told her.

Zeno looked at the two fragments for a moment more and fit them together. A ripple traveled through her. The billion parts of her quivered and settled in their original pattern. She looked down at her hands: smaller, closer in size to Cypher's, more human.

Cypher held out a mirror. Her hair was dark and rich, her eyes like the warm blackness of deep space.

Cypher kissed her slowly. "Do you know what I love most about your first form?" she asked.

"It's not hideous?" Zeno said with a laugh, looking at one slender hand, turning it back and forth.

"No," Cypher said. "It's that I can teleport you now."

She kept one hand on the side of Zeno's face and reached out to touch the wall of the ship with her fingertips. Her awareness went out around them and encoded exactly the ship and herself and Zeno. The real Zeno.

She folded them in on themselves, down to nothing, down to zero.

She divided by zero. Divide anything by zero and you had infinity. They were nowhere and everywhere.

From zero, she relocated them. She put them through the black hole into the universe she'd found—and brought them back from nothing.

Zeno staggered slightly, unused to the disorientation that came with moving through zero. "Where are we?" she gasped.

"We're in a new universe. Well, new to us. It's over 13 billion years old. The Queen can never find us here."

Zeno's eyes widened, her mouth opening in a smile. "That's perfect."

"Oh wait until you see the planet I found. It's out in one of the arms of this galaxy. Pretty little blue-green world with people who look like us. We'll blend right in."

I wiped a hand across my face, smearing tears and trying to clear my eyes. If Blake could find a way to get Zeno and Cypher to safety, into a whole other universe, I had to find a way out of my father's house. It started with calling my mom again and, if I had to, it ended with packing what I could carry and leaving.

CHAPTER FORTY-THREE

I took only a backpack and one big rolling suitcase. No car this time, but at least I'd scraped together enough money for the bus.

When we pulled into the downtown Minneapolis station, I got my suitcase from the stack of luggage the guy was piling up. Cyd texted me that she was waiting by the end of the vending machines. I rolled my stuff in that direction, trying to dodge all the people moving on random paths.

I saw Cyd's red-brown hair and, as I got through more of the crowd, Blake's rough-cut black hair. Before I was all the way to them, Blake came forward and put her arms around me. I dropped the handle of my suitcase and hugged her close. Her head tucked into the side of my neck and I bent my face into her hair.

When I looked up (a million years later) Cyd was holding the handle of my suitcase. I wasn't used to touching anyone in public, to showing anything. Kind of embarrassing. But Cyd was beaming.

"How was the trip down?" Cyd asked and as we headed for the parking lot.

"Pretty nice. I liked not having to drive. Not that I'll be telling my father that. If he ever speaks to me again."

"Your mom?" she asked.

"I called her twice this week, told her I couldn't stay in Duluth anymore. She said we'd talk over the holidays and come up with ideas. I didn't know what else to say. I mean, if I told her I was going to leave, she might have emailed my father."

"You should let her know you're okay."

"Yeah, I will."

When we got to the car, I didn't know where to sit. I didn't want to move any further away from Blake but I didn't want to be rude and have us both sit in the back, like Cyd was the chauffeur. Blake solved that by getting into the front passenger seat and reaching her hand back to me.

I slid into the middle of the back and put both my hands around hers.

"I turned on the heater, but the basement isn't warm yet," Cyd said. "I'm going to stay at my guy's place, so you can sleep in my room if you want. Just…if you do anything, toss the sheets in the wash in the morning."

"Uh." I ducked my head so she couldn't see the blushy smile on my face.

"Thank you," Blake said, like Cyd's offer was totally normal. Was it?

I had a moment of fear. No, panic.

Could this work? If it didn't, I had nowhere to run back to.

We got to the duplex and I carried my suitcase down to the half-finished room in the basement. Cyd was right, I couldn't quite see my breath down here, but it wasn't warm by any stretch of the imagination. I hoped the heater worked a whole lot better than it was right now or I was going to be freezing for months.

Upstairs again, Bear said hi and then headed for her room, saying she had to be up at four a.m. for a sunrise snowshoeing thing that sounded like torture.

Cyd left to stay with her guy. Blake turned into the living room from locking the front door behind Cyd. I was standing in the middle of the room.

"You look startled," she said. "Deer in headlights style."

"It's a lot of new," I told her.

"Yeah. Want to watch a movie?"

"What?"

She said, "You're cute when you get like this."

She took my hand and pulled me toward the couch. I went with her and sat. She looped her arm around my shoulders and I slouched down so I could lean into her.

"Comedy?" she offered.

"Sure."

"Romantic, ridiculous or horror?"

"Horror comedy is a thing?"

"It's a great thing," she said. She flipped around in a variety of menus on the TV until she found what she wanted. We watched a ridiculous, but highly fun movie in which a monstrously large crocodile ate a lot of people and a few hapless cows.

We paused midmovie to get drinks. Cyd had stocked the fridge with Pepsi for me. The process of settling back on the couch and starting up the movie turned into making out for a while, until Bear came out and asked us to turn the TV down (and rolled her eyes at us).

After the movie, I asked, "Do you want to…you can stay. If you want. But you don't have to. I mean, I won't be upset or anything."

"Do you want me to stay?" she asked.

"Of course I do. I'll get you to bed on time, I promise."

She shook her head in mock disappointment and I kissed her cheek.

"I'll text Dad," she said.

After she sent the text, she asked, "Cyd's bed…that's kind of weird, right?"

"Very," I said with a sigh of relief. "Let's see if the basement warmed up."

It was marginally warmer at the bottom of the stairs than two hours ago.

"Come on," Blake said and led the way back up the stairs.

She went to the hall and opened a closet, pulling out a folded quilt that she handed to me.

"Go get that afghan on the couch too and take it down," she said.

I carried the two blankets down and put them on the one thin blanket already on the futon bed in the back room. As I was arranging them, Blake arrived with two more blankets from Cyd's bed. We spread those on the top.

I didn't want to have to take off my clothes in the cool air, but Blake pulled the blankets aside and crawled into the bed with all her clothes on. Relieved, I followed her.

We fit. There wasn't a lot of spare rolling-around room, but we could lie side by side without someone hanging over an edge.

Blake pulled the stack of blankets up to our foreheads. Cold had crept through my socks as we arranged the bed and it lingered in my toes. The top of my head felt like a little, icy hat.

Under the blankets with Blake, I didn't care. She was watching me with her intense look, like my face meant something. Maybe it did.

I kissed her for a long time, bypassing warm and going right to hot. Pulling up my sweater, I disentangled it from the shirt underneath in a shower of static. I managed to wriggle out of it and drop it next to the bed without causing the blankets to slide completely off. Blake was laughing and unbuttoning her overshirt and holding the blankets more or less in place. She kicked off her socks and I did the same even though my feet weren't warm. I wanted to feel the skin of her feet with mine.

She put her hand on my breast over my shirt and bra. Somehow it was more intense than if she'd put her bare skin on mine. She rubbed her thumb around the rise of my nipple. I felt her thumbnail catching on the ridges in the fabric of my shirt, creating tiny waves against my skin.

That went on forever and the other breast was forever. My jeans and shirt and bra had to come off because I was sweating. Blake shimmied out of most of her clothes too. We were both in underpants. She slid her hand under the fabric of mine, exploring before rising up my belly to my breasts again.

If you added this evening to the time in Bear's parents' basement, she'd already touched me more than Sierra had in our entire relationship. My breath stuck hard in my throat. I pushed myself to inhale deeply. The air caught the heat rising through me and blew away the pain.

I kissed Blake, wanting to express everything I couldn't say. And that went on until her hands made kissing impossible.

* * *

The phone rang. The house phone in the kitchen that nobody had the number for. We'd been sitting in the living room most of the afternoon, me and Blake and Cyd, talking about everything. We all stared in the direction of the phone and Cyd got up. When she stepped back into the kitchen doorway, her face had an avocado green tone.

"Lauren, it's your father."

Lake ice cracking, drowning fear pulled at me, but I levered myself up and went to find out how bad this was going to be.

"I know where you are," he said.

"I'm in the Cities. I told you."

He read off Cyd's address. The current address, not the old one.

My knees went shaky and I had to sit down on the kitchen floor. I didn't say anything. He continued talking, "That girl you used to stay with was happy to give it to me. Some friends you have down there. Are you ready to come home?"

"No," I said in a small voice. "I'm not coming back."

Blake slipped into the kitchen, settled onto the floor, and offered me her hand. I interlaced my fingers with hers and held on.

"Yes, you are," my father said. "Do I have to call the police?"

"Yeah," I told him, more volume behind that word. "Go ahead, call the police on me. I'm not going back. I'm not living there anymore."

"Fine. You have twenty-four hours to change your mind and then the police will be involved. You are seventeen years old, you can't run away to—"

I hung up on him.

"He's calling the police?" Blake asked.

"Tomorrow. I have until tomorrow."

"You can stay at my place for a few days. Give you more time."

I shook my head. "Sierra told him where I was. She'll give him your address too, if she hasn't already."

I pulled out my cell phone. He hadn't turned it off yet. Probably sure I'd come home within the twenty-four hours. Probably waiting for me to call him. I called Mom but she didn't answer so I called Isaac.

"Hey, La, what's up?"

"I ran away," I told him.

He laughed. "Good one. Did you join the circus?"

"Isaac, I'm not kidding. I'm in the Cities. I'm not going back to live with him anymore." My voice cracked on the last word and I gulped in a breath to keep from crying.

"Oh shit," he said.

We were both silent for a while.

"Where are you?" he asked.

"I'm staying with friends. He says I've got twenty-four hours and then he's calling the police."

"You actually ran away?"

"Mostly. I mean, I did all my classwork for the rest of the semester and handed it in first. We only had three weeks left."

He was laughing again. "That's my sister, the most prepared runaway ever. You did your laundry first too, didn't you? What's your grand plan?"

"I want to see if I can take my last semester at a high school here. I can live with Cyd and Bear. They've got space in their basement."

"How long have you been planning this? Why didn't you tell me?"

"I've been trying to tell Mom, but I couldn't figure out how. I told her I couldn't live there anymore, but not about leaving. I didn't think...I thought you were busy with school and partying and stuff."

I heard him sucking his teeth, a soft, whistling sound.

"What a mess," he said. "You need to sit tight, okay? Let me talk to Dad. Will you do that?"

"Twenty hours," I said, surprised at the pure metal strength in my voice. "That's how long you've got until I'm gone."

"Lauren."

"I am not going back," I said.

"What's so bad about living with Dad? Is he doing something to you?"

"No. That's just it. There's nothing there. He leaves for days and days. He never listens to me or pays any attention to me. He uses me like I'm there to clean and do the fucking garden. He doesn't care about anything I do. He wants me to be like him and I'm not. There's nothing there! I can't live in nothing, Isaac. I can't!"

I was yelling into the phone, crying. Blake had an arm around me and she took the phone out of my hand.

"Hey, this is Lauren's friend Blake. She's okay but she needs some space. Can she call you back?"

There was a pause and Blake said, "Yeah…yeah…okay. Gotcha."

She hung up the phone and hugged me. I cried on her until I was afraid of getting snot in her hair.

CHAPTER FORTY-FOUR

I packed all my stuff again. It was way too much, so I condensed it down to what I could carry in the hiking backpack Bear loaned me. It sat at the top of the back stairs, where I could grab it and go.

I didn't trust my father to wait the twenty-four hours he'd given me. He would wait for morning. He was sharper mentally in the mornings and I wasn't—he'd use that to his advantage. He'd play this like a court case, taking every bit of high ground he could. If he called the police after his morning workout and breakfast, how long would it take them to get here?

What happened when the police showed up? I remembered a year ago standing in my school, watching the police take that ranting boy out to their squad car in handcuffs. Would they put cuffs on me? Would I try to run?

If I was going to run, it had to be before they got here. I'd told Isaac twenty hours, but I didn't think I should wait that long.

Everyone brainstormed places for me to go. Bear offered her parents' house but Sierra had that address too. Kordell said he'd call his oldest sister and see if I could crash on her couch for a few days. I didn't love that idea, but it was the best I'd heard.

It got late and we agreed to reconvene the Council of Runaway Abettors in the morning. Cyd and Bear went into their rooms, leaving me and Blake on the couch. Her expression was thoughtful and sleepy.

"We should go to bed," I said.

She didn't make a joke. She didn't look at me. Her fingers tapped a pattern on the side of her knee. She sighed and said, "I could call my mother."

"Um?"

"To see if you can stay with her for a while."

I picked up her hand and played with her fingers. "Do you want me to?"

"She's not always good about her meds," Blake said. "If she's not taking them, I don't want you to see that but maybe you should. Maybe you should see what I might be like."

I wanted to say "I don't care" but that sounded dismissive. I ran my thumb back and forth across hers, feeling all the ridges at the knuckle.

"Sometimes I'm afraid of you," I said. "I mean, when I first met you, I was super afraid because you show what you're feeling and you feel so much stuff. But I love that. And, you know, sometimes I'm afraid of myself too. I'd rather be afraid than numb. I'd rather need you and crave you and be afraid for you and be afraid of you and be afraid of how you make me feel and need to feel all that than go back to not feeling anything at all."

I paused and added, "I should have been afraid of Sierra and I wasn't. Because I wasn't feeling anything. And I don't need to be afraid of you. No, that's not what I mean. I feel like I messed it up, I understood it wrong, like what I thought was feeling afraid of you was something else completely."

"A pair of shocks?" she asked.

I grinned at her. "A whole drawer full of shocks."

"Lauren, don't fuck up your life because you think you have to be here for me. I'm okay."

"Hey, I'm the crazy one. You've got a disorder, but I'm the one who's been a robot for most of my life. I mean, when I tell this story to other people I am totally going to blame you for fucking up my life, but in the right way. You fucked up my fucked-up life."

"Double negative," she said.

"Exactly. It needed fucking up. And I'm not saying I never want to meet your mother, or that I don't want to know all that. I do. I'll figure out how to handle it. But maybe not when I'm fleeing the police."

Blake chuckled. "What do you want to do with your last night of freedom?"

"Snuggle."

She raised her eyebrows at me.

"I'm kind of scared," I said. "I mean, I'm terrified. Could we curl up in a ball for a while?"

In the drowsy place between sleep and waking, in the cold basement bed, under the pile of blankets, with my arms around Blake, I thought about Cypher and Zeno. I pictured them in their spaceship. They were close to the black hole they'd teleported through together. Zeno stood in front of the viewport staring into the blackness so deep that no light, no information came out of it.

How long had I been standing there, on the edge of nothing, feeling myself pulled away toward the void?

I thought about Blake being Cypher, the Master of Secrets, the assassin, a girl with equal parts brightness and darkness. Blazing like a quasar and sinking into herself like the black hole.

I wanted to be myself, my true form, whatever that turned out to be, and I liked the person I was around her. I liked trying to follow her when she was talking about infinities, and I liked trying to make her laugh when she was wrapped in foggy plastic-wrap. I liked just sitting with her.

In my near dream, I watched as Cypher came up next to Zeno and touched her arm. "You're brooding," she said.

"I'm looking at where we've been," Zeno replied. "And trying to figure out where we'll go."

"You can imagine, but you can never know," Cypher told her. "The multiverse is an awfully mysterious place."

* * *

I was getting dressed when the bell rang upstairs. I grabbed socks and jammed my feet into them, hunted around for my shoes.

Cyd's voice carried down the stairs. "It's Kordell."

I dropped onto the bed with a sigh, but I kept putting on my shoes anyway, less frantically. It was nine thirty am. I figured I had an hour or two until the police showed up.

In the living room, Kordell was sitting on the couch with Blake. Cyd was in the armchair with a big mug in her hands.

I got a slice of cold pizza and a Pepsi and slid onto the couch next to Blake. She put her arm around my shoulders. We sat quietly for a bit and then she and Kordell started talking about the new cards that had been added to their game.

The doorbell rang again, and a knock, and Isaac's voice calling, "Lauren, it's me."

Everyone turned to me. I got up and threw back the bolt on the door, but when I opened it, Isaac was standing there with our father.

I stepped back. Isaac came in, our father behind him. They were both in suits: Father's was the dark charcoal gray he loved and Isaac's was a navy blue that brought out the unfortunately yellow undertone of his skin. He looked like the tie was choking him. He must have put it on to impress our father, to show that he was on his side.

I wanted to run out the door and keep going.

Blake got in front of me. Cyd and Kordell were frozen, staring, but she moved to put her body between me and them.

She seemed half the size of my father: six inches shorter, compact and slender compared to his broad-shouldered, jacket-enhanced form. She set her feet and put her hands on her hips, like a winged fairy creature getting in the face of a dragon.

He ignored her and took another step toward me.

Blake pulled out her phone. "I will call the cops myself," she said.

My father paused. "I'm not hurting her. She's the one violating the law. You make that call." But he stepped back.

Blake glared at him. He stared at me. I looked at the floor and wondered if I could run fast enough with that big pack of Bear's to get away from here.

In this standstill, Isaac went into the dining room and came back carrying two chairs. He set them down on the floor with the hard crack of wood on wood.

"We are *talking*," he said. "No one is calling the police. Everyone sit down."

He wasn't as big as our father, but his voice snapped in the air like a whip. I went to the couch and sat. Blake came and wedged in between me and Kordell, her phone in her hand.

"Lauren, tell Dad what's going on," Isaac said.

I glanced around the room. In front of all these people? Cyd, who I liked but felt like I didn't even know yet, and the same with Kordell.

"Um."

"You are seventeen," my father said. "You live under my roof. I make sure you have everything you need."

He hadn't sat in the chair. He stepped toward the front window and clasped his hands behind his back. I could see how he came across in the courtroom: both imposing and—not friendly exactly—but someone who could understand you, relatable.

I pushed off the couch. I couldn't sit still.

Pacing between the end of the couch and the doorway to the dining room, opposite my father, I said, "You give me money to buy food and clothes. You treat me like an intelligent dog. You never listen to me."

"You never say anything worth listening to," he countered.

"Dad," Isaac said in a warning tone. He was in the chair he'd carried in and set in front of the television, facing the couch.

The people in the room weren't in exactly the right places for a courtroom, but I got the impression of Isaac in the judge's position with the couch and the armchair serving as the jury. I was the defense, my father the prosecution.

My father turned to face Isaac. "I raised you after your mother left both of you. I taught you to be strong and successful. Look at how well you're doing in college, in your internship. Do you think I mistreated you?"

"No," Isaac said.

Step, step, turn. My father moved and spoke, "You never complained that I didn't listen to you. While you've been away at college, excelling, Lauren has been spending her time in frivolous pursuits: reading comic books and watching cartoons, not getting the grades she could, wasting her time. She needs to learn self-discipline."

"Lauren?" Isaac asked.

My eyes burned, throat tight as a fist.

"They're not cartoons," I said. "They're anime and manga and graphic novels. They're art. And they're a million times more important than those stupid roses and some glossy pictures in a shallow magazine about who has more money. I don't want your life."

He settled his weight back on his heels, tensed and stretched his arms with the hands clasped.

"You may think you don't want it," he said. "But try to get along without my money and see how far you get."

"I don't need your money."

"I'd like to see you do without it."

Cyd put her hand up and said, "Objection."

My father and Isaac stared at her.

Cyd said, "You're telling her she's got to do what you want in order for you to take care of her. But it's a parent's responsibility to take care of their child regardless of whether they're doing life the way that parent wants. Maybe you have to consider that your kids aren't the same. What one needs, well, the other needs something else. That's your job as a parent to figure out."

"Do you have children?" he asked.

"No."

"You can join in this discussion when you do. Until then, Lauren, you're coming back to the house and you are going to finish this year of school and get the grades you need."

I saw in his face how my eyes must look when I'm not feeling anything—when I'm flat. I wondered if Sierra and Blake saw that. When the deep brown lost all warmth and drew light in.

Is that what Sierra reacted to when she said I was cold? Was it hard to connect to me? To love me?

I turned to Blake, her eyes like the kingfisher trapped behind glass, still and moving in a thousand directions at once, haunted, shadowed. Her mouth was tight with fury. Without a smile, her face seemed plain, and not nearly familiar enough, and so right that my chest ached. I wanted to see her face every day until I could recall her perfectly behind my closed eyes.

Did my eyes look like nothingness to her? Did they look like my father's? Maybe we had it backward the whole time and she was infinite and I was zero.

But I didn't need to stay in flat nothingness. Blake had said that flat was how I did sad, so I let myself feel the sadness. How lonely it was in the big, empty house. How much it hurt every day that my father who was supposed to take care of me never wanted to be around me, didn't love me, didn't even like me.

I was still facing Blake as the tears rolled down my face, but I turned to my father without trying to wipe them away.

He took a step back and cleared his throat.

"I need to have friends," I said, surprised that my voice came out a lot steadier than I expected. "I need to be around people who like me. You don't get to ignore me when it's convenient and expect me to show up and be your daughter when you want. You can call the cops and get me dragged back to Duluth and I'll play nice for a few days, maybe even weeks, and then I will lose it, very loudly, very publicly. Maybe at temple, maybe at school, maybe at a work party. I will scream and rant and throw things. If you think you know what embarrassing the family looks like, you have no idea."

"You will not," he said.

I went on talking, evenly. "I hope you do call the cops because I'd like to talk to them about how often you leave me alone. You make such a big deal about how I'm not old enough to be down here on my own but you barely stay at the house."

I glanced at Isaac. He'd given me the idea to research what qualified as neglect, even for a teen. But bringing him up would make it worse. I brushed my hand across my face and squared my shoulders.

"It's neglect," I said. "How would it look to have one of Duluth's top litigators investigated for neglecting his kid? I am *not* going back there. My grades are good enough, I have the credits. Let me finish high school here."

As I talked, his expression went from flat to sharp-lined intensity. My legs were shaking.

He said, "You may be sick of being my child but have you ever thought about how sick I am of being your parent? Do you know what I could be doing if I didn't have you to raise?"

"Then do it," I said.

"You need to learn how hard life is. I'm cutting you off."

Cyd opened her mouth and half-raised her hand, but Isaac spoke before she could. He said, "Wait. La, you have to eat. You should probably be paying rent. You might be able to switch to Mom's health insurance, but if anything happens you'd need cash for the co-pay and all that."

"I'll get a job. I'll figure it out."

"You'll have to anyway," Isaac said. "But hey, you told me there were programs that let high school kids take college courses. Is there one here in the Cities?"

"Yeah."

"Let's see if we can get you into that. Dad, if she's taking a college course, you can tell everyone that she moved down here to do that. You got two smart kids, one of them so smart she's got to move to the Cities and go to college at seventeen. But you don't cut her off."

My father stepped away and stared out the window for a long time. Finally he said, "Lauren lives down here. I pay half the rent and groceries, no more." He turned around and glared at me. "And you come up twice, spring and summer, for events I specify."

"Let me guess. You want me to wear a dress."

"That would be ideal." Humorless. He added, "Someday you'll understand what a mistake you've made."

I wanted to say "fuck you," but one benefit of being raised as a robot is having the self-control not to. I was getting what I wanted, so I smiled as sweetly as I could and said nothing.

"Are we all agreed or do I need to write this down?" Isaac asked.

"We're agreed," my father said. He walked out the front door. I heard the car start and drive away. I turned to Isaac.

He said, "I'm in a hotel at the airport. Flew in last night. Cost a ton. I had Dad pick me up on his way here. He was coming to get you himself, not going to call the cops. At least I don't think so. Anyway, I can take a cab back."

"No offense," Cyd said, "but he is a real piece of work."

"He wasn't that bad a few years ago," Isaac said. "La, I'm sorry."

"He was that bad," I told him. "Just not to you because you're his golden boy. But thanks for…bailing me out."

Isaac shrugged out of his suit jacket and hung it across the back of his chair. The tie came off next, the button-down shirt unbuttoned, untucked, revealing a gray college T-shirt.

"You want a piece of pizza and some Pepsi?" I asked him.

"Yeah. That'd be great." He leaned forward with his hands on his knees. "Man," he said.

I touched his shoulder and went into the kitchen. As I pulled the pizza box out of the fridge, I heard Isaac ask, "So, you're my sister's girlfriend?"

"Yeah, hi," Blake said, her voice rough with emotion.

I paused with my hand on the refrigerator, tears blurring the world.

CHAPTER ALEPH ZERO

I lay in the warmth of the blanket pile and slid my arms more tightly around Blake's sleepy form. I nuzzled into the familiar sweet earth scent of her.

"Cold nose," she mumbled. "Don't poke me."

I didn't move away and she rolled toward me.

"Why is your nose freezing?" she asked, eyes half-open in the dim light.

"Because it's cold out."

"Blankets," she said and pulled the whole stack over our heads.

"Hey."

"What?"

"Good morning," I told her with a huge grin. "I like getting to say that to you from the same bed."

She kissed me hard. A little breathless she said, "Good morning, Goose. I like waking up with you too."

I ran my hand down her side and traced the curve of her hip. She caught my wrist. "Breakfast."

"I can make pancakes."

"Let's go out. We've got university classes soon. We should celebrate our freedom while we can."

"Uh, I've got like five bucks. Total. For the week."

Blake kissed me again. "Good, you'll let me buy. Come on, maybe Cyd and Bear want to come with."

"Bear's out snowshoeing again. Are you texting Cyd? See if she wants to bring her guy. We should check him out."

Blake slid part way out of the blankets and got her phone from the pocket of her pants. I took the opportunity to run my hand over the curve of her butt.

"Cut that out," she said. "I'm hungry. If you keep doing that…"

I stopped and watched her type into her phone. She kept peeking over at me and grinning.

"Cyd says she'll meet us and she's bringing her guy. A few more and we'll have a party. Okay if I text Kordell?"

I nodded. Before I could stop myself, I asked, "If he wasn't dating someone else, would you want to hook up with him?"

"Maybe," she said. "But I wouldn't."

"Because of me?"

"Yeah. I'd never be like, 'I know you moved down here and all, but I'm going to keep hooking up with someone else and expect you to be okay with that.' That's highly shitty."

"Sierra would," I said.

"Forget her." Blake's voice was edged with anger. She rolled onto me, sat up, pulling up the blankets and letting in a blast of cold air. Her hands were heavy on my shoulders as she leaned over me. "What do *you* want?"

"You!" I said.

"Exclusive?"

"Yes! Completely totally yes. I want to be your fucking girlfriend with all the stuff: flowers and candy and singing cherubs."

"You are my fucking girlfriend," Blake said.

I half sat up and wrapped my arms around her as hard as I could. She laughed into my ear and kissed the side of my face. There was more kissing and rolling sideways…and realizing all the blankets were off and we were going to freeze.

We scrambled to get the blankets back around us and ended up sitting up against the wall together.

"We have to get another thing clear," Blake said.

"What?"

"No flowers. You hate flowers."

I laughed. "No flowers."

"And no cherubs, they're creepy."

"Fine," I said. "Numbers and micron pens and funny movies where animals eat people. And you say that you're my girlfriend a hundred more times."

"I'm your girlfriend," she said. "Ninety-nine to go."

"I wish…" I started and wasn't sure I wanted to say the rest of it, but she was watching me so I went on. "I wish you'd been my first. I feel like…what kind of messed-up lesbian am I that I ended up with Sierra? Here I am in year one of being lesbian, of dating and all that, and I've screwed it up already. Like I should get to re-roll my sexual orientation and start over, except I don't want to be anything else. But now I'm always going to be that stupid, stupid person who dated her."

Blake threw her legs over mine and caught my face between her hands. "Hey, she's not your first. I am."

Her eyes were deep water with sunlight shining down through.

"I kissed you first," she said. "I loved you first."

"When I said the thing about black holes?" I asked.

"Nah, then I just thought you were cool."

"You said you kind of loved me."

"I *kind of* love a lot of people," Blake said. "But I don't want to be their girlfriend."

"When did that happen?"

"Over that whole first week you were here. The way you asked questions and were frankly curious about what our answers were. You never asked anything so you could pick a fight, like Roy does, or so you could say your point of view, like Dustin, you really asked. And I thought that if I ever had a shot with you, I was taking it."

She paused and laughed and said, "And in the middle of that I told Kordell, so he already knew when he dared you to kiss me."

"I was a jerk about that kiss. At least in my head."

"You were beautiful," Blake said.

"That was the first time I kissed a girl too," I admitted. "I was mad that it was part of a game, but now it's the best."

We made ourselves get out of our cozy blanket space and find our clothes. As she was putting on her shirt, Blake said, "And there's one other error in your thinking."

"Only one?"

She flashed me a broad grin. "This isn't year one. It's year zero."

"Huh?"

"I kissed you on April tenth last year, so until April tenth this year we're in year zero of your lesbian life. You know like when a baby's born we don't say it's one year old, not until it's lived a year."

"So I get to be a baby lesbian and mess up all kinds of stuff and it doesn't count because it's my year zero?"

"That's more than what I was saying. And better. Let's go with that."

"And after April tenth it's Year One?"

She stood up from putting her shoes on. "If you want, but I think if we're girlfriends it should be more like Aleph Zero."

I scanned back through my brain to the conversation about infinities. I remembered the Alephs because I knew the letter, because it already meant something sacred to me. And zero was the first of them—the first infinity.

"We're infinite?" I asked Blake. "Or irrational?"

"The first," she said. "Because the number line…wait. Are you trying to one-up your Fibonacci joke?"

I said, "You got me. But can you add one to humor? Or is it like love, an infinity?"

RESOURCES

Safer Sex

If you've made it to here, you've probably noticed that Lauren is not having safer sex in this book. (The author has had a talk with her about this and she now knows what to wrap and how.) This can be a common experience for teen girls having sex with girls, in part because good resources are hard to find. If you're having sex with people whose sexual histories you don't know, please practice safer sex. Here are good resources for learning how:

The Scarleteen website, particularly: http://www.scarleteen.com/article/gender/figuring_out_how_to_be_a_lesbian_safer_sexpert

Teensource: www.teensource.org/blog/2011/11/what-'safe-sex'-teen-girls-who-have-sex-other-girls

Allison Moon's *GirlSex 101*, which has great information about negotiation and consent, in addition to safer sex, and is very trans-inclusive.

Bipolar Disorder

Books I read to research this story (all of which were very good):

Welcome to the Jungle: Everything You Ever Wanted to Know About Bipolar but Were Too Freaked Out to Ask by Hilary T. Smith

Facing Bipolar: The Young Adult's Guide to Dealing with Bipolar Disorder by Russ Federman PhD and J. Anderson Thomson MD

Loving Someone with Bipolar Disorder: Understanding and Helping Your Partner by Julie A. Fast and John D. Preston PsyD ABPP

An Unquiet Mind: A Memoir of Moods and Madness by Kay Redfield Jamison

The Dark Side of Innocence: Growing Up Bipolar by Terri Cheney

The Bipolar Disorder Survival Guide, Second Edition: What You and Your Family Need to Know by David J. Miklowitz

Emotional Neglect

Running on Empty: Overcome Your Childhood Emotional Neglect by Jonice Webb (Author), Christine Musello (Contributor)

ADDITIONAL RESOURCES

National Alliance on Mental Illness (NAMI) http://www.nami.org/ or helpline: 800-950-6264

Trevor Project, suicide prevention for LGBTQ youth: http://www.thetrevorproject.org/and 866-488-7386 BP Magazine: http://www.bphope.com/

National Suicide Prevention Lifeline (24/7 across the US): http://www.suicidepreventionlifeline.org/

Boy's Town (not just for boys) a 24/7 helpline for youth and families: http://www.boystown.org/

Bipolar Burble, Natasha Tracy's site and blog: http://natashatracy.com/topic/bipolar-blog/

Bella Books, Inc.

Women. Books. Even Better Together.

P.O. Box 10543
Tallahassee, FL 32302

Phone: 800-729-4992
www.bellabooks.com